Also by Frannie Watson with Doug Watson:
Mirrors: Real Stories of People Who Transform Pain to Joy and Turmoil to Peace

Also by Frannie Watson:
Pursued but Shielded
KIRKUS REVIEWS
"Police search for a serial rapist whose urges escalate to murder in this faith-based detective novel."
"A mingling of spiritual insights and chilling crime."

SNATCHED BUT FOLLOWED

Stephen & Olivia,
Merry Christmas,
Love you guys!

Jan. 1, 2017
Lawrenceville, GA

Frannie Watson

FRANNIE WATSON

LifeRich
PUBLISHING

This is a work of fiction. All of the characters, names, incidents,
organizations, and dialogue in this novel are either the products
of the author's imagination or are used fictitiously.

Scripture quotations taken from the New American Standard Bible® (NASB),
Copyright © 1960, 1962, 1963, 1968, 1971, 1972, 1973,
1975, 1977, 1995 by The Lockman Foundation
Used by permission. www.Lockman.org

Scripture quotations marked (NIV) are taken from the Holy Bible, New
International Version®, NIV®. Copyright © 1973, 1978, 1984, 2011 by Biblica,
Inc.™ Used by permission of Zondervan. All rights reserved worldwide.

Author's photograph taken by Greg Watson

LifeRich Publishing is a registered trademark of
The Reader's Digest Association, Inc.

LifeRich Publishing books may be ordered through booksellers or by contacting:

LifeRich Publishing
1663 Liberty Drive
Bloomington, IN 47403
www.liferichpublishing.com
1 (888) 238-8637

Because of the dynamic nature of the Internet, any web addresses or
links contained in this book may have changed since publication and
may no longer be valid. The views expressed in this work are solely those
of the author and do not necessarily reflect the views of the publisher,
and the publisher hereby disclaims any responsibility for them.

Any people depicted in stock imagery provided by Thinkstock are models,
and such images are being used for illustrative purposes only.
Certain stock imagery © Thinkstock.

ISBN: 978-1-4897-1042-0 (sc)
ISBN: 978-1-4897-1043-7 (hc)
ISBN: 978-1-4897-1041-3 (e)

Library of Congress Control Number: 2016918178

Print information available on the last page.

LifeRich Publishing rev. date: 11/30/2016

ACKNOWLEDGMENTS

....

It has been with great humility that I have had this opportunity to write about sex trafficking. To the quality people I have interviewed for the details in this story but to whom I cannot thank by name, I say thank you and I could not have written this story without you.

It has been one of my greatest honors to have met you and I commend you for all that you have accomplished and will accomplish to heal and then help heal those devastated by sex trafficking.

Although I do also want to thank so many by name: Nancy Addison my very talented editor, thank you, I could not publish without you. Nancy Thompson, such a wonderful friend for many years, thank you for your support and brilliant ideas, help, and editing skills on the beginning of this book. Greg Watson, who reads the manuscript to give us his astute insights and who is the photographer of my author's photo, thank you. Doug Watson, my husband and friend, thank you for your keen eye for details that rescued my story countless times.

Regarding the story's essence, once again I want to thank each of these kind people who gave me their time and experience during their interviews, thank you: Michele Rickett, author and president of the international ministry – She is Safe. Dana Ridenour Endorf, author of *Behind The Mask* - retired Special Agent Dana Ridenour of the FBI gave me her perspective of law enforcement. Her experience in sex trafficking legitimized my story. I also interviewed others who are in the category I began with above, thank you.

The remaining people I want to thank are the many prayer warriors who prayed for me throughout these last eighteen months. Some of them also were helpful with their feedback about this story.

One of my WDA team members warned me that I would be attacked spiritually if I wrote about sex trafficking and she was correct. I am so thankful she told me this, so I could ask people to pray. So thank you so much for your prayers: Jan Wolbrecht, Renata Dennis, Nancy Thompson, Mary Bowman, Jane Neall, Hollie Kent, Shan O'Neal, Janet and Stephen Meeks, Doug Watson, Nancy Addison, our churches and my WDA teammates: Jack Larson, Margo Theivagt, Lee Tolar, Nancy Higgins, Joseph Hobbs and Beverly Keller.

I so appreciate the wonderful feedback I received from my readers of the first novel, *Pursued but Shielded*, thank you. Your insights and encouragement were priceless, thank you.

I want all my readers to know that victims who escape from sex trafficking will need a great deal of support for a long time. This story, because of the time restraints of a novel, can only show a condensed time period for the characters. In the recommended readings at the back of the novel, I have mentioned just a few real life examples of what each victim must push through to make a new life for themselves. I only wrote generally about the atrocities of sex trafficking out of respect for the Christian audience that I target. Please realize that some of the information I recommended is graphic about sex trafficking.

I know I have probably not mentioned each of the people who helped me with this project, so I now thank each of you. I hope each of my readers will be moved by this story as well as entertained.

DEDICATION

This book is dedicated to each snatched child and her family, as well as all the workers who provide a sanctuary for the girls who have escaped sex trafficking.

Atlanta Journal

MONDAY, April 21, 1997

Girls' Vanishings Bewilder Police

By John Smith
Staff Writer

Atlanta's finest admit they are perplexed by the disappearances of a large number of juvenile girls over the past several months. "We have every available officer searching for the source," said Sex Crimes Unit Captain Bill North. "Of course the Atlanta Police Department continues to follow leads that have come to our attention, but there have been an overwhelming number of calls, draining our manpower from finding the source or crime boss." The human trafficking method of operations (MO) varies, although there is usually a female recruiter and a male counterpart working together to kidnap the minors. Parents and guardians must remain observant and vigilant.

Local Newspaper Article – Alma's folder for L.R.

The handler was beginning to see his profession in another light - helping to create businesses that sell sex to men. The high demand for underage girls created businesses that snatched them from their innocent daily routines and forced them into the deadly under-world of human trafficking. He reflected on the most gut-wrenching aspect of this sex trafficking business, which was how quickly, with no warning, it took captive the most treasured gift of any parent -- their child.

FRIDAY, MAY 9, 1997 - AFTERNOON

Clay Stevens and Alma Hernandez were checking the human trafficking numbers on a balcony overlooking the warehouse that housed their company's main offices. This large warehouse was north west of Atlanta, where L.R. Gomez had worked for over thirty-five years building a variety of worldwide illegal operations.

Clay and Alma were working at a long table next to the railing because their boss was yelling so loudly in his closed office they could not hear each other speaking. The yelling became louder. They turned and looked through the glassed office as an angry L.R. burst out of his private office. Clay and Alma moved farther back on the second floor balcony as L.R.'s two bodyguards stood to follow him. Both of the bodyguards stood almost a foot higher than L.R. but he was just as tough.

L.R. rushed out of the main office cursing, "Nobody steals from me, do you hear me?" Everyone in the warehouse stopped in their tracks to respond one by one, "Yes, Boss!"

L.R. made a beeline toward the steep stairs of the warehouse exit while his bodyguards, Face and Tiny, followed closely on his heels. An unknowing José Ramos rushed by Clay and Alma, and turned directly into the path of L.R., "Boss, no matter who I talk to, they all tell me that the trucks carrying the cargo from Savannah will be late." Without any warning L.R. erupted like a volcano. Using all his strength he grabbed José and hoisted him over the railing. He fell onto the concrete floor below, breaking his neck. He was dead on impact.

3

WEDNESDAY, MAY 7, 1997 - EVENING

Thirty-six hours earlier

Patrick Rafael Cordero, Senior Account Manager at a large investment firm, was clearing his desk and planning for his future millions. He glanced one last time through a list of his investors. Patrick's profits and experience had earned him some very important and high profile investors. Patience, professional good looks and timing had been his keys to success in Florida and they would be again, but this time without the mistakes that had driven him north.

Earlier he had visited the bank and collected the money. He had put the duffle bag of money in his car trunk for his payment to Clay. The night before, he had completed all the details of transferring the money from his largest and newest investor, Learco Raul Gomez, who had written that he preferred to be called L.R. He had never spoken to L.R. since he was a new addition to his client list, making him the easiest client to steal from. But now it was time to meet Clay at the bar and grill.

Patrick arrived and saw Clay waving him over. As he weaved through the crowd he tried to reassure himself as he thought about the stolen funds. *The stolen money in my trunk will be re-deposited into L.R.'s accounts once the money begins coming in from the girls I will manage.*

Clay was Patrick's contact to set up his new pimping business in human trafficking. Clay and Patrick had come together earlier and

5

it was at that meeting Patrick had committed to another illegal plan to gain a great deal of quick money. He had stolen money from one of his investors and was about to put it into the lucrative business of sex trafficking.

Patrick walked up to the booth and asked Clay, "How long have you been here?"

"Just long enough to finish my beer. Order what you want, it's on me tonight."

Patrick ordered a scotch on the rocks and they just sat looking around at the crowd, until the waiter returned.

Patrick thanked the waiter and took a sip of his drink.

"Do you have the money?"

"Yes. It's in my car trunk ready to move over to your car. This means we are ready to get started, right?"

"No, not yet, but things are shaping up. Listen, Patrick, I'm not tending to your business, but do you want to be so exposed by using the bank where the money can be tracked?"

"It's OK. I've set up ghost accounts before and no one will be able to track the money flow. This is not the first time that I've done something like this. So don't worry about me."

"Great, because I work for someone that doesn't tolerate mistakes. Just remember that going forward. So getting back to the next step, my boss wants to go over a few things with you. What about Friday night at dinner -- the boss's treat?"

"Wow, sure thing. Tell me where and what time and I'll not be late."

"I'll have to let you know later, OK? I'll call your mobile phone and leave you the information."

The waiter came over to take their order. They ordered a second round of drinks.

"Look Patrick, my boss is very intimidating so just answer his questions with short answers and keep your mouth shut. Do you understand?"

Their drinks arrived and Patrick took a swallow. "I understand, Clay, I've worked with these kinds of people before."

"Good." Clay finished his beer and stood up. "Sorry Patrick, I've got another meeting, so let's go and swap out your package." Clay paid the server enough for whatever Patrick could order as well as a nice tip. Patrick told the server he would be right back. He led Clay to his car, took out the duffle bag full of the stolen money and handed it to him. Then Clay said, "See you Friday night."

As Patrick watched him disappear in the shadows he thought, *I'm going to make so much money. I'll be able to help out my sister and niece. They've really had to struggle and some of this money would help them out.*

He then turned, went back to the grill, walked to his booth, and finished his drink. Then he ordered his meal to go. Once his meal arrived, he went home, ate and went to bed.

As Clay drove home he thought, *What are you doing Clay, hooked up with L.R. and his goons? You are a fool! No money is worth dealing with these kinds of criminals, no money!* Clay shook his head. His boss was one of the oldest, most vile crime bosses in the world, and this guy Patrick was totally clueless about L.R.'s brutality. Patrick was about to be just one more of his latest greedy recruits who would soon manage the fifty or more young girls between twelve and fifteen. Each of these recruits would become pimps, providing sexual activities to their wealthy associates for an extremely high price. They were responsible for the motel accommodations split between them. Each pimp would make about $21,000 per week – an amount well over whatever they were making in their white-collar day jobs. And since it was all in cash, there was no paper trail to report to the IRS. This juicy income completely overcame the fear of being caught.

THURSDAY, MAY 8, 1997

While on lunch break, Liliana Cordero Phillips hurried to pick up her thirteen year old daughter, Mai, at school. The school nurse had called her saying Mai had a fever and needed to go home. As she drove through Atlanta's midtown, Liliana argued with herself about her career change. For the last couple of semesters Liliana had been attending night classes in counseling. She was torn between giving Mai the mother-daughter relationship that she needed and deserved, or committing the time to take required night courses to further her career. It seemed like there was no way to balance the two.

She drove up to the front of Mai's middle school where she was waiting.

"Mom I'm so sorry you had to come and pick me up!"

Liliana quickly replied, "Mai, it was no problem at all. I love you and I'm just so sorry you are not feeling well. Do you want me to stay with you the rest of the day?"

"No mom, I'll be OK once I can go to sleep. You need to get back to work and you've got class tonight. Don't worry, OK?"

"Mai, you are so strong and forgiving. Thank you for understanding so many things." Liliana reached over and squeezed her daughter's hand. "You are wise beyond your years."

Liliana did not often show her emotions to her daughter – maybe today she was just too tired to hold everything in as she usually did. Mai's father had been the one to say tender and encouraging words to their daughter. It was his way, but not hers. She glanced over at her daughter, thinking about how she was so much like her father. Mai was tall like her father but looked more like Liliana's mother and brother. She had long, golden red hair and blue eyes the color of her Irish grandmother's. Her skin was pale, and she was clearly a beautiful girl. Liliana almost chuckled. Mai had definitely not inherited Liliana's short, full figured frame, or her dark brown eyes and oval face that marked her as half Cuban. But she did have one of her mom's characteristics: a strong and self-confident temperament.

They both were silent for the rest of the ride home. Liliana made sure Mai took some medicine and was as comfortable as she could be, with a fever over 100 degrees. Then she kissed her daughter goodbye and drove back to work.

Del Thomas was originally from Wales, with the blue eyes, ivory skin and dark hair common among the Welsh people. Her boyfriend Will said she stood out in a crowd like a shooting star. Del sat and ate her lunch, reflecting about Will Evans and all the memorable times that they had spent together during the past several months. When he had come back to Atlanta, it had been the first time she had seen him since middle school. Her family had moved from England right before the beginning of that first year of middle school and even as a young teenager, Del had been attracted to Will. A year later, his father was transferred to California and so Will moved with his family to Los Angeles.

Several years later, Del had completed college and finished her Master's degree, and had returned to Atlanta to work in social services, counseling people who did not even want to meet with her. She had always wanted to make a difference professionally, to really help people. Unfortunately, her social services position had not provided many opportunities to see changes in the lives of her clients. During the court-assigned meetings, she felt that she was just another box checked off on her clients' "not go to jail" checklist when they left her office. In most cases she felt ineffective and useless.

Soon she began as a part time consultant at the Atlanta Police

Department. It was while she was consulting with the APD during the previous fall that she had reconnected with Will, a private investigator. Will's younger sister, Elizabeth, had been sexually assaulted and severely beaten, and this terrible crime had brought him back to Atlanta from Los Angeles. He had gained many years of law enforcement experience with the LAPD. Del was thrilled that she and Will had been reunited – one of the few bright spots that happened during Elizabeth's serial rapist case with the APD.

Del felt an increasing attraction to Will as she watched his steady commitment to solving the case that had affected his sister in such a way. Del had known that she was falling in love with Will as they worked together on the case, but reservations tugged at her heart. Her faith was a driving force in her life, but Del had questions about Will's relationship with God. She also had to admit that while they worked on the case, he had not seemed very interested in her. Although Del understood that his attention was rightfully directed toward apprehending his sister's attacker, she wondered if there was a possibility for a future relationship. When the rapist had been arrested and Will was less distracted, the two began spending significant time together, and after a while, Will had become very clear about his growing feelings for her.

Del knew that she had fallen in love with Will, yet her love for her Lord was very important. *When I start to commit emotionally to him, doubts tug at my spirit and I continue to question his spiritual condition. There is no indication that he has any opposition to God, but does he really know what he believes? Would we be committed to the same priorities in life? Seeing Will struggle through his sister's case last fall and then spending so much time dating him has shown me so many of his exceptional qualities. I've known I loved him since we were schoolmates over twenty years ago. I just need to trust God that He knows both of our hearts.* Del knew God would show her the answer in time and patience would be her friend.

Later that day, Del finished her class homework between appointments. She was taking classes for a graduate degree in counseling. But before she could start her graduate classes, she had to fulfill the Atlanta University's prerequisite undergraduate classes that had not been required for her psychology degree.

As she walked to class, she looked up into the Atlanta sky to see if she could still see the Comet Hale-Bopp. It had been one of the brightest comets seen in a long time and she had been enjoying it many evenings as she walked to class since January. No, she could not see it anymore, but she would remember it with affection because Will had pointed it out to her.

After work, Patrick went back to the bar he had gone to the previous evening. He sat at the bar and ordered a scotch on the rocks, followed by another drink and then another. For whatever reason, Clay's warnings brought back thoughts of the lowlifes he had known from the Florida massage parlors. This unnerved him. He ordered a burger and fries. By the time he left the bar he was feeling no pain.

Liliana waited for Del after their Thursday night counseling class. After they greeted each other she told Del that she was sorry she had missed her calls. She told her that her daughter was sick, but other than that, everything was fine. They visited for few minutes and set up a study time for next Thursday's exam. Liliana thanked Del for being concerned about her and they both left.

FRIDAY, MAY 9, 1997

Patrick's boss, Jason Hill, had been to his desk several times that morning to ask him about the withdrawals from the investment accounts of his new elite investor. This was the first platinum investor assigned to Patrick and now his boss was regretting his decision. Each week a report was generated for the investors' activities. L.R. Gomez had withdrawn an unusually large sum of money from each of his accounts. The sum of the withdrawals was over the limit of his restricted withdrawal amount. Jason's weekly report flagged it. He had to get some kind of explanation from Patrick. Before leaving Patrick's desk, he wrote him a note to come see him about the Gomez accounts. Since Jason could not find Patrick, he decided to call Mr. Gomez to confirm the withdrawals.

After returning to his office, Jason called Mr. Gomez's work number, and he left his name and company name, as well as a message asking him to please return his call. A few minutes passed and Jason's phone rang. It was Mr. Gomez.

Jason explained the situation to him but before he could confirm the withdrawals, Mr. Gomez cut him off with swears and threats. Jason tried to reassure him that the company would resolve the error but Gomez only wanted the name of the person who was responsible for his accounts. Jason tried to reassure Mr. Gomez that the company would replace the withdrawn money but Gomez hung up on him with another threat. By law, Jason could not reveal Patrick's identity, but he needed to cover himself in case the situation escalated. He called the VP of Investment Security and gave the details of how Gomez had responded to this call.

Patrick rode the elevator with his eyes closed, trying to control the nausea from his over drinking the evening before. He was an hour late and knew he would have to see his boss about making up the time. When he saw his boss's message on his desk, he grabbed a couple of files and a few personal items, pushed them into his briefcase and then walked back to the elevator, taking the opposite path from the one that led to his boss's office. He made it to the elevator without being noticed and out of the building without seeing anyone following him.

He left the parking garage by the back exit. He had to get hold of Clay before his boss called the police. He had to try and stop the process of this new business so that he could return the investor's money. Clay did not answer so he left a message that this deal had taken a terrible turn and the money must be returned to him immediately. He would not be meeting them for dinner that evening. Patrick knew he could not go to his apartment so he headed to his sister's place. He could kick himself for being so short-sighted. Patrick could not believe that the money had been flagged by his boss. He had to find Clay!

During Liliana's lunch break she called Mai to see how she felt. That morning Mai had argued to return to school even though she still had a fever. Liliana had always been so proud of Mai's commitment to her attendance and studies. Her dedication so far had been rewarded with a grade point average of 4.0. When Liliana had awakened Mai, she could tell that she was feeling better and that her fever had broken. There was no class that night so she would treat Mai to a home cooked meal with her favorite dishes.

Clay had picked up the phone message from Patrick and as he walked into the warehouse off Howell Mill Road inside I-75, he looked up to where L.R.'s office was located. He had to let L.R. know that dinner would have to be re-scheduled. He he was halfway up the metal stairs against the wall when he saw Alma waving at him. As soon as Clay heard L.R. yelling in his office, he knew that they would be working out on the balcony that morning.

Alma Hernandez was one of the few employees who had worked for over ten years for L.R. She was of Cuban ancestry, plain, tall with reddish brown, curly hair pulled back into a bun. Alma was the glue that held the Atlanta warehouse together. Clay sometimes wondered why a smart woman like her was working for L.R.

They had just begun going over the numbers when it had all happened. When L.R. had burst out of the office, they had picked up their papers and moved back into the shadows on the second level. Then they both watched with horror as those terrible events took place leaving José Ramos dead. Clay could hear Alma crying softly and then he heard L.R. call out his name. He stepped forward, moving slowly to where L.R. was standing.

L.R. screamed out again as he walked away from the railing. Then he saw Clay walking toward him. Clay quickly glanced over the rail at José's dead body, as L.R. shouted, "Nobody steals from me and lives to tell anyone! Clay, clean this mess up and cancel that dinner meeting tonight." L.R. and his bodyguards went down the stairs and left the building, as Clay and Alma just stared at each other.

The warehouse normally could be extremely noisy but, as Clay asked someone to help him carry José's body out to the company pickup truck in back of the warehouse, it was completely silent. There were only a few tearful remarks or whimpers from José's closest friends.

As Clay started to descend the stairs his eyes focused on Alma still standing in the shadows. He tried to mouth that he was sorry to Alma. But Clay was not sure she saw him. Then he remembered that he had seen Jose and Alma several times holding hands when they must have thought they were alone. L.R. did not tolerate dating in the workplace. The guy helping him with José's body almost dropped him but Clay caught and steadied them both. When he looked up to spot Alma again she had gone.

Mai had called a classmate to get her assignments the night before. She did not want to fall behind in her classwork. She wanted to keep her high grade point average from dropping. As Mai finished up her homework she could smell the wonderful aroma flooding her room from the kitchen. Her stomach growled with anticipation of her favorite dishes being prepared by her mom. She missed the home cooking each night but more than the cooking, she missed her mom.

Mai thanked her over and over for the delicious dinner Liliana had prepared for her. The meal included pot roast with carrots, onions, and potatoes -- her favorite. They had both enjoyed the evening of eating together and catching up with each other's activities. Mai had not expressed her feelings out loud about Liliana's demanding evening schedule, but Liliana could see in her eyes that Mai was lonely.

Once again Liliana felt guilty for the time spent at school instead of with her daughter. But she knew at her present job she could not save the money she would need for Mai's college years. Mai would understand when she was older; at least this was what Liliana told herself.

Driving José's body to the river, Clay drifted back to the first time he had met his boss, L.R. Gomez. Someone had told him the L was for Learco which means "Judge of his village" and the R was for Raul which means "Wolf Counselor" and Clay found he was as intimidating as the meaning of his name. L.R. was a distinguished man with a stocky build and thick, curly silver hair, standing just under five feet five inches. His powerful, piercing eyes cut straight through Clay as L.R. gripped his hand like a vice. Clay had never before met anyone who immediately instilled fear and projected spellbinding evil. Once again Clay was definitely doubting this new business decision.

Clay had known José Ramos for some time. José was a really nice guy who had worked for L.R. for several years. Before José started working for L.R., Clay had worked with him on several enormous Dunwoody mansion burglary jobs, where they had walked away with some valuable goods. Although the money was great, these kinds of break-ins were becoming more difficult as a result of the new high tech security systems. These security systems had affected his number of jobs as a full time thief. These declines left him broke. So he had called in some favors and now he was only a thief part time. For the last several months his full time job was working as the middleman for L.R. He had been recruiting new corporate white-collar executives. They were recruited to manage and streamline the trafficking of underage girls. But now José was dead and for what? Clay's thoughts were interrupted by his truck falling into a huge pothole on the rough terrain. The death of José from L.R.'s rage sickened Clay. José had been an OK guy and now he was dead. Clay found a fairly secluded area to pitch his body into the Chattahoochee River. Clay was careful to wear gloves and old clothes he had retrieved from his car.

Once Clay was back on the road he stopped into the closest bar to get a beer and to sit quietly so he could try and get a hold of himself. Clay had been dealing in crime a long time but he had never witnessed a murder, and he had never been told to dump the body. The waiter served him the beer, interrupting his train of thoughts. Clay asked the waiter for another beer and before he could return Clay had finished the first one.

As Clay finished the second beer, stood, and paid the cashier with cash, he decided that this killing had been the last straw. He must find a way out of this job and he must tell Alma that he was so sorry for her loss and for not helping José. His nerves were still going crazy even after the beers. He thought it would be a good idea over the weekend to find some easy burglary jobs so he could put some extra cash away in case he had to leave town.

While Del drove to meet Will, she began to think about the steps that had led to her consulting job at APD and seeing Will again. Her parents Brian and Carys still had siblings back in Wales, but they did not see them as much as they would have liked. Del missed the extended family but she liked her parents living in Atlanta. She seemed as if she would have a wide circle of friends but in reality she only had her church, Liliana and her sweet Will. After graduating she learned that her university had just added a certificate in Criminal Justice/Forensics, and it was no coincidence that she sensed God directing her to add this to her graduate degree in Psychology. When she had applied for a consulting position with the Atlanta Police Department, their personnel assistant had told her that the certificate had given her the edge she needed to beat out her competition for the APD consulting job. APD Sex Crimes Detective, Victor Jones, had also put in a good word. Victor and his wife Amy had been friends since childhood. They were the main reason she had returned to Atlanta after graduate school. She wished she could see them more often, but Victor's job made his free time unpredictable, and Amy's job as a science teacher took up many evenings and weekends with planning and grading papers.

Del arrived at her favorite restaurant across from Lenox Mall and saw Will waiting in the area by the bar, watching the baseball game on their television. She paused at the door and thought, *Just look at him. He is great looking --- that muscular build, those blue eyes and blond hair. What else could I want? Why do I struggle so? Just get to know him and stop over thinking the 'what ifs.' Believe God and enjoy your time with him!* Then Will saw Del standing at the entrance. He walked over and gave her a quick hug.

"Sorry to keep you waiting."

"No problem. I was watching the Braves game. How was your day?"

But before Del could answer the hostess called Will's name to be seated. As they followed her to the table, Del thought, *I just need to trust God and focus on getting to know Will better, and I'm going to start right now!*

L.R. had reached out to every one of his contacts but none of them had the connections to find out who had stolen his money. This was extremely frustrating for someone who had always been able to find his man and destroy him. He was not worried because time had taught him well. There would always be someone he could persuade; either through money or bodily harm, L.R. will find this thief.

Clay sat in his dark apartment willing himself to forget the complete horror on Alma's face as he turned to walk down stairs, to pick up José's body and carry him out, and the awful sound of José's body hitting the water. But no matter what he did the sound continued to echo and Alma's sorrowful eyes pierced him again and again. Then Clay reached out and turned the lamp on, opened up the table drawer, and took out a Bible. Many years ago this book had changed his life but then he had walked away from all that it taught. Once again he opened the Bible to verses that had always meant a great deal to him. Clay read out loud the words of King David who had ordered the killing of one of his soldiers because the King wanted the soldier's wife:

"¹Have mercy on me, O God, according to your unfailing love; according to your great compassion blot out my transgressions. ²Wash away all my iniquity and cleanse me from my sin. ³For I know my transgressions and my sin is always before me. ⁴Against you, you only, have I sinned and done what is evil in your sight, so that you are proved right when you speak and justified when you judge." Psalm 51:1-4 (NIV)

Clay closed his eyes and prayed, *Oh God, it has been a long time since I read your words and I'm sorry for that. Please forgive me for what I did to José's body today. I was afraid of L.R. and what he would have done to me if I had refused. Please help me to know what I should do about working for this evil man. Thanks for listening and for always being a part of my life even when I'm not living out the plan you have for me.* When Clay opened his eyes he began to feel a peace that he had forgotten that he had had so long ago. The sorrow from his intense day was replaced with powerful feelings of God's love. Yes, this was the love he remembered from God, way back in high school. But it had been a long time. Clay shook his head, thinking of all the evil he had done. God had forgiven King David, but that king was a pretty special guy. Clay was just . . . he shook his head again. He could feel the love of God, but he could not shake the feeling that he was not worthy of it. But if he remembered what his old youth leader had said, that was not a problem for God. He took a deep breath and opened the Bible again.

Patrick decided not to approach his sister, especially after listening to the message from Clay. He sounded very upset and had emphatically told him there was no way that any of that money could be returned. At least the dinner had been called off.

Patrick found a cheap motel not far from his sister's neighborhood in Grant Park. He knew what a terrible situation he was in as he sat in the dimly lit motel room. He unconsciously pushed his fingers through his hair as if some knowledge could be triggered about what he should do next. All of this was just too similar to what had happened in Florida. This knowledge only depressed him more as he left his room to find a liquor store.

SATURDAY, MAY 10, 1997

Alma sat at her kitchen table reading the Atlanta Saturday newspaper. She was crying as she searched each page for any information on her lover and friend, José Ramos. For the past couple of months he would bring coffee and the newspaper each Saturday morning. They would drink their coffee and read the paper at this same table. She finally submitted to the waves of grief allowing her head to drop into her cupped hands. Even though she had seen that vile man throw José to his death, she just could not believe he was dead.

After the intense grief lifted somewhat, she began to think about her life working for L.R. She had been a young illegal immigrant from Cuba when L.R. had found her in Miami and hired her. He had given her legal documents and had paid her to look the other way at whatever he was doing. But José's murder had changed everything. Her loyalty had ended with José's life. She had always known L.R. was evil, but it had been too easy just to take his money and not think about that part of it. Those days were gone. She had worked in his office long enough to know his one weakness: his most precious keepsake, his mother's brooch. He kept it in his office where he could look at it every day.

L.R. had another little secret that Alma knew – he was wanted in England for murder. L.R. had been able to bribe the cops here in Atlanta, but it had been a different story in England – he had barely escaped with his life ten years ago. She just needed to get him to England . . . and the brooch would make the perfect bait.

Alma smiled. The plan could work – she just needed to keep cool for the next couple of days. There were still a couple of angles to work on – she didn't have a passport, but if she could hitch a ride on one of L.R.'s ships, that would be even better. But L.R. seemed to have an evil sixth sense and so her plan must include patience, time, and discipline as well as be executed perfectly.

She had to bury her emotions for José for now. There were many steps to perfect as she went about her duties at L.R.'s office. She thought, *Once I steal the brooch, I'll tell him I'm in England where he was almost captured. It's the only possession that he has any emotional attachment to. He'll have no choice but to follow me!*

Clay had left several messages on Patrick's mobile phone. It was really unusual for him not to return his calls. This was not a good sign but he would have to wait for him to call before these feelings of alarm could be confirmed. Clay would continue running his Saturday errands and just wait.

Patrick was awakened by housekeeping at eleven. He was very hung over and pleaded with the lady to allow him to take a quick shower. She said she would clean the next room but he had to be out by the time she was finished. Patrick thanked her and quickly showered, dressed and checked out before she returned.

He found a fast food restaurant to sit, drink coffee, and figure out his next step.

L.R. had given Face and Tiny the weekend to find out the location and the identity of the investment company's executive who had stolen his money. They knew if they did not have the name by Monday L.R. would kill them like José. L.R. had given them his boss's name, Jason Hill. They would start the search with him.

Liliana took most of her Saturday to study for her final exam the following Thursday. She wanted to be prepared when she would meet with Del on Monday evening. Del was really smart and Liliana wanted to be able to keep up with her. She was also enjoying having a friend she could talk to, about pretty much anything. Liliana didn't have much in common with anyone at work, and nobody seemed to care about her there. Most people in her apartment building just wanted to keep to themselves after work, watch TV or whatever. Liliana hadn't realized how lonely she had been until she had begun the friendship with Del.

Liliana sighed. She had so much to do, but she had promised Mai to take a break so they could go out and do some shopping. She was about to clear her things off the table when there was a knock on the door.

She walked over to the door and looked through the peephole. She could not believe her eyes, it was Patrick, the brother who never showed up unless he needed something. She opened the door and just stood there, taking in his wrinkled clothes and unshaven face.

"Aren't you going to let me in, Liliana?"

"What do you want, Patrick?"

"Let me in and I'll tell you. Please I can't be seen!" So Liliana stepped back out of the way, allowing him to enter.

"Do you want something to drink?"

"Do you have a beer?"

"No just water or a soda."

"I would like some water."

As Liliana went into the kitchen to get Patrick's water, Mai came into the living room and said, "Uncle Patrick, I thought I heard you." Mai went over and hugged him. As Liliana walked back from the kitchen, she was struck by how much alike they both looked – and definitely from the Irish side of the family. Liliana gave him the water and asked Mai if she could give them a few minutes alone. Mai would know that something was wrong – Patrick only showed up when he needed something. He was always getting into trouble and asking her to bail him out, but Mai did not need to know all the details. This was just like when he moved to Atlanta from Florida and stayed with them until he found a job. Mai did not know what he had been running from in Florida, and Liliana thought it better not to tell her. She waited until Mai had walked back to her room before she asked him what he wanted, this time.

Del had really laughed and enjoyed her time with Will the evening before. He had been so sweet when he insisted on going with her to the car. She had parked on the street beside the restaurant. Now she reached over and took her Bible from her bedside table and opened it to one of her favorite verses.

"[11]For I know the plans that I have for you, declares the Lord, plans for welfare and not for calamity to give you a future and a hope. [12]Then you will call upon Me and come and pray to Me, and I will listen to you. [13]And you will seek Me and find Me, when you search for Me with all your heart." Jeremiah 29:11-13 (NASB)

Del closed her Bible and bowed her head to talk with the God who just promised her that He had a plan for her, "Lord God, thank You that You have a plan for my life! I so appreciate You writing it down so I can read your promise to me over and over, so I won't forget. You see I struggle so with trusting You. I'll believe You for the big picture. But when I think about Will and his spiritual condition, I totally lose sight that Your plan also includes Will's spiritual condition. Please forgive my lack of faith in Your total plan for me and for Will. I love You Lord Jesus and I thank You for bringing me to the cross and forgiving me for my sins. Amen." Del took in a deep breath, opened her eyes, and grinned. Then she climbed out of bed to shower and to start cleaning up her apartment.

Tiny and Face had found the home of Mr. Hill. All they had to do now was to follow him around until they could beat the information out of him. Then they could call L.R. with the name and they could actually make their regular Saturday night poker game. But too bad for Mr. Hill, L.R. said he should not remember their encounter.

Mai heard the front door close and then her mom ask if she was ready to leave.

"Mom, what did Uncle Patrick want?"

"The same as what he always wants, money."

"Why is he always getting into trouble?"

"I don't know, Mai. I get so mad at him and yet, I also feel really sorry for him. All he can think about is getting rich. He doesn't want to take the time to earn money slowly, like everyone else. He just wants more and more, faster and faster, and you know that only leads to trouble. He is his own worst enemy and because he has no one else -- I gave him the money he wanted. He seemed really scared this time, even more than before. But he wouldn't tell me what was happening. Mai, we just need to pray for him."

Mai nodded. "I will, but are we still going shopping?"

Liliana laughed. "Yes, we still have shopping money. And enough to eat out. Close the windows and the blinds and we'll be ready to go. After we get back we can study the rest of the weekend."

Patrick looked in every direction before darting to his car. He had decided to get out of town. He knew of an inexpensive place north of Atlanta near Lake Lanier. He had received a couple of messages from Clay, but he was not going to call him until he was somewhere safe.

Will drove over to Del's apartment, after he finished running and working out at the gym, to eat lunch at her place. Del let Will in and told him she would be right back. She had left the water running in the kitchen. Del had prepared a couple of turkey deli sandwiches and drinks – diet soda for her and beer for Will. When they sat down at the kitchen table, Del bowed her head and Will said, "Del, I'll bless the food with a short prayer if you would like?" Dell nodded her head in approval.

"Lord, thank you for this food and for the good time we had last night. Amen."

When Will looked up, Del had a big smile and her eyes were glistening.

"What's wrong, did I do something wrong?"

"Oh no, Will. It was perfect." She looked as if she was going to say something else, but just started eating.

"What's on your mind, Del? Whenever you try not to say anything, it lets me know that you really need to talk about something."

Del did not know whether to go ahead and talk to Will about his spiritual condition since she had just given God everything about it, even her confusion about waiting. So she prayed, *Lord Jesus is this You showing me that this is the time and all I need to do is just talk it through with Will? I know he loves me as much as I love him but I'm not comfortable telling him with the concerns I have. Please guide me ...*

"OK, Will. I've been praying about the right time to talk with you about something really important to me. Since you're asking do you think this would be a good time to discuss it?"

"Sure, I always think it's the right time to talk about anything with you. I think we have talked a lot during the past few months and you know I'm open to hear whatever is on your mind."

Del's anxious spirit relaxed after hearing Will's positive response to her needing to talk something through with him. "Will, you know how much you mean to me and how my heart is little by little opening up to you, but I've been concerned about something, and so here goes.

"We've talked about our faith in God many times. I want you to know how much I respect you and trust your judgment. I also understand your limited knowledge of God because your parents never took you to church while growing up. I also believe that when Elizabeth started her relationship with God, that had an impact on you. Forgive my ramblings. I believe an intimate relationship between a man and a woman should be grounded in a common belief in Jesus. So this is my concern that you are still thinking through what you believe. In no way do I want to put pressure on your spiritual journey…" Will interrupted her.

"Del, I want to put you at ease about my belief in God. You are right about how much I've learned about Jesus from Elizabeth. But I've also learned a great deal from you, and from reading the Bible that Elizabeth gave me. I, too, believe that a couple should have common beliefs. Del, I'm not sure about everything I believe, I'm not at odds with your beliefs in Jesus. In fact I'm sure that what you and Elizabeth believe is correct. I just need more time to work everything through about my faith. When you grow up with absolutely no awareness of God as a part of your life, it's very strange to include God in how you think things through. Does that make sense? For Elizabeth it had to be a natural flow for her to turn to God after her sexual assault. But for me, it's awkward to trust someone other than myself. Reading about the struggles of the men who followed Jesus has helped me understand more. Del, I've been touched deeply by all I've seen and learned about the Christian walk. Please know that God is working in my life. It's just taking me a while to understand." He leaned back in his chair, but then jumped up and put his arms around her when she began to cry. "Are you all right? I'm sorry if I said anything to upset you!"

Del shook her head. "It's just tears of joy!" She hugged him back. "Thank you so much for trusting me with your truthfulness and encouraging words about your spiritual journey. I can't tell you how much it means to me and how it puts my spirit at peace."

Del silently thanked Jesus for answering her prayers, replacing her fears and anxieties with a sense of confidence about their relationship. They finished eating what was left of their lunch and Will turned on the Braves game. They sat on the couch, Del leaning against his chest as he put his arm around her, and they both smiled.

Face and Tiny were not having a great deal of luck. Jason Hill was a real family man and he had not left the house the whole time they had been watching. They were beginning to doubt if they would make their poker game.

Clay had just spent most of his day trying to re-establish contact with his informants he used to pay to tell him which houses were worth stealing from. If he was to return to his old profession of thievery, he would need each of his old informants.

Clay had not eaten all day, and suddenly realized he was hungry. Eating did not occur to him when he was out doing errands. He threw on some old grubby clothes and went out to get a well-earned meal. As he drove away from his apartment, he wondered once again why Patrick had not returned his phone calls. Something definitely must be up. But he was much too hungry to try to call again.

Will had some work to do and Del needed to study for her Thursday's exam. So when the Braves game was over, Del walked him to her front door and opened it. Will turned, looked into Del's blue eyes, leaned down and kissed her lips with tenderness. He pulled back and said, "Del, don't worry about God and me. He's got that and our relationship covered. OK?" Del smiled and hugged him tight before closing the door. Will turned and whistled the rest of the way to his car - something he had done since a kid when things were going extremely well.

He had not felt this good in years – not since his wife had still been alive. Her death had hit him hard – she had been murdered by some lowlife druggie needing a fix. He had not dated a woman since then, and had never felt attracted to anyone, until he had come back to Atlanta and found Del again. Her smile, the warmth of her touch – he had needed this, and he had found it all in Del.

Finally about nine o'clock Mr. Hill dove out of his driveway alone. Face and Tiny followed at a reasonable distance. He pulled into a dimly lit parking lot and went into the liquor store. The two men looked around and then walked over to shadows near Mr. Hill's car. When he walked around the corner he did not even know what grabbed him. Face had a vise grip around Hill's neck and pressed him up against the store wall as Tiny grabbed the bag of booze.

As Face tightened his grip, Tiny asked, "Who worked the investments of L.R. Gomez? Choose your words carefully because they may be your last."

"His name is Patrick Cordero." Face loosened his grip and Tiny hit him hard in his stomach. As Hill's knees buckled under him, Face hit him on the side of his head with a billy club and pushed him into the wall. They took a quick look around them – no witnesses. They quickly got back into their car and pulled out of the parking lot.

"Well, Face, that only took a couple of minutes and we got some free booze as well. Maybe we can make the poker game after all. But you should call L.R. now, so we don't have to keep looking over our shoulders." They put their call through and drove over to the bar where they had the Saturday night poker game in the back.

SUNDAY, MAY 11, 1997

Patrick woke up abruptly, throwing the sheets off of him and jumping to his feet. He did not recognize his surroundings. Then he remembered that he had driven up to Lake Lanier the night before and this was the room he had rented. Patrick was amazed that it was Sunday already. The past few days had been very difficult and he could not believe that he was in trouble once again.

Clay had visited his gym earlier that Sunday than he normally did. He wanted to lift and run even more than before if he was to get in better shape to steal from the bigger homes. On the way back to his apartment he once again left another message on Patrick's mobile. Clay was genuinely worried about Patrick.

L.R. sat at home in a drunken stupor that year's Mother's Day. He had been drinking through the night and yet he still was not drunk enough to escape his emotions. No matter how many years went by, Mother's Day was heart breaking for him. His mother's love was the only good emotion he could remember. When he was four she had died suddenly. The pain of his grief was over-whelming and he never wanted to feel that again. So he buried the love he had felt from his mother deep down and chose instead to focus on the hatred from every one of his father's beatings. L.R. did not have any proof that his father murdered his mother, only his father's boasts, but his suspicions fed his anger and revulsion for his father until he died. He had learned from his father the Gomez legacy to command with fear, cruelty and intimidation. Then he took one last big swallow of liquor which finally brought him what he had wanted; L.R. passed out.

Del had enjoyed her time at church earlier in the day. She had asked some of her friends to pray for her time with Will later that day. They had spent a lovely evening together last night, and he would be coming over that afternoon. When he arrived, they realized how tired they both were. Will took the couch, falling asleep immediately. She gazed at Will sleeping so soundly on her couch. How was she ever going to open her heart to him? Sometimes she wished she had not spent her childhood in Wales where generally the people do not open up easily. She really wanted to experience the joy and love she felt more openly with Will. Maybe she would share these cultural conflicts with him soon. But now she had to study.

MONDAY, MAY 12, 1997

Alma arrived at the warehouse office very early. She wanted to get in the office to make some calls to Miami. There were a couple of people still working in that office she could trust. They would book the passage on the freighter leaving New York this coming weekend for her. She knew they were very smart because she had seen them do things like this when she had worked in Miami. They would book passage for her in a way that it would not come back to any of them. Alma had also met some of the men from the freighters when they came into the office but most of them were gone. Once she was in the Atlanta office she only saw a few of those men when she would be there working on a special project for L.R. Her plan to revenge José's death began to take shape.

Del was as delighted as she could possibly be. The time spent with Will over the weekend had been so much fun and revealing. She still had many concerns but she had left them with God. He would help her get to know Will and leave Will's future with God. She got up and took a shower. She put all her class materials that she would need for that night's studying with Liliana into her car. Then she drove out to face her half an hour morning commute to work.

Tiny and Face had been staking out Patrick's apartment since yesterday. There had been no sign of him the whole time. When the sun came up and still no Patrick, Face said, "We need to check in

33

with L.R. and he will tell us what to do now. This guy has left town or something. He's not going to come back here."

"Yeah, OK, let's call L.R. ..."

Patrick had finally talked to Clay the night before but he did not tell him much. He just lied and told Clay something had come up and he would be out of town for a couple of days. Patrick took another swallow of coffee and turned another page of the newspaper. He had been sitting at the same booth in one of the few restaurants in town all morning. The money that Liliana had given him was running out and he still did not know what his next move should be. Maybe he should confide in his sister.

The VP of the investment firm had called a meeting with all of Jason's team. Jason's wife had called him earlier that morning to inform him that Jason Hill had been violently attacked late Saturday and had not regained consciousness. He had asked her if the police had been notified and she told him the police were the ones who notified her. He had asked Mrs. Hill for the name of her police contact and his phone number.

The VP calmly told Jason's team about the attack and then introduced the other account manager who would temporarily manage the team until Jason's position could be filled. Once questions had been answered the VP returned to his office and called Mrs. Hill's police contact to tell him what had happened between Jason and Patrick's investor, L.R. Gomez, the previous Friday. He also informed the police officer that Patrick Cordero had not shown up for work that morning and that the investment company would be filing criminal embezzlement charges against Patrick Cordero, once his lawyers had been brought up to speed. The VP had concerns that this investor had been somehow involved with the attack on Jason because he would not reveal Patrick's information.

The officer thanked him for calling and gave him the direct phone number for the lead investigator, Detective Rankin. Then the officer asked if his lawyer could call Detective Rankin, once they were ready to file charges against Patrick Cordero. He agreed and they hung up. Then the VP called his law department and explained everything that had transpired.

L.R. had given Face and Tiny another job to go take care of. For some reason the name Patrick Cordero seemed familiar. He felt like he had known that name in Miami. Then he remembered and picked up the phone.

"Hey Sal, do you remember that guy who worked a few of our massage parlors a few years back, Patrick Cordero? Yeah, that's the guy. Can you find his file and send me any contact information you have on him? Yeah, thanks …"

Del had a message from Liliana waiting for her at work. She called her to confirm their time to meet at their normal place in the university library at seven. Del was glad Liliana had left her this information confirming their time to study for their exam. She was going to miss her interaction with Liliana once their class together would be finished that week.

Clay dropped by the warehouse late that Monday, as he wanted to see if he could find any more details out about L.R.'s plans to meet Patrick. On the way into the warehouse he ran into Face and Tiny. Clay greeted them and Tiny stopped him and said, "Look, Clay, this might not be a good time to talk to L.R."

"Why, is something up?"

"Well, maybe. Face and me found out the guy's name who stole from L.R. last week. But we can't find him. It's like he's totally disappeared and L.R. wasn't happy about that."

"Maybe I can help you guys out. You know I can ask around for you. What is this fool's name?"

Face said, "Tiny, I'm not sure we should say nothing else."

"It's OK, Face. Clay can help us out. His name is Patrick

Cordero. Why don't you ask around and give me a call tomorrow to let me know what you found out."

Clay held his facial expression blank like in a poker game when he had just been dealt a winning hand and said, "Sure Tiny, I'll ask around for you and then get back to you tomorrow." Then he walked to the back of the warehouse and started talking with some of the guys. He quickly looked back over his shoulder at Tiny and Face who were still arguing over if Tiny should have said anything about this guy. But Clay saw Tiny had won him over as they walked out of the warehouse.

Once they left, Clay told the guys he had to take off for an appointment. As soon as he got in his car he called Patrick and told him he had to get back in touch with him as soon as possible. That he had just found something out that was life or death for him.

Clay could not believe that Patrick was the same guy L.R. was after for stealing his money, because Clay had given that same stolen money to L.R. last week to get Patrick set up as a pimp. This was the craziest thing he had ever been involved in and Patrick was in a great deal of trouble. When he set that dinner meeting up last week, Clay could not remember if he had mentioned Patrick's name. Clay's time at the warehouse was also becoming risky and he needed to connect with his informants so he could set up some kind of theft job. If things started falling apart he needed some money to get out of town. This job with L.R. had become too dangerous for him and Patrick.

TUESDAY, MAY 13, 1997

Patrick checked out of the motel early Tuesday as he had spent all the money he had. His only option left after hearing Clay's message about life or death was to come clean with Liliana. He was hoping she would know what to do. He could not call Clay until he had talked through everything with his sister. Patrick would take the scenic route back to Atlanta so he would reach Liliana's after she had arrived home from work.

Sal had called L.R. early that morning with the name and address of Patrick's sister. L.R. gave Face and Tiny the information and a command not to come back until they had him. Tiny and Face found the place as well as a perfect view of the front entrance and the apartment. They had already entered the building and found out the apartment was on the third floor above the front entrance. Since neither of them had ever seen Patrick or his sister, they had to watch to see who went through the front entrance and to see the lights come on and blinds open at that apartment. This was not the first time they had found someone using this exact method.

Patrick's investment company had already filed charges against him for embezzlement and the night before the APD had put out a BOLO (Be On the Look Out) for him.

Del had reached work that morning refreshed from a great night of sleep after studying hard the night before. She needed to discuss something with Will, but first she had to study for her Thursday night exam. She and Liliana had accomplished a great deal for their last class that night. Their last time to study together would be at the library the following night. She would be glad when this class was finished. She did not know when she could squeeze some time into her week to see Will, but she would do it somehow.

Del called Will during her lunch break. They decided to eat a late dinner together after she finished her class. They would meet at the restaurant near Del's apartment because it had serving hours until two o'clock the next morning. Del told Will she would call him once she finished with class and talking to Liliana about the next evening's study times. Then they just talked until Del's lunch hour was over.

Liliana called Mai when she arrived at work early that morning. She told her how sorry she was that the whole week would be dedicated to studying for the Thursday night exam. Mai said she understood that she would not see her much through the week but Liliana could hear the disappointment in her daughter's voice. Liliana promised she would take her daughter to a very special dinner that coming Friday. She told her it was hard for her as well not to spend the amount of time together as she wanted. She asked her to be patient through the process, told her how much she meant to her and then she hung up.

Clay dropped by the warehouse to tell Face and Tiny that he had not been able to find out any information on their thief. Alma told him that L.R. had sent them on an errand earlier that morning. Clay thanked her and then told her how sorry he had been about José. She thanked him and returned to her desk, trying to keep her emotions in check. Clay turned to leave the office and stole a glance at Alma. The pain on her face tore at Clay's heart and he prayed that Jesus would comfort her and forgive him.

When Clay left the office he tried to find out from the guys on the floor if they knew where Face and Tiny had gone, but no one knew. Clay walked out to his car and tried to get in touch with Patrick. He still did not answer and so Clay left another message begging him to call him back as soon as possible.

His phone rang. *This had better be Patrick!* Clay quickly picked it up, but instead of Patrick, it was one of his informants. *Well, if it couldn't be Patrick, at least there might be some action here.* The informant told him about this great mark over by the zoo. Clay got the details and told him if it worked out, he would give him a nice bonus. Clay got on the interstate connector to go check this house out.

Clay got to the zoo, found the street and then drove by the house. He whistled and then spoke out loud, "Well this is not bad and he said the owner of the home was out of town for the whole week. Not a bad neighborhood either, close to the Atlanta Zoo, so there will be people walking around."

One more circle around the house and Clay made his mind up. He mentally started putting a plan together and it needed to be soon. *What about Thursday evening when the zoo was still open? Yeah, Thursday would be a good day for a quick score!*

Clay drove out of the neighborhood and headed to his apartment. He had to work quickly to get everything together by Thursday. The timing could not have been better because he had to get as far away as he could from L.R. Another plus was that the word had gotten out about him getting back into the business. He was once again paying his informants well for any information on homes that would be worth the risk.

The day at the warehouse was almost over and Alma had been successful in hiding her grief over José for the past two days. She had been determined not to seem any different. In fact L.R.'s secretary had commented that she must have had some needed rest the past couple of nights because she was in great spirits. This comment would help her plan at the end of the week and she was very excited. She had used this comment to help set up his secretary to gain access to L.R.'s office to steal his most prized possession - the brooch that belonged to his mother.

Her plan was another step closer to taking shape. Alma knew everything hinged on the timing of the shadow box's removal as well as the timing of L.R. signing for the package containing a note - the shadow box minus the brooch later that week.

She also needed to bribe the company's semi-truck driver with enough money for him to allow her to go with him that weekend. She knew he was taking the company's cargo to the freighter in the New York port. The bribe had to be enough money to overcome the driver's fear of L.R. Her friends she had worked with in Miami had also left a message confirming that she had been booked for passage on this same freighter to England.

Tiny and Face had staked out the sister's apartment building the whole day, but none of the people entering the building went to her apartment. They were discussing who was going for dinner when things started getting interesting.

Mai walked home from the bus stop and arrived home about five. She was getting ready to go in her building when her uncle Patrick joined her at the entrance.

"Hi Mai, I was wondering if I could go up to your apartment with you? I need to talk to your mom."

"Sure, come on in." They climbed the steps and Mai opened the apartment door. Patrick followed her in after taking a quick look down the stairs to make sure no one had followed them. The apartment was hot and stuffy, and Mai went over to the front windows, raised the blinds and opened the windows. As she was turning away from the windows, she saw two really large men point to her and get out of a car from across the street.

"Uncle Patrick, do you know these men?" He hurried over and saw the men entering the building.

"Mai, I've gotten myself into a real mess and I think those guys are here to kill me. I don't have anywhere to go, can you help me hide?"

Mai said nothing but took her uncle's hand, grabbed a key off the wall and led him to the back of the apartment where she opened a door off the hall. She pulled him through the door and quietly shut it. She then turned on the light and motioned for him to follow her. They followed the hall to another door that led to the outside stairs or fire escape.

"Uncle Patrick, see that door at the bottom of the steps? That's where each of the apartments has a storage area. Here's the key, go in and lock the door behind you and don't open it until either mom or I knock on the door. Hurry!" She pushed him forward and quietly closed the door. He scrambled down the stairs and then inside the door she had pointed out. He found the door with their apartment number and put the key in. It opened and he quickly went inside found the light and then locked the door behind him.

Mai was back in the apartment in a flash. She emptied her book bag onto the kitchen table and got a glass of water before she heard a knock on the door. She went to the door slowly while taking deep breaths to settle herself down.

When she got to the door, she asked, "Who's there?"

"We are friends of Patrick Cordero. Could we come in for a minute?"

"I need to call my neighbor to come up as I'm alone. Please be patient and I'll be right back." Mai called her neighbor and waited until she heard her knock on the door. Mai opened the door as her neighbor stepped in front of Face and Tiny, blocking their entrance.

The neighbor, Mrs. Baines, turned toward them, holding a sawed off shotgun. "Can we help you boys?"

They both stepped back and Tiny said, "We know Patrick from work and we needed to get in touch with him about something. Do you know where we can find him?" Mai could see that Face was looking at her and trying to see into the apartment, but Mrs. Baines was such a large woman that he was not having much success. She was starting to raise the barrel of the shotgun, when Mai said she had not seen her uncle this week. Mrs. Baines stepped back and shut the door.

Tiny yelled through the closed door, "Thanks and if you see Patrick tell him we would like to talk to him." They shook their heads and started down the steps swearing loudly all the way to their car. Mai rushed over and closed the blinds. She watched them get into their car and after a short time they drove away.

"Oh, Mrs. Baines, thank you so much for coming up so quickly! I was really scared. But when I saw you had brought your shotgun with you, I knew I was OK."

"Oh, Miss Mai, honey, who were those men? They were only here to make trouble. I've seen those kind before. Do you want to come down and stay with us?"

"No. I saw them leave and I don't know who they are. But I think you are right when you said they are trouble. I'll call my mom once I know her class is over. She'll know what to do. I can't thank you enough, Mrs. Baines!"

"OK and you're sure you don't want to come down and stay with us?"

"You're so kind but I have so much homework, I'd better stay here." Mrs. Baines stared at Mai for a minute and then turned and went out, closing the door behind her.

"Miss Mai, latch the dead bolts and call me if you see them coming back." Mrs. Baines waited until she had heard the dead bolts latch and then went back to her apartment.

Mai would have to wait until it was night and that she was sure those guys were not coming back before she could go down and tell her uncle he could come out.

Del and Liliana were setting up a time to study the following night when Liliana became restless.

"Del, I'm sorry, I just remembered something important and I need to go. I also must stay home with Mai tomorrow so I won't be able to meet with you. I'm sorry but I have to get home and I promise to explain all of this to you later. I'll see you Thursday night."

Before Del could respond, Liliana was briskly walking toward the parking lots. Then Del left to meet Will for dinner. She did find it unusual for Liliana to cancel their study time, but it must have been important.

Patrick was still waiting for someone to come and say the coast was clear. What could be taking them so long? He had looked at his phone several times to call Clay but he did not have very good reception. Just then he heard his sister knocking on the door.

"Patrick it's me. Open the door!" Patrick opened the door and stared into the eyes of his sister. He had seen her like this before -- she was angrier than a hornet. He turned the light off and locked the door.

"I'm sorry Liliana, really sorry."

"I don't want to hear it, Patrick! You came here and put both of us in terrible danger…"

They walked up the fire escape and toward her apartment. Patrick took his phone out and checked for reception. It was good and so Patrick told her he would be right in. She just glared at him and slammed the door behind her.

"Clay, this is Patrick. You're right. I'm in a bad fix. I'm at my sister's and these two thugs almost got me. If it hadn't been for the quick thinking of my niece, I think they would have killed me. What am I going to do Clay, I'm really scared?"

"Look, Patrick, those thugs won't quit hunting you. So this is what you're going to do …"

Del walked out into the cool night air, looked around at the beautiful flowers and allowed herself to see that her love was blossoming just as they were. Then she realized how hungry she was and called Will to let him know she was on her way. She would meet him at the restaurant. He said he was also hungry and he was looking forward to their date.

After Clay told Patrick what to do, he put his phone in his pocket. Patrick then opened the back door and walked carefully into the living area. Liliana was pacing back and forth. Mai was at the kitchen table staring at her homework. Patrick started to speak but Liliana put her hand up and shook her head. Patrick just sat down on the couch and waited for Liliana to cool off.

Tiny and Face had gone to get some dinner. When they came back to the sister's apartment they parked at a different place. Tiny had checked his phone messages and he only had a message from Clay saying he had not found anything out. They ate their dinner in silence, glad that L.R. had not left a message.

After a time, Liliana told Mai to go to bed. She could finish her homework in the morning. Mai hugged her mom, and then Patrick. She turned and went to her room but left the door ajar.

"Look Liliana, I didn't know those guys were after me and I'm sorry I put you and Mai in danger. But I know how you can resolve this. Pick up the phone and tell the cops your brother wants to turn himself in. I'm sure they will come and get me and these thugs that came here will see the cops take me away."

"You want me to call the police? Are you crazy? You'll go to prison!"

"Prison is better that death. Believe me, this is my only way out and it'll get those guys away from you and Mai."

Mai could not believe what she was hearing. But sure enough she heard her mom calling the police. Mai ran down the hall crying and hugged Patrick. "I'm so sorry Uncle Patrick. I thought I helped you today and now the police will come and take you away."

Patrick hugged her back and said, "Look, Mai, I've got to do this and it'll keep you and your mom safe. Here, take my mobile phone. It was paid for by my company, so use it until the service runs out. Put it in a drawer or something until the cops have gone." He hugged her tight and then motioned for her to go back to her room.

"Patrick, I'm really sorry all this is happening. Maybe you are right saying this is your only option but I wish it could have been something other than prison." Liliana then walked over and hugged her brother. Soon there was a hard knock on the front door, "This is the Atlanta Police, please open the door!" Patrick got down on his knees and clasped his hands behind his head as the officers walked toward him with their weapons drawn. They pushed Patrick to the floor, hand cuffed him and read him his Miranda Rights. One of the officers helped Patrick to his feet, pushed him through the door and down the steps. The other officer stayed to question Liliana.

Tiny and Face could not believe their eyes! The air filled with their cursing as they watched the police put Patrick Cordero into their car and drive away. Face started beating the steering wheel as Tiny called L.R. While the phone rang, he looked over at Face and said "He might kill us for this."

Clay arrived home and quickly ate the take-out he had bought. He finished his beer and said out loud, "I'd given anything to see Face and Tiny calling L.R. with the news that the cops just picked up Patrick Cordero." Clay could not stop laughing as he began putting his things together for Thursday.

WEDNESDAY, MAY 14, 1997

Mai was still upset with her mom when she got out of bed Wednesday morning to finish her homework. She felt like her mom could have done something more but maybe she was right to call the police. They had prayed God would work in her uncle's life and maybe this was it. She was just sad that she would not see her uncle for a while but glad she would not be seeing those mean men again. Mom told her that she was not studying that night with her classmate. So they would go out and eat together when she got home from work.

L.R. did not kill Face and Tiny but he was really angry with them. Since he would be delayed on getting to Patrick, he would show that niece of his not to butt in to other people's business. L.R. had a job for Face and Tiny that would take them to Miami but when they returned they would take care of the niece. L.R. was grinning with that evil glint in his eyes as he thought, *It will take me some time to get to Patrick because I will have to call in some favors. But Mr. Cordero, I will kill you.*

Will really enjoyed himself the night before. He felt like she had a great time as well. Before he left she asked if he could let Victor and Amy know that they would make their party this coming Friday night, and tell them what dish they were bringing to the party. He told her he would. They were good people, combining Elizabeth's acceptance to Art School in Paris with their daughter

47

Annie's birthday party. He and Del still had to nail down their congratulation ideas for Elizabeth.

Face and Tiny had picked up the two briefcases of cash and were heading toward the Miami warehouse. L.R. had told his best recruiter, Gayle Simpson, to wait there through the afternoon. Tiny had only met her once or twice but Face had never met her. Gayle had mainly recruited the underage girls in Miami and Los Angeles. She had been recruiting young girls at pools and beaches for a couple of years. L.R. had noticed her soon after she had been recruited when he had been taking care of a problem in his L.A. warehouse. He had been impressed with her monthly high-end call girl dates and recruitment numbers and then he saw her abilities of persuasion while flirting with the warehouse workers.

Tiny had heard L.R. explaining why Gayle had such high recruitment numbers. She knew the girls who, like her, had come from dysfunctional families would be easy to manipulate. Unless their numbers were critical, Gayle knew to stay away from girls from stable families because they were more self-confident and not as easily influenced. At an early age, Gayle had instinctively developed her abilities of persuasion in dealing with her broken family with their addiction issues.

L.R. rewarded these abilities with money, drugs, an apartment, clothes, makeup, and a car. Coming from a background without any gifts or love, Gayle like so many others thought her pimp loved her. Together with her male partner, she would work pools near middle schools, sometimes kidnapping or promising a career in modeling or movies, recruiting ten to twenty underage girls a month.

L.R. would move Gayle around to different coastal cities in California and Florida to make sure his prime money-making girl would not be noticed by the local police. He was also careful with her, making sure she got good medical care, like birth control pills, vitamins and physicals, and that she only used drugs and alcohol recreationally. The other girls without these protections would die before they reached twenty.

When they got to the warehouse Tiny told Face to go to their favorite barbeque restaurant and get some food to take back to their motel, while he delivered L.R.'s message to Gayle. Tiny found her waiting in the office and told her that L.R. wanted her to escort a couple of high-end girls to England because his regular escort was ill. He needed her in Atlanta by Saturday morning and to pack warm clothes. He then turned to the office manager and told them to make sure Gayle was on one of the trucks going to Atlanta by Friday. Tiny turned back to Gayle and she nodded that she understood her assignment. Tiny left the warehouse as Face drove into the parking lot.

Alma continued to bury her feelings as she went through her daily activities, although the closer the weekend loomed, the more nervous she became. She missed José so much that it was becoming more difficult to control her emotions. She had to use those deep emotions to keep her focused on her plan against L.R.

Patrick was questioned through the night by the detective in charge of his case, Paul Rankin. When they took him back to his cell, he allowed himself to blow off some steam by pacing around. He was really upset that his boss Jason was in the hospital unconscious. He bet the same guys that came after him at his sister's apartment had attacked him. But unfortunately he was being charged for his assault as well as the embezzlement of L.R. Gomez's money. He did not even make any money off of that deal.

Del drove to the university library from work so she could finish studying the remaining material for her exam the following night. As she walked through the garage she was smiling broadly and thanking God for helping her find the time for her studies. After Del finished studying, She went home and checked her panty for the ingredients to prepare the dish she was taking to the party. Will had volunteered to go grocery shopping the next day for both of them and so she called him and let him know what she needed.

THURSDAY, MAY 15, 1997

When Liliana left that Thursday morning for work she had a real sense of danger. Mai had promised her that she would take extra precautions. She also told her to give the whole crisis to God. Liliana was always surprised when her young daughter would say things like an adult. She took her daughter's advice and started praying during the rest of her drive to work.

Alma was pleased with her progress. All the steps of her plan were falling into place nicely. She would need to prep L.R.'s secretary today about needing to take some time off after Friday, because someone in her family had fallen gravely ill. She was pretty sure no one had suspected any difference in her behavior except when Clay had said those kind words to her. But L.R. and his secretary had not been in the office when Clay had spoken to her. Alma did not blame Clay for following L.R.'s orders. She would one day tell him so but now she had to finish preparing for her departure.

Clay had all his tools and equipment in the trunk of his car. He had already driven around the house he would rob that night. There was no activity in the house and with the cover of the people who were visiting the Zoo by early evening he would be gone with his loot. The weather would be a plus as well, clear and cool. He went over each step again in his head and then headed to a fast food restaurant to get a late lunch.

Del was trying to study for her exam during her lunch break but she was excited about getting together with Will to prepare their dish for the party the next night. She was beginning to relax and enjoy Will's company doing the everyday routines that couples do together. But now she had to pull her attention back to studying for the final exam that night.

Face and Tiny had returned from Miami that morning and were waiting for L.R. to finish his phone call. He had told them to be quick about getting back to the warehouse because he had an important job to do. His secretary told them they could go into his office.

After he hung up the phone, Tiny told L.R. that he had delivered his message to Gayle and that she would get here by the weekend. L.R. told them to go get Patrick's niece.

Patrick had only slept a few hours before Detective Rankin started interrogating him again. He had told him everything he knew except the part about Clay. Clay had saved him from those two big bruisers and he would never tell the cops about Clay. He owed him his life. He would just sit there and answer all of Rankin's questions again. He did wish Liliana would come by and let him know they were all right.

Mai stood on the bottom step of the school bus and looked both ways before stepping onto the sidewalk. She walked quickly to her home, letting her eyes move from one side of the street to the other. She had told her mom that she would be careful and only relaxed when she arrived safely at her home. She spread her books out on the kitchen table and started doing her homework. She wanted to be finished by the time her mom got home from taking her final exam that night.

Tiny and Face had parked further back than before but they still saw the girl enter the apartment building. L.R. had told them to make no mistakes, so they would stay in the car for a little longer. They had not eaten anything since their breakfast on the plane, and their stomachs were making noises. L.R. told them they could eat after they dropped the girl off at the warehouse. Somebody would meet them and take her to where the other girls were waiting for their trip to the New York harbor Saturday night.

Del stopped for something to tide her over until the exam was over. By the time she had arrived and walked to her classroom, the food had done its job and she was ready to take her exam. When she walked in she saw Liliana and waved and mouthed good luck. She waved back and mouthed you, too.

Will was glad Del's class was almost over. He had missed her and wanted to spend more time with her. He bet she was really tired. She had been working and doing this class for almost three months. He then remembered that Del had asked him to pray for her exam. He looked at his watch and realized she was already taking her exam. So he quickly asked God to help her. He had really seen a change in her the past few times they had gone out together and he was glad.

Clay Stevens parked on the other side of the zoo and walked over to the house. He walked slowly so he could make mental notes about the way to the house because it would be dark when he walked back. Clay was stealing from one of the larger homes owned by a celebrity in an eastern suburb of Atlanta. That night he was going to make the most money ever in his ten-year career, and he was excited. The sun had dropped behind the tall, old trees of the Grant Park neighborhood. He had timed his journey perfectly. He went around to the back of the house to let himself in the back door. He quickly but carefully went through the house, helping himself to all that he thought would sell quickly.

A block away, while Clay was completing his job, Face and Tiny were going over the final details of their plan to kidnap Patrick's niece. Face was going to stay in his Buick while Tiny went up the back fire escape to grab the girl.

Once Tiny reached the back of her apartment he tried to open the door but it had a lot of locks. He began hitting the door with his shoulder. It took him several times to hit the door before he broke through, so he knew that the girl had heard him.

Once he got through he realized he was not in the apartment but a hallway, going left and right. At each end was a door. He remembered when he looked at the apartment building from the front that the sister's apartment was on his right. He hit the door on his left hard enough to break through on the first hit. He ran through the apartment – it was empty, with the front door opened. He ran through the door, slamming it shut. He ran down the steps and out of the apartment building.

Mai had been working on her homework in the kitchen when she heard the noise at the back of the apartment. She hurried back to her mother's room and peaked through the blinds. She saw one of the men who had come to the apartment earlier that week. She ran out the front door and down the steps to Mrs. Baines' apartment. Mai started banging on the door, looking up the steps, ready to run if she saw that other man. No one came to the door. *Better get out of here, fast.* She turned and ran. Just as she pushed through the outside door she heard a door above her slam and then him coming down the steps. She ran toward the neighborhood store screaming for someone to help her.

Face saw the girl run out of the building. He grinned as he watched her run down the street. He drove to the entrance just as Tiny came out and pulled away as soon as Tiny had gotten into the car. They drove down the street until they caught up to her.

Face said, "Tiny, grab her fast and shut her up before someone calls the cops."

"I know what I'm doing. Where do you think she's going?"

"I don't care, just grab her. There can be no mistakes tonight!"

They drove up beside her. Face threw the car into park as Tiny jumped out of the car. He picked up Mai, holding her with one arm as he opened the back door and threw her in. She sprawled onto the back seat, screaming, and Tiny jumped in with her. He slammed the back door and Face hit the gas.

Just as Clay was getting ready to leave, he glanced out the huge front windows as an old blue Buick stopped in front of the house. For an instant he froze. The owner wasn't supposed to return that night. Then he saw the pretty girl in her early teens running on the sidewalk, screaming her lungs out. Quicker than he could have believed possible, a big guy jumped out of the car and grabbed her, throwing her into the back seat. She was fighting and screaming for help but Clay recognized the guys in the car as Face and Tiny. He knew not to mess with them.

Mai was still screaming as they sped away. The huge man driving turned toward her and gave her a scary stare as the other man quickly put tape over her mouth. He tied her hands together and then her feet. Once she was restrained the driver stopped the car long enough so the other man could get back into the front seat.

She sat in the rear of the car, trying to listen. She was so frightened that she could do nothing but cry. Yet she knew she had to listen carefully so she could come up with an escape plan. She slowed her breathing, concentrated and willed all her senses to work. The two men did not even act like she was in the car.

Clay could feel the anger rise in his stomach. He unconsciously pushed his long fingers through his curly red hair as he paced back and forth. He looked at the empty sidewalk where the young girl had just been kidnapped, "It's 1997, for crying out loud, and in a good neighborhood! How could something like this happen?" He was so upset he didn't even realize he was screaming out loud. He slowed his breathing, forcing himself to be quiet. He was still on the job.

Why am I so disturbed about this kidnapping? It's just another girl, just like the girls in the warehouse. He leaned against the wall, his breathing slowly coming back to normal. *Maybe it's because this is the first time I've actually seen the snatch. But she didn't fit the profile of the other girls I have seen at the warehouse.* He willed himself to return to his present job before someone caught him.

He quickly looked at his watch and grabbed his loot, checking to make sure everything was in its correct place, and then he walked to the back of the huge old home in Grant Park. He made sure the alarm and locks were turned on and positioned as he had found them. Then he left.

He carefully retraced his route through the Atlanta Zoo to get to the street on the opposite side of the zoo where he had parked his car. He got in his car and just sat, thinking about what he had just seen.

He threw his stolen goods onto the back floor and banged his fists against the steering wheel, "What is wrong with you? This kid means nothing to you!"

Yet he knew down deep inside why he could not let it go. She looked like his kid sister when she had been that age. It had not been too many years later that she had been in that terrible car accident. She had lingered for a couple of months before she had died from her injuries.

He looked at his watch again, cranked his car and threw it into gear. Still mumbling under his breath, he drove away from the area.

Mai knew her usual routine of checking in with Mrs. Baines on the nights her mom was in class had been stopped. She had told her she would be celebrating with her mom after her exam. That was why no one had answered when she had banged on their door. Until her mom returned from class no one would know something was wrong. No one would know to contact the police. Her mom would return from taking her final exam and would not find het at home.

By then it would be too late to find her. No one would know where she was. At this, she started to cry once again. She was not strong enough to escape from the two large men who had taken her.

The two men in the front seat were yelling at each other. Mai was not sure what the argument was over but she thought it had to do with where they were going to take her. They had been driving around for some time now and Mai was hungry and scared.

Face had heard that they should take the girl to the place where the other girls were being held. But Tiny had heard L.R. say to bring them to the warehouse and someone would meet them. They were both so hungry they started yelling at each other. This debate continued for several miles.

They finally decided to go to the warehouse first because if it was the place someone would be waiting for them. Also there was a really great barbeque restaurant close to the warehouse.

Del and Liliana talked a little about the exam and they both felt they had done well. Del told her she would leave a message about her final grades at her work phone. Del saw Liliana was about to leave and before she turned Del gave her a quick hug and told her she was praying for them. She smiled and said she would see her next semester and they left.

When they arrived at the warehouse, Tiny went in to see if anyone was waiting for them. He did not see anyone but he heard one of the guys on the floor in back telling him that someone called and said they were running late. Tiny went back out to the car and told Face.

Del met Will in Buckhead for a late dinner. She was feeling more relaxed after the exam and was looking forward to her date with Will without the pressure of the course. He was waiting for her by the bar and they gave each other a hug. They stood there for a few minutes.

"How was the exam?"

"It was a long test but both Liliana and I talked about it and we thought we did OK. We'll see next week. How was your day? Have you decided what clients you'll be taking on?"

The hostess said their table was ready and they followed her to their table. They both ordered before saying anything else.

Then Will answered her question, "Not yet. I'm sort of taking some time to rest up after my last case. I was glad it was over so I could take a break."

"I know it's crazy they sat us here tonight." Del reached across and took Will's hand and squeezed it. "Will, we're being recognized by the staff as a couple. It's so exciting!"

"Yeah, I know. I've been thinking they've noticed us here a lot. Here comes our food, real quick. I'm so happy we're making routines of being together. You know?"

Del smiled. "Yeah, and that's OK with me." They were silent as the waiter set their plates down. When he left, Will took Del's hand and thanked God for the food and for Del.

When Liliana saw the front door was unlocked, she knew something bad had happened. She slowly opened the door. The apartment was not the way she had left it. Mai's books were pushed away from where she had been sitting. She could see the door to the fire escape opened. Her heart rate was climbing fast.

She called out Mai's name but there was no answer. The lights that she normally turned on were not on. Liliana switched on the hall light and she could see that the opened door was damaged. She screamed out Mai's name and then ran into Mai's room turning on the light. She was not there. Her eyes were welling up and tears were falling to the floor, her kind and brilliant daughter's floor. She thought, *Oh please God, don't let anything happen to my only daughter. Please God.*

She ran out of the apartment and went down to Mrs. Baines'

apartment and knocked on their door. When she answered Liliana asked, "Have you seen Mai tonight?"

"No, but we went out earlier to the store. What's going on, Miz Phillips?" Mrs. Baines saw how panicked she was, so she grabbed her sweater and went back to Liliana's apartment. They both examined the hall door and then the busted door to the fire escape. They came back into the apartment and looked for any sign of a note or if there was blood on the floor meaning there had been a struggle, but everything was where it normally was except for the scattered books and broken doors. Liliana finally gave in to her worst fears. She plopped down on the couch and started sobbing uncontrollably. Mrs. Baines sat down beside her for moral support. They sat there for a while and then Mrs. Baines asked, "Is you going to call the police?"

"I don't know what to do. Mrs. Baines, do you think those men that you confronted last Tuesday would have some reason to take Mai? How am I going to secure these doors without the manager finding out? The manager will want to call the police. I'm just not thinking too straight right now."

"I'm not sure. But I know they was mean men, and those kinds of men that came here are usually up to some kind of evil deeds. Don't you worry about the doors. We can help you. Why, do you think they would hurt Miss Mai if you called the police?"

"I'm not sure of anything. But I know my brother was involved with terrible people. I'd never seen him as scared as he was the last few times I saw him. Maybe I should go ask him. What do you think?"

"I don't know, either. But if you go see him those cops record everything."

"You're right. I don't want to give the cops any more information that could hurt Patrick. Wait, my classmate's boyfriend is a private investigator. His name is Will. I know they are good people and not the cops. What do you think?"

"That's a good idea because those PI's know how to find out

information without people knowing about it. Yeah, why don't you call them?"

"I'll have to wait until tomorrow because they were going out for a late dinner. Oh, Mrs. Baines, what are they going to do with my sweet Mai?" Then she just leaned her head over on her shoulder and sobbed.

After a little while Mrs. Baines went down and got her some of their dinner's leftovers and brought a plate back to Liliana's.

"Miz Phillips, do you want to stay with us tonight?"

"Thanks, Mrs. Baines, for the food and your help, but I think I should stay here in case anyone calls. I'll call in sick tomorrow and call my classmate, Del. I'll let you know what she says and thanks so much for your kindness."

As Mrs. Baines was walking out the door, she said, "I'll be sending up lots of prayers for Miss Mai and you. Call me if you needs to, no matter what time it is." She shut the door and called, "Miz Phillips, can you lock your door?"

Liliana struggled with the door, pushing and shoving, but she finally got the locks to bolt. She spoke through the door, "Thanks for helping me, Mrs. Baines. I'm very thankful for a neighbor such as you."

Liliana put Mai's books in her book bag and cleaned up the kitchen table. She just stood there staring at the book bag. She was desperate to do something to find her daughter. But what could she do? She had no family except Patrick and he was in jail. The only other person she thought she could turn to was Del. She really did not know her very well, either. Totally frustrated, she just walked back to Mai's room, fell down on her bed sobbing and then turned to God as He was all she had. She cried out for His strength and protection until she fell into a restless sleep.

After grabbing a bite to eat, Clay drove to his midtown apartment. He could not get the young girl out of his mind. He knew those guys who kidnapped her. They were cruel and ruthless. They were the heavy-handed part of the human trafficking business in Atlanta. But the whole idea of taking these young girls was now not as appealing. He had only been a part of the business side which had shielded him from what he had just seen. But now something was happening that had not happened in a very long time -- Clay's conscience was driving him to call this crime in. He was sure what this innocent girl was about to experience. She would become a victim of human trafficking, and it was driving him to a very dangerous decision.

He had moved up the criminal ladder and was the middleman and recruiter for his ruthless crime boss who was the driving force behind these terrible crimes as well as many others. Clay knew it would be very chancy to call the cops and give them a report. He did have a personal connection, someone he had gone to high school with, an APD detective, Victor Jones. Maybe he would get a break if he called Victor.

The more he thought about what those young girls were going through, the more he knew he had to make the call. Even if it did get him into trouble he had to tell Victor. He picked up the phone and dialed the number for the APD and asked to speak to Victor Jones. He was not there, so he left him a message letting him know he witnessed a kidnapping and needed to speak with him as soon as possible. He gave him his mobile phone number.

After Clay hung up his disappointment of not talking to Victor turned to desperation as he knew how horrible Tiny and Face would be to this girl. Clay knew that time was running out to find her before it was too late. Clay grabbed his keys and headed out to see if they had taken the girl to the warehouse. He drove into the lot next to the warehouse. He would be able to see them but they could not see him. There was a shallow rise from L.R.'s property to the one he was looking down from and Clay could see their Buick was just sitting there. He wondered what was happening, and tried to find a better angle to see if he could see into the car windows.

As he was moving into a better position he ducked down as another car was driving onto the property. A man he had never seen got out of the car and met Tiny. They had some words, and then transferred the young girl to the other car. Clay backed away carefully and drove down to the entrance. He knew this new guy would be taking the girl to another location and he wanted to see if he could follow him.

Face and Tiny had waited much longer than they had wanted to when the man that was L.R.'s contact for them finally drove into the warehouse lot. Face blindfolded the girl and cut her leg restraints. They both lifted her out of the back seat and walked her over to this guy's car. He opened the back door and they pushed her onto the back seat and slammed the door.

He said, "Thanks guys, I'll take care of her from here." They waved and got back into their car, stomachs growling, and headed to the barbeque place to eat.

The man drove the girl to the house where they held the kidnapped young girls before they shipped them to their destination. Clay followed the car several car lengths behind.

Clay parked down the street from the place the man parked in front of - a run-down old house. The man dragged the girl out of the back seat. She was fighting him, so he slapped her hard. Then he pushed her toward the house and they both went in. Clay pulled out slowly and drove down the street.

As he passed the place he wrote down the color, make and model of the guy's car as well as the tag number. Then he saw the house number on the mailbox and wrote the street name and number. With real sorrow he drove off without trying to go in there and take her back. Clay knew how L.R. worked and knew he would have had no chance if he had tried to go in there on his own. But he saw she was still alive and he had gotten the information off the guy's car as well as the location of the kidnapped girl. He prayed for God's protection for her and for the other kidnapped girls. He was sure they were also in that house.

Once inside, the man gave the girl to the woman in charge. She pushed her down to the ground and told her not to move. The guy said, "She hasn't eaten, if you have anything left. Boss told me this one was important that nothing should put her into danger or damage her, understand."

She replied, "I understand." She pulled the girl up and nodded to the man as he left. She led her into a room, took her blindfold and restraints off and pushed her down on a bed. She turned and left the room, locking the door behind her.

The woman went to the kitchen and heated up some of the leftovers from supper. She had seen many of these girls come and go. They were mostly shy and timid from low self-esteem. This new girl was different. She had stared directly into the woman's eyes when the blindfold was removed. The girl had then held her hands out confidently, as if challenging the women to remove the restraints. The woman had only seen a handful of girls like her. When the other girls like her were raped through the night they were still defiant. They would have to put them through the raping process several times before they would not fight back anymore. Fortunately the boss had commanded that this girl stay pure.

The food was ready, so the woman fixed a plate and put a glass of water on a tray. She unlocked the door and placed the tray beside her. She once again looked at the girl, who was still defiantly staring at the woman. The woman just shook her head, turned and left the room, locking the door behind her. As the woman turned and walked back through the house she thought, *This girl is even stronger than the others. She is most definitely not like the rest of them. She's even more confident and smarter than the others who had been defiant. I wonder what the boss wants from her.*

When the woman left Mai pushed herself back with her feet and leaned up against the nasty wall. Her efforts not to touch the dirty mattress with her hand had been successful.

She then looked around the smelly room. There was only an old, marked up rickety wooden chair and the single mattress she was sitting on. She heard the door being unlocked and she sat up straight. The woman brought in some food and water and put it on the bed. The woman stood staring and then she left, locking the door.

Mai took the tray and placed it on the chair but took the water. She then pushed the chair with her foot far away from the mattress. The smell made her stomach churn even more than it had been doing. She was terrified and she wanted her mother. At the thought of her mom she started sobbing and praying to God for help and protection. She leaned up against the wall and stayed like that for a long time until she finally fell asleep, exhausted.

FRIDAY, MAY 16, 1997

Clay left his apartment early to go back over to the house where he had followed the man with the young girl the night before. He had not yet received a call from Victor Jones. Once he drove by the house, he would go over to the warehouse and see if he could hear any gossip.

When he arrived at the house he could see immediately that no one was there anymore; the blinds were opened, there was no movement inside the house, and there were no cars around the house. He had heard that L.R. was very diligent to keep the underage girls moving so the people around the homes did not get suspicious. They would move them at night when the neighbors were sleeping. Clay was almost overcome with disappointment, but realized he had to try even harder to find out any information he could at the warehouse. *Maybe I should talk to the guys working on the production floor packing and unloading the trucks? Maybe I can tell them L.R. sent me to get the information about the girls' shipment.*

Liliana waited until seven to call her boss and left a message about her not coming to work. She did not sleep much and she wanted her day cleared before she contacted Del.

After leaving her boss a message, she called Del at work and left a message asking if she could meet her as well as Will as soon as possible. She gave Del the number of the mobile phone that Patrick had given them and hung the phone up. She collapsed onto the couch, sobbing uncontrollably, closed her eyes, prayed and fell asleep.

Alma arrived early to catch up on the rest of her work in her in-box. Once everyone had left the office that afternoon, she would steal the shadow box. Once she got to New York, she would take the brooch out, take the empty shadow box to a priority delivery place, and make sure they delivered it to L.R. on Thursday.

There could be no mistakes on her last day working for L.R. Gomez. The following week, L.R. would receive the empty shadow box after looking everywhere for it. Then on the outside of the shadow box he would see the taped note.

She would tell him she stole the brooch and was on the freighter bound for England. Waiting until the end of the week would give the freighter more time in its crossing of the Northern Atlantic. But she would also challenge him to enter England one more time if he wanted the brooch back. He hated England because it was the only place in the world that he was almost captured.

Del arrived at her office refreshed and dreaming of her Will. Once she reached her desk, she got a cup of coffee from the break room. She noticed her message light blinking on her phone. She picked up the message and then dialed Liliana's mobile phone.

"Liliana, this is Del. Are you OK? Because I could really hear that your voice was different."

"Hi, Del. Yeah, something has happened to Mai and I was wondering if I could meet you and your boyfriend, Will, today? It is really important so if it could be as soon as possible."

"Sure, we can meet you. Where and when do you want to meet?"

"Do you know the hot donut place on Ponce? How about meeting there at 10:00?"

"We'll meet you there at 10:00."

Del looked at her clock. It was just a little past nine. She looked at her calendar; her appointments for the rest of the day were few.

She also noticed that Victor's party was that night at six; she made a mental note and then dialed Will's number. She knew he was home between clients and told him that something had happened to Liliana's daughter and she wanted to meet with them. He told her that he would meet them, and she gave him the time and place. That done, she started calling her clients. Her clients were always ready to re-schedule when it was Friday.

Del quickly worked to clear her desk and then sent an e-mail to her supervisor letting her know that she would be taking the rest of the day as vacation time. She took a quick glance around her desk and then headed for the elevator.

Clay arrived at the warehouse early enough that L.R. had not arrived yet. He walked back to where the guys he knew were packing. He was asking how everyone's Friday was going, when one of the guys stepped closer to him.

"Hey, Clay, L.R. was asking us last night if we'd seen you. So you'd better check in with him, OK?"

Clay nodded, but was determined to find out about what time the truck would be leaving before he went back upstairs. "Thanks for reminding me. L.R. wanted me to confirm with you guys about the time the truck with the girls would be leaving this weekend?"

Clay just stood there and watched as the guys looked around at each other. Then the same guy that told him about L.R.'s message said, "Well that's odd but the truck leaves here tomorrow night sometime around nine."

"Thanks. I'm going to go and let L.R. know right now."

Clay walked over to the steps and climbed them two at a time. He looked down at the guys and waited until they started packing again. Then he carefully walked to the entrance stairs, looked around and shot down the steps and took off in his car. Clay thought, *Man that was close! Well, I wasn't sure if L.R. had been missing me but now I know. I've got to get with Victor because L.R.'s goons will be coming for me!*

Del and Will arrived at the donut place first and waited in Del's car for Liliana to arrive. When they saw her walking toward the entrance they got out of the car to meet her. Del could tell she had been crying.

"Hi Liliana, this is Will Evans. Would you like to go in?"

Liliana held her hand out to shake Will's and responded, "Hi, Will. Actually no. I just asked you to meet me here in case someone was listening in. Can we just sit in your car?"

Del was glad not to eat the donuts because she had eaten too many sweets over the weekend. She said, "Sure, we can go sit in Will's car because there is more room."

Will led the way and opened the front passenger door for Liliana and then opened the back door for Del. Once everyone was inside Will's car, Del asked, "Liliana what's going on?"

Liliana started crying and Del passed her a box of tissues. Del and Will sat quietly and waited for her to gain enough composure to speak. Then she told them what had happened over the past several days starting with Patrick leading those two goons to her apartment and finishing up with the smashed doors leading out to the fire escape and Mai not being at home when she returned from class. Once she stopped talking, her head dropped into her opened hands.

There was a pause and then Will asked, "How can we help you?"

Liliana seemed to be revived with Will's question and she said, "Thank you Will, for such kindness in your voice. It really means a great deal after feeling so alone last night. Del has told me you are a PI and I feel since Patrick was just arrested, somehow I don't want the police mixed up in this. So I wanted to see if you could help find Mai." Again she started sobbing and Del reached over and put her hand on her shoulder.

"Yes, of course. But Liliana, had you ever seen these two goons before?"

"Actually I never saw them. They had come to the door when Mai was alone, and she had called our neighbor Mrs. Baines this past Tuesday when I was in class. But Patrick told me before he was arrested that he thought they worked for someone who was the investor that he'd stolen a large amount of money from. He told me this man's name and that he had no idea that they had identified him. He said if he had known he was being followed he would have never come to the apartment to talk to me."

"Liliana, can you remember the name Patrick told you?"

"No. But I think if I heard it again, I'd know it."

Will sat thinking for a few minutes and then said, "Look Liliana, I'm going to look into this. I know you don't want to involve the police but since there is so little information that you know, I'm probably going to talk with a friend who works for the police. Del and I have known this man since we were kids.

"I want to be honest with you from the start about the people I will need to talk with concerning your case. Trust is very important in my business. So that you can understand each step, I'll be updating you as I find out new information. This process can take some time but with each lead I tell you about, that's how you'll know I'm in your corner. OK?"

Liliana smiled and said, "Thank you. Will, I'll trust you with whatever information you need to help you find Mai."

"OK then." He saw the fatigue in Liliana's face and body language so Will decided to postpone any other questioning until later. He realized she did not know a whole lot more and he could better use his time interviewing the brother and neighbor. Liliana would be more comfortable giving Del the rest of her basic information.

"Look, I've gotten what information I need for now so I'm going to take off. Del will get the details from you. Like Mrs. Baines' information and Patrick's full name. Also all of your information -- address, phone numbers, a photo of Mai, you know information like that."

Both Del and Liliana got out of Will's car and walked over to Liliana's car. Then Will drove out of the lot.

"Liliana, are you hungry? Let's go to a restaurant so we can talk, OK?"

"OK. I know a place not too far from here. You follow me and I'll lead you to it. Thanks so much Del, for you guys dropping everything and coming to help me right away." Liliana started crying again and Del gave her a hug.

"We're going to do everything we can to help you out with this. OK?"

They got into their cars and headed out of the lot to the restaurant. Once they got to the restaurant and parked, Del got into Liliana's car and took all of the information that Will wanted. When she finished she could see how drained Liliana was after all of their questions. So Del suggested that they postpone eating for now with all that she was going through. Liliana thanked her for coming and especially for their support. Del told her to call her anytime. Then they left and returned to their homes.

Detective Victor Jones with the Sex Crimes Unit of APD had left a couple of messages for Clay. He was returning his call from yesterday's message. Victor found it odd that Clay would call him now when he had not seen him since high school. Victor would leave his desk, only to return and see his message light blinking on his phone. Clay and Victor were just missing each other's calls. It was lunch time so he would have to catch up with his old school buddy once he returned.

Later that day after he had all of the information from Del, Will called Liliana at home. He asked her if she could please call ahead to her neighbor as an introduction for him. When Will called her, he was able to see Mrs. Baines right away. She was great because of all the details she gave him.

He went back to his apartment and put together a time line of all the events he had gathered surrounding Mai's kidnapping. He saw from the time line it would be very important to question Patrick Cordero. Will would first need to talk to Victor before he could set that up. Once he had interviewed Patrick he would confirm all the facts he had with Liliana.

Victor had just returned to his desk after processing a couple of crime scenes when the phone rang, "Detective Jones."

"Victor this is Clay. Boy, am I glad to talk to you. I've got some important and delicate information and I was wondering if I could meet you somewhere?"

"Sure, Clay. But it will have to be later tonight. I'm already running late and there is a party at my house tonight. Is this your mobile number?"

"Yes."

"I'll call you when I can come and meet you." They decided on a late night restaurant and then hung up.

When Victor arrived at his house most of their friends were already there. Victor and Amy had both loved the quaint neighborhood of Ansley Park. So after saving for several years they had bought the yellow two story wood framed house with white wraparound porch. They had invited both friends of their daughter Annie, and Elizabeth's brother, Will, as well as Del.

Fortunately for Victor, the light hors d'oeuvres were being served so he had not missed much. He moved through the house until he came to the kitchen. Amy was working hard to keep the food in the dining room supplied. She saw him come through the swinging door and said, "Victor, where have you been? Del has been helping me but how could you be so late?"

"Amy, I'm so sorry! I couldn't get off the phone with someone who had been calling me all day. Tell me what you need me to do."

Amy looked at Victor and realized once again his job was not predictable. She smiled at him and said, "I'm sorry for being so impatient. Let's get the rest of this food out on the table. As soon as everyone has eaten, we can light the candles for Annie for her birthday song. Once the cake is cut the children can go watch the video and we can celebrate Elizabeth's acceptance to Art School and her departure next week to France."

Victor was glad to see everyone but he kept looking at his watch wondering what was so urgent that Clay Stevens wanted to see him so badly. Fortunately the time flew by fast catching up with everyone. It was also great to actually see Will and Del, as they mostly just spoke to each other on the phone. He knew Amy would be disappointed once again when he would have leave so he could meet with Clay.

FRIDAY, MAY 16, 1997 - LATE

The office had cleared out early except for Alma. Her vacation had been approved by L.R. and she told everyone she was staying to clear her desk before leaving. She moved around the office looking as busy as she could, but what she was really doing was making sure no one was on the office level. Then she reached into her desk and took out her tote bag and went inside L.R.'s office. She quickly took down the shadow box. She stood back and looked at the empty place on the wall. As she placed the shadow box carefully into her tote bag she thought, *Yes, I think L.R. will be cursing so loud that the whole warehouse will hear him once he sees this has been stolen. I wonder if he will suspect me before he receives the empty shadow box and my note.* Alma could not stop herself from grinning ear to ear.

She cracked his door, looked out to see if anyone was around, then quietly slipped out, gathered all her belongings from her desk and left the office for the final time. No one even noticed her as she left the warehouse. She had done it. But there was still one more hurdle. She had to come back tomorrow night with enough money to convince the semi-truck driver to allow her passage to the New York harbor. She surely could not leave the country any other way without a passport. She had already arranged passage on the same freighter the girls would be on to Southampton, England.

The freighter was owned by L.R. so she had suggested to his logistics manager that he had wanted her on board. As Alma walked to her car she thought, *This plan will definitely bring L.R. to England where he can be prosecuted, since the corrupt cops here wouldn't touch him. I know that this brooch I'm carrying out of the warehouse belonged to his beloved mother. It was the most important thing he owned and he will have to follow me to England once he receives my package. I have burned all my bridges – this job, taken all my money out of my bank account, never to see my family again but it's OK. I live only for L.R.'s takedown and nothing beyond that matters.*

Victor waited at the bar watching for Clay's arrival. It was almost midnight. He nursed a draft beer and then saw Clay at the door. He had not changed much with age but he did seem nervous. Victor grabbed his mug and went over to shake hands with Clay. Then they were led to a booth in the back of the place. Clay asked about the party and Victor told him it had gone well. The conversation remained light, just catching up, until the server brought Clay's draft beer.

Then Clay began telling Victor about the girl's kidnapping the night before. He only wanted to tell him what he personally knew were facts so he thought carefully about what he wanted to reveal as well as keeping some key information as insurance. He then came sort of clean with him about his own illegal activities with the sex trafficking over the past couple of months. He told Victor what a mistake it had been. He told him that he knew the goons who kidnapped the girl because they worked for the same guy he had been working for until earlier that day. Clay told him he had to show his hand to find out the time and place this girl and others would be trucked out of town the next night. Victor just sat thinking over the deliberate details Clay had left out and then looked intently at Clay to see if there was any body language that would show he was lying.

"Clay, I can see that you needed to report this, but why did you call me? We haven't really had anything to do with each other since high school. I mean we've run into each other through the years, but why me, what's your angle?"

"Look Victor, if I just went to APD's missing persons and told them about this girl, they'd fill out their forms and send it onto whomever. But with you, I could tell you about my connection with these people. I was hoping you would use me as an informant and not throw me in jail. Also these people I work for move these girls fast and I knew you'd understand that."

Victor just sat thinking and tapping his fingers on the table. Clay waited. "OK Clay, what do you think we should do?" Clay relaxed some with that question because it meant Victor was willing to go with the informant thing. Clay told him about how he witnessed a murder and that he was told to dump the body by his boss who had murdered this guy. He told Victor that this crime boss was paying off many people with great power and influence in the United States and especially in Atlanta. That he had been paying off others in many countries for over thirty years.

"Victor, I've never met anyone like this guy. He's powerful and evil. I've been on the wrong side of the law since high school but I've never met anyone that I immediately feared like this guy. I've seen him kill without any hesitation and now I'm next. That's why I've come to you, because I'm out of options and I need your help."

Victor sat tapping his fingers on the table again and Clay waited. He was really trying to think through his options, *I'm not sure I can trust this guy that I haven't seen since high school. If what he says about individuals on the take inside APD is true, I don't want to know any details about this until someone I trust can check out Clay's story - see if he is telling the truth. That's how I can handle this without getting too involved with the details of the case. I can get Adam Jeffords in homicide, who I know I can trust, to look into it. I can also ask Will's take on it once Jeffords checks out the dump site.*

"Look Clay, I've got to think this through and talk to a PI I trust. So you disappear, don't go home, or anywhere someone might know you. You stay there until I call or you hear from someone I've told to call instead of me. From what you've told me, I'm not sure who I can trust at APD or higher, meaning I don't need anyone at APD knowing I'm in contact with you. So here's my mobile number and you stay alive and wait to be contacted."

As they were finishing their beers to leave Victor said, "Clay before we go please write down the name of your boss and the name of the person he told you to take care of, and the place where you dumped him." Victor handed him his pocket notebook and Clay wrote down the information.

He returned the notebook to Victor and they shook hands, "Thanks, Victor. Thanks for everything and I'll be waiting for your call." Then they left.

SATURDAY, MAY 17, 1997

Driving home, Victor called Jeffords and left a message with his informant's tip about José Ramos. He asked Adam to keep him in the loop, but anonymously. He did not know whether to believe Clay or not especially when it could mean his job if there were people in high places at APD on the take. Victor had to make sure Clay's story was confirmed before going forward with any type of investigation. If APD personnel were compromised with bribes, he had to stay as far away from Clay as he possibly could. Homicide would be the best place to start because a murder with a witness would be eagerly supported by the prosecution's office. It would possibly bring the dirty officials out of hiding. These would be the facts he would need to have before he pursued Clay's story.

Alma got an early start on that Saturday morning. She had many things to accomplish but the main item was to find a funeral home that would promise to bury José once the police found him. She had been calling different ones all week and the list was down to two homes. She would visit them both and then make up her mind. She had cleared out her savings account earlier that week and she would use part of it to bury José. They had promised each other to take care of any arrangements because neither one of them had many family members in the United States. Alma's parents were in Miami but the family they could call on did not have money enough to bury him with dignity. The man she loved deserved that.

Del had asked Liliana to come to her apartment and eat lunch with her. Del was up early to get everything ready. She prayed all morning for Mai and Liliana. Because of her training, Del did not want to be too negative, but she wasn't sure how she could say anything that would be positive. She knew that most of the girls who had been kidnapped and forced into human trafficking were completely stripped of any emotional self-reliance or certainty. In the first hours they were repeatedly raped by multiple men, told their families will be harmed if they do not obey them, and then they were drugged with narcotics.

She asked God to show her the best way to support Liliana as well as for His wisdom for Will during his investigation into Mai's kidnapping. Del could see Liliana was in pain, but was not giving in to her emotions. Del could not imagine how hard something like this would be for any mother. She needed to hurry as she only had a couple of more hours to clean her apartment and to shower.

Will had left a message for Victor late last night after their party, but he had not heard back from him. He really needed to talk to Patrick. None of his informants had heard anything about the kidnapping. Will felt like his time was running out - there was usually a 48 – 72 hour window for these kinds of cases. The forty-eight hours would end that evening. Will thought, *Victor where are you? Call me, time is running out!*

Victor kept looking at his watch at the breakfast table. Amy asked, "What's going on, Victor? You've probably looked at your watch fifty times since we've been up this morning."

"I'm sorry. You know how some cases are more time sensitive than others. If it's that obvious, maybe I should go ahead and get to the office. Thanks for being so patient with me."

"You should go ahead because I haven't seen you like this since you worked Elizabeth's case. If it's anything like that you must focus everything you know how to do so it can be resolved!"

Victor leaned over and hugged and kissed his wife. Then he hurried to shower and leave.

Clay paced back and forth in his cheap, rundown motel room. He still had not heard from anyone about what to do next. He stopped pacing and sat down at the table by the window. He picked up his Bible that he had been carrying around in his car. He turned to some verses he used to read a great deal. "Come to Me, all who are weary and heavy-laden, and I will give you rest. Take My yoke upon you, and learn from Me, for I am gentle and humble in heart; and you shall find rest for your souls. For My yoke is easy and My load is light." Matthew 11:28-30 (NASB) Clay bowed his head, closed his eyes and then prayed, *God, please forgive me! My life has not honored you as I had thought it would in high school. I'm not that kid who wanted to follow You but a man who followed evil men who said what they had would make me rich. Please help me to save this young girl, to follow You once again and give me rest. In Jesus' name I pray.* When Clay opened his eyes the peace he had once known was back and he was not afraid.

He decided to pay for another night, and went over to the front desk and got that taken care of. He then went to buy some food. He really needed to return the jewels he had stolen. He would have to think through how to do that but he was too hungry for details like that. He would eat and then God would show him what to do and how to earn some money, not steal it.

Liliana followed the directions to Del's apartment. She was early but she just could not stay at her apartment any longer. She arrived at Del's complex and found her unit number. She was about to knock on the door when Del opened the door and invited her in.

At any other time, Liliana would have looked at the apartment to see how Del had decorated it, but this morning she was too anxious about Mai to even glance around her. She blindly followed

Del through the small living room with its off white carpet and walls, the comfortable furniture and brightly colored paintings.

Del led her into the kitchen where the kitchen table was set for two. The kitchen was a nice size, painted yellow, with baby blue accents, but all Liliana could see was a table set for two, just as she set her table for Mai and her. Del walked over to the counter to finish preparing lunch. She looked over her shoulder and saw Liliana just staring at the table. Del spoke softly, "I've been praying a great deal for Mai and you. Are you feeling any better today?"

"Thank you, Del. I can't tell you how much it has meant to me, the way you and Will have supported me in this awful and difficult place. You know you hear in the news about children being kidnapped and other horrible things. But you never think it's going to be your child." Liliana paused, gathering what courage she had left. "What's going to happen to my Mai? What's going to happen to me without her?"

Without warning she collapsed onto the kitchen chair, sobbing uncontrollably into her hands. Del stood silent for a moment, then found a box of tissues and put them down beside her friend.

"Liliana, no one can answer your questions. So I won't even try. But I can take your hand and we can pray together and ask God for His help and guidance."

Liliana reached out and took Del's hand. "Yes, please say to God what I cannot." So that was what Del did.

Victor had been going through the combined APD files from all the different departments' cold cases. He was trying to find any file that mentioned Clay's boss, L.R. Gomez. He was not having any luck, so he looked at his watch to see how long he had been there. He was shocked to see that hours had passed. Too many hours without checking in with Adam, hopefully he had had a break looking for the body, if there was a body. Victor put everything back and then went back to his desk. His message light was flashing.

He had a few messages. A couple were from Will saying he

needed to talk to him today and then Adam saying they had found a Hispanic male's body down river from his informant's dump. They had him transported to the morgue and would call him back once he knew more information. That was what he had needed to know for sure, so he dialed Will's mobile phone to set up a time to talk with him as soon as possible. Clay's kidnapped victim was running out of time.

Mai had been moved three times since her capture. Her fear had turned to anger that led her to a silent but determined mindset to flee. She had seen a pattern in their movements. This was a good thing because she saw a flaw in their procedure that she could maybe use to escape. She would have to be absolutely sure that she had it figured out, because she would only have one chance to make it work.

Del had driven to Will's apartment. She was talking through her visit with Liliana when they heard the doorbell. Will went to the door - it was Victor. They walked back to the living area where Del was sitting. They were both talking non-stop but neither of them was listening to the other's story.

Del held up her hand. "Time out, boys! Victor, you called this meeting, so you go first." They both looked at each other then sat down.

"After you guys left the party last night I met with Clay Stevens. Del, you might remember him from high school. He was a tall, lanky guy with curly, red hair that always seemed messy. Well anyway, I had not talked to him much, except when I had run in to him periodically since high school. Then I get these messages at work that he had to talk with me as soon as possible. So we set up a time after the party.

"I had no idea what I was walking into, but he sounded really scared. Clay starts telling me about this very young girl that he sees kidnapped this past Thursday evening. He says he knew the kidnappers because he works for the same guy that they work for. About this time he starts looking around, like he's getting ready to bolt. So I try to calm him down. But then he says that he needs to know if I'm going to use him as an informant or am I going to arrest him."

Victor kept looking at Will and Del because they could not seem to sit still and they kept looking at each other like they already knew what he was saying.

"So I tell him that yeah, you can be my informant. Then Clay gets real serious and looks around again. He then tells me about this boss of his at work and how he saw him kill this co-worker there and that his boss then tells Clay to get rid of the body. He also tells me that his boss moves these young girls around for sex, human trafficking. His boss runs a transportation company and pays off leadership and cops. Clay then gets real quiet and just looks at me. So I tell him to lay low while I check into his story giving him my number and to use that mobile number only. He gives me his boss's name and where he dumped the body and the guy's name.

"I gave a trusted buddy of mine, Detective Adam Jeffords in homicide, all this confidential information last night. Today he left me a message telling me that they found a Hispanic male's body and he would give me more details once he gets them. All of this to say Clay was telling me the truth and I need to find this kidnapped girl outside of APD."

Will and Del had gotten very quiet. Then Del looked at Will and told him to tell Victor. Will shook his head in disbelief.

"Victor, this is going to sound crazy because Del's friend, Liliana Phillips, from her night class called her Friday morning asking us to meet with her. I had never met her before but Del had told her I was a PI. Del knew she must be in trouble and took the rest of the day off. We met her and she asks me if I could investigate something she couldn't go to the cops with. I said sure, and she told us that her daughter, Mai, wasn't home the night before when she returned home from her night class exam. Her apartment had been broken into. She then told us about her brother, Patrick Cordero, who had been arrested earlier in the week. But before he was arrested he had told Liliana that he had stolen a lot of money from one of his clients. Earlier in the week, two goons had gone to Liliana's apartment to try to find Patrick, but Mai hid him and called her neighbor to help her. The goons were not able to get Patrick, or even get into the apartment to search for him. He thought those guys had been sent by this same client. I talked to their neighbor, Mrs. Baines, who had helped Mai with these two goons. I've run down every other lead and struck out until now. Victor, we think those guys took Mai. We think Clay saw Mai's kidnapping!"

They just sat quietly, trying to take in each detail they had heard.

"Look Victor, that's why I've been calling you because I need to question Liliana's brother, Patrick Cordero. Now I think we both need to question him!"

Del spoke for the first time, "Wait, you guys! Patrick isn't going anywhere. Mai is the one you need to focus on. She's the one who is in real trouble. Victor, you need to get a warrant to search this business. Wait a minute. What's Clay's mobile number? Will needs to call him for the business's address. Victor, you need to stay out of this for your own safety. Let Adam get the warrant to search the office regarding the murder by Clay's boss. Then it's your informant who is providing the information, not you. Then the warrant could also work to find Mai." Victor took out his pocket notebook and gave them Clay's mobile phone number.

Del continued, "What do you guys think? Do you think Adam will go for this, Victor? Because it's Saturday meaning it'll take longer to get a judge to sign off on a warrant. But what else can we do? Is there anything we can do for Mai right now?"

Victor shook his head. "I hate this part of it. The way things stand right now, with the laws we have, we can't really address directly what Mai has been caught up in. Right now we don't have the laws to deal with what is going on. We have to pursue other venues for prosecution to remain within our present laws on the books. To get Mai back, we have to go through Jeffords' homicide case or something else instead of addressing the real problem of sex slavery that can only be recognized under immigration of human trafficking."

Del looked shocked, and Will nodded his head to confirm what Victor had been saying. "I ran into this in California, as well. Even when we did recognize that a crime scene involved sex trafficking we'd still have to turn it over to Vice, which handled prostitution. And yes, we all know that sex trafficking is not the same as prostitution, but right now the laws do not make a distinction between underage or adult sex trafficking and prostitution."

Victor added, "Sometimes it's also hard to get concrete facts from the victims. They have been so brainwashed and controlled by their pimps that they are too terrified to say anything against them."

Suddenly Del's face crumpled as if she had just remembered something. "I just read an article at work that included this statistic, there are between 700,000 to two million women and children trafficked across United States borders per year. What an incredibly huge number of victims! I hardly can wrap my brain around it. Do you mean we really can't do anything about Mai?"

They all just sat there until Victor said, "Yeah, you're right, Del. Right now we can't do anything directly for Mai. The sex trafficking subject is a difficult one for all of us but regarding the warrant, I don't know. I trust you guys, because I've known you for a long time. But with all of these complicated turns in this case, especially not knowing who in APD and higher might be taking money under the table, I'm not sure I can even trust Captain North. I'm not sure if anyone else would even believe this crazy story. I don't know how to approach Adam with this warrant business. Will, why don't you go with me and we'll see if Adam has left me a message at the precinct." They stood to leave but they saw that Del was struggling with their decision.

Will said, "Look Del, we're all concerned about Mai's safety and time constraints, but we need to make sure what will be the best way to approach Adam about this warrant, especially it being the weekend. We can't tell him about Mai because Victor hasn't told Adam about Mai being kidnapped. We also don't know who in APD has been bought out by L.R. and if Victor told him now that would compromise him. We need more facts and Patrick can help us get those. Give us the rest of the afternoon. We need Adam to pull the right kind of police support, so we can't make any mistakes. I'll call you as soon as we know anything. So until I call you please hang out here, OK?" Then they left.

Del watched them leave the apartment, speechless in her unbelief. She was still struggling with her emotions. Their commitment to law enforcement procedures made it seem as if they were indifferent to Mai's abduction. How could they just ignore Mai, brush her aside as if nothing might be happening to her! Even now, she might be . . . but Del forced herself to stop this line of thought. *Breathe*, she said to herself. *Breathe and pray. And try to think of what I can do to help.*

As soon as they were in Victor's car, he turned to Will. "I know Del and you have a heightened urgency because of all that took place with Elizabeth last fall, but you know I can't press Adam, although I probably can get you in to see Patrick without any alarms going off. No one at APD could have possibly put it together, that these cases are connected. We'll work something out before they take Mai anywhere. You know, why you don't give Del a job that will allow her to feel like she's helping out. Call her and get her to call Clay to find out the location of where the truck will pick up the girls and when."

"Good idea, and giving her this job will make her feel better because she'll be working on details related to Mai. She also knew Clay in high school and maybe he'd tell her something he hasn't told you." Will and Del had given each other a key to their apartments a couple of months earlier so he knew she could lock up if she needed to leave. He gave Del a call with her new assignment.

Alma was really packing fast, as wrapping the shadow box package with her note to be delivered to L.R. late Wednesday and finding a funeral home that would take care of José's body had taken more time than she had thought. The sun was going down and she wanted to leave her car in a public parking area and walk to the warehouse. She had two pieces of luggage - a large canvas backpack and a medium canvas bag with wheels and a shoulder strap.

The night before she had taken the shadow box, she had bought a fine jewelry felt bag with a tie pull to store the brooch. When she first took it out of the shadow box it was so heavy. She then understood the high value of it, besides the sentimental value to L.R. It was so beautiful, shaped like a number eight. Half of the figure eight, on opposing sides, were four rows of large rubies. On the other sides were various sizes and shapes of diamonds embedded in white gold. The diamonds were rectangle, rounded, and square in shape. Alma had never seen anything so beautiful. She just sat for a minute and gazed at all the beautiful lights reflecting off of the brooch. She then carefully wrapped the brooch in the felt and placed it into the jewelry bag. Then she placed the empty shadow box wrapped with bubble wrap and her note to L.R. into the shipping box she had gotten earlier in the week.

She needed to keep the brooch on her at all times, but how? Then she remembered the flat pouch her mother had given her. It was made from satin and tied around the waist. She could put the brooch in it as well as her driver's license, credit cards, and cash. She then finished packing, looked around the apartment one last time and left.

Victor called in a favor to get Will in to talk to Patrick. Will was surprised at how readily Patrick answered all his questions. Patrick had been genuinely upset about Mai's kidnapping and that it probably had to do with the mess he had started by stealing his investor's money. Once Will had gathered all the information,

Patrick made Will promise that he would tell Liliana how sorry he was. Will told him he would tell her.

Del had called Clay, and had convinced him to come with her to his work place that she now knew was a warehouse. Clay had jumped at the chance to get out of that motel room, and was eager to help in any way he could. They had waited until after dark, then had driven to a parking lot near the warehouse. Clay and Del quietly got out of Del's car. Del was not sure what she was about to see but just in case something happened she knew her identity must not be known. She went around to the passenger side of the car and opened the glove box. She put her wallet, mobile phone, and checkbook into it and closed and locked it. She then locked the car and gave the keys to Clay. She could not plan much past these actions but she knew she had to be ready to do anything to protect her friend's daughter.

"What are you doing, Del?"

"No time to explain now, Clay just think through what I told you on the way over here. Now just lead me to the place you told me about. The view where we can see the warehouse."

Clay turned on his small pocket flashlight and led her to the ridge overlooking the warehouse. When they arrived they got down on their bellies and inched forward. There was some type of commotion taking place in the parking lot. A young girl was being dragged toward the back of a semi-truck. She was screaming and fighting with all her strength. The big man who was dragging her slapped her hard, picked her up and put her in the back of the truck.

"Del, I think that was your friend's daughter. The guy is called Face."

Without warning, Del, overwhelmed with Mai's danger, impulsively slid down the hill and ran toward the back of the truck. Clay moved quickly to the farther end of the hill so he could get a better view. Del ran to the man who had slapped Mai, and started pushing him as hard as she could but he was much bigger up close. It looked like she was trying to get a better view of the inside of the truck but it was not working. He tried to push her away but then Del tried to go around him. Then, apparently frustrated with the crazy woman, Face said something, picked Del up, put her into the truck and closed the doors. Clay was stunned. He had no idea what to do next.

Before he could come up with anything, he saw Alma climbing up into the passenger's side of the truck's cab. He thought, *What are you up to, Alma?* Then the truck eased out from the warehouse. The truck was too far away for Clay to be able to read the license plate. He thought, *Maybe I can take Del's car and follow the truck and call Victor to let him know the tag number.*

He ran over to her car and tried every key on her keychain but none of them went into the door's lock. Then he shined his flashlight onto the keys and saw the one that looked most like a car key. He finally got it into the lock and drove out to the road, but the truck was nowhere to be seen. He drove over to I-75 and pulled into the parking lot of a fast food place that he knew Face and Tiny hated and called Victor's mobile. As the phone ring, Clay thought, *Why did I let Del talk me into this? Del could always talk me into anything in high school and once again I let her do it to me! I'm going to be in some hot water with Victor.* Then he heard Victor say, "Detective Jones."

When Victor finished getting the information from Clay he hung up. Then he put in a call to Adam to see how much more time before he would have the warrant. Then he just sat there trying to figure out how he was going to tell Will that Del had been kidnapped and put on the same truck with Mai. Clay was unable to provide enough information about the semi to put an APB out on the vehicle but he said he would meet Victor at the donut store on Ponce. Victor knew Will would be returning soon so he had to come up with something to say, and fast.

Del looked around the trailer. There was very little light, only two battery dome lights. But at least there were some lights so they could see each other, the surroundings and the cargo pushed to the rear so they would not trip over anything. The boxed cargo must need some type of ventilation as the trailer had several vents on the walls at the ceiling.

Then she looked at the five young girls sitting across from her. She had to be careful with words and her actions so she could connect with the girls. She knew her opportunities would be limited so she prayed for God's help and for His wisdom.

Mai's mouth was bleeding and her cheek was swelling from the slap, but she was the first to speak to Del. "Who are you? You look older than the other girls."

Del smiled and said, "Are you Mai Phillips?"

"How did you know my name?"

Del tried not to look directly at the other girls. "My name is Del and I go to night school with your mother, Liliana. She knew that I had a boyfriend who was a private eye, and when you were kidnapped, she asked me to see if we could find anything out about you. We found out some information that brought me to the warehouse, where I saw you. So here I am."

"Is my mom OK? I've been so worried about her!"

"Mai, she's been worried about you as well. That is why I'm here. She wanted you to know she's praying and that she loves and misses you." Del could see the other girls wiping away their tears – good, that meant that her words were having an effect on them. Mai got up and sat beside Del who was sitting alone. Del put her arm around Mai. There was silence and no more questions, just quiet whimpers from the girls until they fell asleep. There was only one of the girls who appeared older and who did not show any emotion. Del made a mental note of this girl's appearance and response.

Her thoughts drifted once again to her training. *I will not have too many opportunities to win these girls over so I need to choose my words very carefully. Their pimp or who they called their boyfriend would terrify the girls to never speak to outsiders, or if they had to speak then lie to anyone associated with the criminal or mental health systems.*

If they disobeyed, they were beaten. The pimp's method of psychological manipulation has proven to be very effective. Each girl will have her own story, God, please help me!

Del had to stay mentally sharp to take advantage of her small window to make an emotional connection with these girls. Without this connection she would not gain their trust. Their trust in Del would be the only way that any of them would open up enough to share their stories, first with her, and then later with the police.

The girls' safety would always be her highest priority but with limited knowledge, Del had also created the crime that Victor could act on, her own kidnapping. She knew that Victor's hands had been tied with Mai's kidnapping, but now with her kidnapping and the testimony from the girls, Victor would have some concrete facts to work with.

The facts gleaned from their stories would be the building blocks needed to support a criminal investigation. If Del wanted the charges to stand up in any future court case, she had to earn the girls' trust to gain the proof or facts she needed to help them as well as Victor. Del asked God's help for such an important undertaking that she had stumbled into.

Gayle acted as if she was sleeping but she was watching this intruder. She knew this woman's capture was dangerous. She must figure out how to contact her boss, L.R. Gayle thought that L.R. would blame her, so she wanted to contact him as soon as possible about this woman and her PI boyfriend.

Alma had been chatting with the driver of the semi off and on as they headed up I-85 to New York City's Harbor. The driver's name was Joe and he was fairly social for one of L.R.'s drivers. He was especially talkative once she paid him $250.00 for allowing her to catch a ride to the ship she had booked passage on to England. In fact he was so appreciative that Alma talked him into stopping the truck for a bathroom break for the girls., as long as she made sure they would all return and that nothing would be said to L.R. All the women were able to wash up as well as go to the bathroom. They all thanked Alma as they returned to the semi with no one trying to escape, but she noticed there was one woman who was older than the others.

Victor told Will to bring his file with all he had gathered from his investigation along with him because they had to leave to meet someone. Once they were in the car, Victor told him about Del's capture. He had never seen Will so upset.

"I'm sorry, I know you are dating – and you looked pretty happy together at the party last night, but I guess I didn't know how serious you are about each other."

"Well yeah, Del and I have been dating quite seriously."

Victor had never seen his friend look so miserable. "Oh, Will, I had no idea you were getting that serious. I am really sorry I had to tell you that."

"That's OK. You had no way of knowing we have been getting together more regularly. Where are we going again?"

"To meet Clay Stevens. Remember, he's the guy that gave us all the information. Del and I went to high school with him, that's how he knew me and why he called me when all this started happening." Victor paused a moment, then said, "He was with Del at the warehouse."

"Victor, did you just tell me that this Clay was with Del and he didn't do anything to help?"

"Hold on Will! You've got to promise me you won't hurt Clay until you hear his whole story. If you can't, then I need to drop you off at your apartment."

"OK, Victor, you've got my word. But he'd better have some really good reasons that kept him from helping Del!"

SUNDAY, MAY 18, 1997

Victor and Will arrived at the donut shop just after midnight. Clay was sitting at a table in the back. This place filled up quickly in the early morning hours. It was one place that was open, inexpensive and a semi-safe location in that part of Atlanta.

Clay stood up and reached out to shake their hands. "Hi, Victor. Hi, I'm Clay Stevens. I'm really sorry for this mix up. I should've known something was up, when Del was so insistent about going over to the warehouse without you. But Del has been talking me into jams since high school. Sorry that I'm going on so. It's just that I really wanted to do something but then I would have been captured and not be able to tell you what happened."

Victor nodded toward Will. "Clay, this is Will Evans, Del's boyfriend. Look, just tell us what went down from the beginning." They sat down, Will glaring across the table at Clay.

"Sure. OK, Victor." Clay unfolded each detail from Del's phone call to when he had called Victor.

They ordered some coffee. Victor could see Will was getting ready to jump on Clay, so he said, "Look, Clay, it isn't what we want, but it's what we have to deal with." As Clay seemed to relax a little, Victor looked at him more sharply. "But maybe you can help us out with more information about the truck and its destination because I am pretty sure you've held back some details as insurance."

Will got more control over himself after that and sat back into his chair. Victor followed up with, "Did Del say anything to you that seemed out of place?"

Clay had straightened up in his seat. "Yeah, you're right about the insurance but this is different. It was on the drive over she told me that many different scenarios could happen once they got to the parking lot overlooking the warehouse. She told me everything was up in the air and we couldn't plan any real strategy. Yet she had worked through different possibilities and with one of them, there was a chance you, Victor, would be able to come after her legally. It didn't make any sense to me even when I thought it through, so I just forgot it until now. Do you understand what she's talking about?"

Victor looked over at Will and said, "She's clever! Crazy but she's got some guts to give me something I can run with." Will just sat there shaking his head from side to side, mumbling to himself.

"Victor, I'm still not following. What do you mean?"

Will spoke up, "See Clay, legally our hands were tied because no one went to the cops about Mai. Victor didn't know which cops were on the payroll of L.R., so he couldn't take the chance of officially reporting it. Reports could be seen by a variety of people and if just one of L.R.'s people saw the report they would then go after Victor. But Del knew once she had been kidnapped by those creeps, Victor could now open up an investigation into her disappearance with L.R.'s group. Even if the charges of the human trafficking of minors doesn't stick, kidnapping would. Oh Del, what have you gotten yourself into!?" Will let out a sigh and started rubbing his forehead with his hand.

"OK. She's given me something to run with, so let's get going fellas!" Clay and Will followed Victor's lead. Will threw down enough money to cover their bill as they walked out of the donut shop. Clay handed Del's keys to Will and then he ran after Victor yelling back over his shoulder.

"Will, all of Del's things are locked in the glove compartment."

Will watched Victor drive away as he walked to Del's car. He opened the driver's door and slid behind the wheel. He then bowed his head and prayed, "God I'm not sure what I believe but I know Del believes in You and Your miracles. So I ask that You look after Del and the girls and bring them home to us. Amen. Oh, one more thing, help me to know what to say to Del's parents and Elizabeth. Thanks."

Victor and Clay went through the APD Sex Crimes outer doors. It looked as busy as the middle of the afternoon. "Wow, Victor, is it always like this?"

"No, something big must have happened. Go sit at that desk, I'll come back once I check in with my Captain."

Victor stuck his head into Captain Bill North's office, "Cap, if you're in the middle of something, shake your head, OK? I've got some bad news, so give me a call when you're finished. Thanks."

Victor turned to walk back to his desk, when he heard Cap say his name.

"What's going on, Victor?"

"Del Thomas has been kidnapped. We think she's gotten mixed up with one of Atlanta's worst scum, L.R. Gomez." Victor searched Cap's expression as he thought through what Victor just told him. There was no sign of anything but concern for Del. Victor was very glad for that.

"How did Del get hooked up with that low life?"

"Will was hired by a friend from Del's class to find her daughter who went missing last Thursday night. Del and her friend were taking their final. When she returned to her place, her daughter was missing and their apartment had been broken into. Will found out with the help of one of my informants that the girl was kidnapped by L.R.'s thugs. Del went over to his warehouse earlier tonight and was thrown onto the same semi-truck as her friend's daughter."

"How did you find out about all of this?"

"My informant."

Victor waited for Cap to decide how he wanted to handle this. While Victor was watching Cap go through something in his drawer, he thought he should go ahead and tell Cap about the other related cases.

"Cap, I think I need to give you a couple of more details related to Del's kidnapping. Very early yesterday morning I called in a possible homicide that my informant had seen to Homicide Detective Adam Jeffords. I also know that another Detective Paul Rankin is handling a related case, the brother of the woman that hired Will."

Cap stared at Victor. "Let me get this straight, you're telling me that there are two other APD departments investigating related cases?"

"Yes. Detective Jeffords did find a Hispanic male, fitting the description from my informant's story. For both Detective Rankin's case against Patrick Cordero and Detective Jeffords' dead body, neither of them are aware that the three cases are related. I thought you should know about the related cases before you make your final decision, sir."

Cap shook his head. "I swear, Victor, if I didn't know you, I'd think you were making this up!" He sat back in his chair and gave a nod. "OK, since you seem to have more information than I do, how would you like to handle this?"

"Well, maybe you could ask Detective Jeffords' captain to allow Will and me to accompany Jeffords when he is issued the warrant to search L.R.'s warehouse. We would only be there initially as observers. But once we see how the search goes and how L.R. handles this, that we would ask Jeffords to look through their trucking records. Maybe we could get lucky and find the truck that Del and the kidnapped girl are on and its destination."

"OK, Victor, I'll follow your plan up to a point and call Jeffords' captain to see what he says. But if I run into any kind of roadblocks with him or whatever, we'll have to re-evaluate your plan. You know the homicide captain probably won't pick this message up until he checks his messages in the morning. Also we'll need to talk about why it took you a day before I was notified about all of this." Cap waved for Victor to leave. Relieved, Victor walked over to where

Clay was sitting. Clay would stay with him until his safety was not threatened anymore.

About daylight, Alma talked Joe into stopping one last time outside Washington D.C. for a bathroom break for her and the girls. Joe told Alma that L.R. better not find out about these stops. She assured him no one would ever find out.

Alma had returned to the truck's cab when she saw a young man trying to talk with the girls. She could see him move in on one of them just as the older woman came out of the restroom. The young man was beginning to get rough with one of the girls while the others were trying to intervene. The older woman quickly pushed her way between the girl and man with some loudly spoken threats. When the woman told the girls to get into the truck, the man slapped her to the ground and started kicking her in the stomach.

Alma saw Joe coming back from the station and she yelled to him about the scuffle. Joe ran to the truck, and when the man saw the huge frame of Joe running toward him, he ran away. Joe helped the woman to the truck, looking all around to see if anyone witnessed the assault, but it was still early.

Joe was upset and afraid that L.R. would find out about the attack. Alma assured him that she would take care of any problems if they came up. She also told him she would increase his payment to $300.00 and so he just drove and stopped complaining.

Will called Liliana early that morning. He told her that he had talked to Patrick and that Patrick wanted her to know that he was sorry. Then he told her about all the events that had taken place since her lunch with Del the day before. He told her to pray for everyone involved and then hung up.

Victor received a call from Detective Jeffords around eleven to meet him over at the warehouse and gave him the address. Victor called Will but his call went to voice mail. So he just left him a message about the warrant and where to go. Victor hung up and thought it was strange that Will did not answer. He knew Victor would be calling about the warrant but Victor had to hurry to meet Jeffords.

L.R. listened to his voice mail for the fifth time from one of his men in the factory's shipping department. It was about Clay asking him for the destination of one of the freighters. What did Clay want with something so unrelated to his job? L.R. called Face and Tiny and told them to pick up Clay and bring him to the warehouse. Then he shaved, dressed and left for his warehouse.

The semi-truck pulled into the terminal where L.R.'s ship bound for England, The NY Derby, was anchored. They had made the fourteen-hour trip in just over twelve hours. Joe had made up the time from leaving Atlanta late. He backed his semi up to the front apron, the area behind the wharf shed, where his cargo would be loaded onto the ship.

When Joe and Alma climbed down from the truck's cab, she asked, "Joe, where will the girls be taken?"

"I don't know. You could ask that guy over there. He's a longshoreman who'll be loading L.R.'s ship. Take care and be careful who you trust going over."

"Thanks for everything, Joe!" Then Alma walked over to the longshoreman and got the information she had wanted. From handling the paperwork for so long in L.R.'s office, she knew a lot about the ship, but seeing it up close was totally different.

L.R. had purchased his break bulk cargo freighters from China in the late 1970s. Their Handysize range was 3-5 cargo holds that held his dry goods contraband and shipped them all over the world. The NY Derby was one of the smaller vessels with the bridge, cabins, and crew area on the stern, the crane on the bow and the three holds in the ship's center, meaning the height of the deck there was close to the ocean in that center section.

The girls would be taken to the lowest deck, and housed in a large room with three sides made of smoothed steel and the fourth chained off with a locked gate. This area was always left empty of other kind of cargo so the human cargo would be secured. He also told her the Derby would leave within the hour. She picked up her bags, found her way to the gangway, and then to her room.

Alma's room window faced the dock and she could see the girls being herded like sheep into the door that led to the lower deck. She noticed that one of the girls was helping the woman walk and guessed she had been hurt worse than she thought.

She turned away because the reality of the scene was so dehumanizing. She had been L.R.'s customs broker for over ten years, but her nausea came from the reality of what she had experienced over these past several days. It was the memory of José's death and then how these girls were herded onto the ship to be sold to the highest bidder once they reached Europe. L.R. had to pay for all of his crimes either legally or otherwise even if she went down with him. No matter what, L.R. would not hurt anyone else.

Alma was almost finished unpacking when she heard the motors from the ship come to life. She went over to her window and saw the longshoreman releasing the restraints. Then the tugboats bumped up against the vessel and the huge freighter began to slowly move out of the harbor. Just as she was turning from the window she saw a man running from a taxi.

He was a nice looking man, tall with blond hair and very muscular. His whole body was moving as he waved and yelled as the ship was pulling away. Finally the longshoreman approached him and they started walking toward the terminal. Alma wondered if this man was somehow connected to the unknown woman with the girls. Then she dismissed the scene to finish unpacking.

Will assured the longshoreman that he would leave without any further disruptions. He was frustrated, angry, and afraid of what might be happening to Del, but he couldn't do anything else here.

Now he just looked out over the harbor as The NY Derby moved out toward the Atlantic. He had almost gotten there in time. He started walking back to his taxi. He told the taxi driver to take him to the airport and sat back, allowing his emotions to surface. He dropped his head into his open palms, took a huge gulp of air, and openly moaned. "Oh Del how will I get you back?"

The cab driver asked Will, "Hey buddy, are you OK?"

L.R. drove up to his warehouse and got out of his car. Face and Tiny were waiting for him.

"Where's Clay?"

Face answered, "Boss, he wasn't at his apartment. So we asked his neighbors if they had seen him. One of them said that he hadn't seen him since Friday." Face looked at Tiny and then they both looked down at the ground until L.R. told them what to do next.

Suddenly the whole place was crawling with cops. An unmarked car pulled up behind their cars blocking any exit. Three plain clothes detectives, Jeffords, Jeffords' partner, Detective Dennis, and Victor, got out of the car. Jeffords walked over to L.R.

"I'm Detective Jeffords. Are you L.R. Gomez?"

L.R. nodded his head, and coolly answered, "Yes. How can I help you boys?"

Detective Jeffords handed L.R. the warrant and then waved his team to enter the warehouse for their search.

"Mr. Gomez and you fellows remain where you are until our search has been completed," Jeffords demanded.

Victor took this opportunity to walk to the back of the warehouse. He asked one of the workmen where they kept their shipping manifest log and he pointed over to a desk in the corner. Victor walked over and started looking for trucks that left Saturday night. There were five. He took out his notebook, wrote down all the information that log had for those five trucks, closed the log and walked back to the front where Jeffords was standing. Victor felt someone looking at him, and looked up to see Gomez staring

100

straight through him. Victor held his gaze until Gomez looked up to his office.

Then Victor remembered that Clay had told him that Gomez had thrown José from the second floor near the steps. Victor crossed over to where the steps were and started looking for what could possibly be the scene of José's murder. Victor looked up to find the rail and then pushed some boxes away from the area.

"Hey, Jeffords, maybe you should get some of your guys to look over here." Victor pointed out an area of the floor that was stained. Jeffords called over a couple of officers from his team, told them to collect anything in this area and to tape the area off as a crime scene.

Victor looked back over his shoulder. Gomez was on his phone, probably calling his lawyer. Jeffords smiled at Victor and they both knew they had found what they had come for, the place where José was murdered. Jeffords saw Gomez lean over and tell his goon something. He knew he had to act now or this guy would order many more killings. As Jeffords passed Victor he said, "You'd better hide your informant or these goons will kill him."

Jeffords cuffed Gomez and his goons while giving them their Miranda rights. Then he ordered his team to take each of them in a separate squad car and to keep them separated once they reached homicide. Victor thanked Jeffords for allowing him to come along and then got one of the uniformed cops to drop him off at his car.

Once Victor was in his car he called Will. Once again the call went to voice mail, so Victor told him to come by his house to pick up Clay to take him to his apartment. He relayed the events of Gomez's arrest and said that Clay was in extreme danger. Victor then drove home to spend what was left of the weekend with his family.

Del and the girls were taken to the lowest level of the ship. Everyone was very tired and weary from being in the truck for so long and Del was in real pain from her beating. There was a lot of grumbling as the surroundings became darker and damper with strong mechanical and mold odors.

The crewman led them into a more lighted area that seemed to be some type of large workshop area on the free side of the fence. The wire fence was from floor to ceiling and had a gate in it. The crewman opened the gate with his keys and stepped back to allow the women to pass through. He then locked the gate and said, "A steward will bring you clean sheets and sleeping bags for warm covers on the bunk beds as well as some hot food." He had just turned to walk away when Del asked if she could get some ice and alcohol for her injuries. He nodded and walked back into the stair well.

The area was totally enclosed with steel. The ceiling was steel girders about fifteen feet high. The area was well lighted and ventilated with two restrooms near the wire fence. There were bunk beds on each side of the steel walls as far back as the rear wall, about a hundred feet. The area was cold, damp and reeked of mildew. A couple of the girls just sat down where they had been standing and started crying. Del felt like joining them in their tears especially hurting like she was, but decided it was time to continue the connection she had started on the truck.

Del said, "I know this isn't a five star resort but with a little work we can clean up and arrange things a little better. Now that we can see each other better we can introduce ourselves. I'll start." She waited for the girls to respond, and when they raised their eyes from the floor to her face, she continued. "As I said on the truck, my name is Del, and I'm taking classes with Mai's mom." Del knew she must wait for them without showing any impatience but it was hard to not show how much pain she was in. Now that she could see each girl really for the first time, she could see how young, tall and beautiful they were.

Mai said, "Del just said my name, Mai. Are you OK? You don't look too good. Anyway, I would like to help you out with this area, Del."

Then one by one they spoke. "My name is Kendra and I'll help. And thanks for stepping in to help us at the truck stop. I'm sorry you took such a beating."

"My name is Tameka and I'll help too."

The last two were more reserved, then, "My name is Gayle and this is Rose."

Del had real concerns for the last two girls, especially Gayle, but for now she needed to take the minds of the other girls off this terrible place and her. "OK then, let's check the area for some cleaning products and something to clean with." Del led the way, looking, searching each open door and under the stored boxes.

Kendra came out of a bathroom holding a bucket with several items inside and said, "I found some spray cleaner and cloths." Mai and Tameka went over to Kendra and started discussing who would do what and where. Gayle and Rose just sat and stared at their surroundings with very little emotion on their faces. Del joined the girls who had already begun cleaning and prayed, *God, please keep us safe in this place. Please help Gayle and Rose with whatever they are struggling with. Thank You for keeping us safe so far, amen.*

They had about finished the cleaning when the fence rattled as the gate opened. There were several stewards carrying food, water and linens as well as ice and medicine for Del.

They whistled when they saw the girls but Del stepped towards them and they quickly stopped. They put down their loads and left. The last man, who had led them before, said, "That switch by the bathrooms turns off the high lights. But the lights in the shop will remain lit." Then he left.

The girls ate, made up their bunk beds and then climbed into their beds for the night. Mai was on the top bunk bed above Kendra, and Tameka had the top bunk next to it, end to end. Tameka, Kendra and Mai watched Del shut the door to the bathroom. Tameka turned so her head was at the foot of her bed, close to Kendra. She whispered Kendra's name, and saw her sit up in bed.

Tameka said, "Kendra, that was the second time this lady has stood up for us. Does it feel as strange to you as it does for me to have someone care after these past months that have been so terrible?"

"Yes it does. She must be really hurting from the beating this morning, but didn't seem to give it a thought when she did it again tonight. It's been such a long time since I've felt something that is anything like what I had with my grandmother and people I knew at church. I had almost forgotten how great that feels. I really think that she's a person who cares or she would not have protected us or come after Mai." Kendra poked her head over the side of the bed so she could see Mai. "What do you think, Mai?"

Mai looked up at her new bunkmates. "I know Del is a great person who really cares for all of us. My mom couldn't stop talking about her when she would return from either studying with her or from their class together. Mom told me how smart she was and also how much she loved growing in her faith through her church. I know you guys haven't known me long but I know Del is a kind person who really cares for us. I trust her and I think you should, too."

There was a short pause and then Tameka replied, "You know Mai, I think you're right. I'm with Kendra, it just feels nice to have someone like our family taking up for us after all we've been through." Then the bathroom door opened, so Tameka quietly turned around in her bed as she heard both girls agreeing with her.

After Del cleaned, iced and treated her wounds, she quietly came out of the bathroom, turned off the light switch and found her bed. The warmth of the linens was the best thing she had felt since leaving Atlanta but it was difficult finding a place on her body that she could lay on that did not hurt.

Will arrived back in Atlanta from New York after dinner. He checked his messages. There were several from Victor, Liliana and Elizabeth. He was so depressed he really did not want to deal with any of them but once he got to his car, he called Elizabeth and Liliana as he drove toward Victor's house.

At the precinct, Detective Jeffords and his partner questioned L.R., Face, and Tiny for several hours. Jeffords did not get any information but their names, addresses and ages. L.R.'s lawyer arrived and there were no more questions allowed. Detective Jeffords had them detained in the precinct's lock-up until their bail would be set the next day.

MONDAY, MAY 19, 1997

The precinct's lock-up was crowded. It was after midnight when the three men arrived but Patrick saw them before they entered. He recognized the two big goons and was terrified. He was able to hide at the opposite end of the lock-up area. There were several large men sleeping on the benches on that end and he slid down to the ground behind the benches and leaned his back against the bars. He then pulled his collar up on his neck and dropped his head between his bent knees. Between his knees Patrick watched the three men find an open bench near the entrance. For the time being, Patrick had been spared.

Victor and Will were at Victor's house, in the den. It was late, rather very early in the morning, so Amy went on to bed because she knew Victor and Will had to work. It had been a long weekend without Victor, but with her workweek starting in just a few hours, she needed to get as much sleep as she could.

Will stopped pacing around the room and dropped into a chair. "Victor, I almost got there in time." Will's voice was shaky with emotion.

"Will, what are you talking about? Where did you go?"

"I flew to New York City last night and spent most of the morning trying to find L.R.'s ships. I spent a great deal of money bribing the longshoremen but the freighter that Del and the girls had been loaded on was just pulling away from the dock. It had pulled too far away for me to jump for it. Then this dock worker told me if I didn't leave he was going to call the cops. I can't lose Del like I lost Julie, by some lowlife's trying to grab some money and power!"

Victor shook his head. "Oh, Will, I'm so sorry! We probably should have listened to Del when she told us the girls should be our first priority. Sorry about that, my friend.

"But, wow that was great investigative work you did and in such a small amount of time. You did a lot better than the department. I could only find the times of the semi truck's departure Saturday night from the warehouse. But Jeffords did arrest L.R. and his two goons. I wish you could've seen L.R.'s face when I followed Clay's details of the murder and went to what I thought might be the point of impact. Sure enough there was still some evidence left on the warehouse floor."

The details of the search pulled Will out of his depression and he added, "The ship that was leaving the dock, I saw the name, 'The NY Derby.' But we can't do anything because kidnapping falls under another department, doesn't it?"

Victor jumped to his feet and pounded his friend on his back. "Sorry to be so excited but you just gave me the missing link! I had followed all the leads I had gathered from the warehouse and now ol' buddy you've given me the name of the freighter. Now we can ask for her cargo manifest and find out where she's headed.

"We'll talk to Cap as soon as we get in the office to see if he can reach out to his contacts. We'll do what we can until he can work something out. But for now you need to go home and get some rest. Also, Clay is really being tracked by L.R's crew, so he needs to stay with you for now, if that's OK." At Will's nod, he added. "I'll go wake him." They left Victor's house with little conversation and drove to Will's apartment.

Del was awakened by crewmen working in the workshop. Her chest was hurting whenever she took a breath. She sat up and that helped her breathing. Once they left, she decided to go over the information she had on the girls so far.

Tameka had spoken after Mai about wanting to help out. She was young, tall, with light mocha skin, a wide smile and sharp facial features. Her shoulder length hair had tight curls, was combed back and was parted in the middle. She had a thin frame and narrow medium brown eyes.

Kendra had spoken next and was the one who found the bucket in the bathroom. She seemed older and more emotionally stable. She was tall also, with mahogany skin and a rounded face with big, dark round eyes. She had straight black hair that hung elbow length. Her figure was more hourglass, but still thin. She seemed to want to help but was more reserved.

Gayle had spoken for the last two girls. She had pale skin, and was tall and full figured. She had thick, straight blond hair, with darker roots, that fell below her shoulders. Her face was sharp, with big, diamond shaped, dark green or blue eyes. Gayle seemed to be the oldest, more controlling and unfriendly. From the little Del had seen, she probably should not be trusted. Gayle resembled many of her hardest cases at work and most of them would do anything to get what they wanted.

Rose had not spoken or even looked up, and seemed to follow Gayle's lead. She seemed to have India mixed features and was the youngest. Her straight, dark brown hair fell to her elbows, and she had wide diamond shaped brown eyes that were closer to her sharp cheeks than her nose. She was the tallest and had the slightest figure of all the girls.

Sleep was becoming too hard to fight with the rocking motion of the ship, even with her aching body. Del submitted to the movement of the freighter and fell into a restless sleep.

Victor, with very little sleep, arrived at the precinct early but there were still a large number of officers working their early morning emergency. He needed to work out what and how he was going to present to Captain North. He wanted to finish his report before Cap, Will and Clay arrived. He pulled out his forms and began working on his report of the events from yesterday.

Alma woke up with the sun shining through her window. It was colder than she thought it would be and she had not brought her winter gear. The Northern Atlantic cold seemed to come right through the window into the cabin. She turned over in her warm bedding and fell back to sleep.

Clay had gotten up early and fixed some coffee. He was in the living room reading through some of his more encouraging Bible verses when Will came out of his room.

"Hi, Will, did you sleep OK?"

"No, not really. I smelled the coffee. Thanks for making it for us."

"I'm sorry to hear that. Is there anything I can do for you?"

"No thanks." Will went into the kitchen to get some coffee.

Clay thought Will wanted to be left alone so he went back to reading. He knew he was returning to reading the scriptures because he was afraid that L.R. was going to kill him. But nevertheless he was really enjoying the peace that the word of God was giving to him.

He felt Will's presence close by and looked over as Will sat down on the couch..

"Is that a Bible you are reading? I didn't figure you for someone who would have a Bible."

"Well, I was really committed to Jesus when I was in high school. I went to the same church as Del and her parents. But then I graduated and couldn't find a decent job and I'm not very academic so college wasn't an option. Then I met this guy at a bar one night and he told me he could use me if I didn't mind breaking into wealthy houses. I was young and stupid enough to think that it was a great opportunity. So he taught me the trade of being a thief and I read my Bible and attended church less and less. Finally my faith in God just got swept away."

Clay hesitated to see if Will seemed to be following him and asked, "Did you hear about knowing God when you went to church as a kid?"

"No because my family didn't go to church. Did you think God was OK with you stealing things? I only ask because I have heard that one of the Ten Commandments is that you don't steal."

"That's a good question. Yes, I did know it was wrong to steal but I just pushed those feelings way down deep until I didn't think about it anymore. I also missed the people I had gotten to know at church but I also pushed that away and thought about all the money I had.

"It was when L.R. told me that I had to get rid of José's body and heard his body hit the water, I just couldn't shake it. No matter what I did I couldn't get that sound out of my head. When I got home I just picked up my Bible and started reading it. It was like coming home." Clay glanced over and saw Will nodding his head. He was getting it. Clay went on, "Then things got worse and I realized I was reading the Bible almost every day. Through reading the Bible and all these hard things hitting at once, I saw that I really needed Jesus back in my life. So I prayed and told Him how sorry I was for all the years of crime and not worshiping Him."

Clay paused and Will leaned forward, then asked, "Wonder what it was that hit you so hard? You had worked for L.R. for a while, right?" Clay nodded and Will went on. "So you knew the kind of stuff he did. What was different about this? If you don't mind me asking."

Clay closed his eyes a moment, remembering. "I'm not sure. I think maybe because it was José. He was someone I connected with and that I had known for a while. I had never seen anyone die before and then I was made to dump him like a piece of garbage. It really made me think of my own death and what that meant. It made me take a good look at my life.

"Everything I've been going through has gotten worse, but after praying and asking Jesus to help me, I have that peace and confidence I used to have in high school, that God is with me and that He has a plan for my life. I was just too stupid before but now I know that I need Him. I got in touch with Victor and I've been reunited with Del and met you. I don't know what's going to happen but I know I'll never turn my back on Jesus again. I'll never forget my friend, José, and that God used his senseless death to help me come back to Jesus."

Will grinned. "Thanks, Clay. That's some story. It's strange how God works but how do you know what God wants? I mean what if I'm not sure I know Jesus the way Del and you do." He paused, and Clay waited. "What if I'm not good enough for God to accept me?"

Clay slapped his knee. "Come on, Will! After I just told you about all the terrible things I've done? No one is good enough to know God. The Bible says, '10 as it is written, There is none righteous, not even one;' Romans 3:10 (NASB) But it also says that, '16 For God so loved the world, that He gave His only begotten Son, that whoever believes in Him shall not perish, but have eternal life.' John 3:16 (NASB) You see that's the whole point, that none of us are worthy of God because God is holy and we aren't." Clay saw that Will was looking at him intently, drinking in every word. He had never talked about God like this before, but he had been reading the Bible so much that the words were all there, just waiting for Clay to say them.

"But God sent Jesus, His only son, to pay for our sins. Once Jesus died on the cross and took upon Himself the world's sins, now we can have a relationship with God, once we believe that Jesus died for all the wrong stuff we've done - believe that Jesus took our sins on Himself that terrible day men killed Him. But you see, it wasn't just that Jesus died that terrible day, it's that God raised Him from the dead three days later. Jesus is still alive and when we understand that He lives with us, and we believe in what He did for us, we can't quit thanking Jesus for dying so we can have a relationship with God. It's the most amazing gift that we could ever receive!"

Will nodded, a faraway look in his eyes. "It makes a lot of sense, what you told me. It gives me many things to think through. Maybe we can talk later once I've had chance to think about it some."

"Sure, no problem. Will, you know Victor has told me I can't leave here, don't you? Are you OK with that?"

"No, he didn't tell me but it's OK. I've got books and videos over there on the bookshelf. So help yourself to the books as well as what's in the fridge. But I've got to shower and get down to the precinct." Will left to shower and Clay thanked God that he had the chance to talk to Will, and that he had said the right things. Clay asked God to help Del and him for His strength and wisdom in these hard times.

As Will showered he thought, *Oh God, I miss Del so much. Please help and protect her. Thanks.*

Del was at the rear of their quarters, reading the small New Testament with Psalms she always carried in her jacket. She wanted to help the girls but she really did not know where to start. As she read she prayed for God to show her how to reach out to them. She was reading in the book of Galatians at the end of chapter five. The writer is comparing men's qualities to God's. She heard someone walking toward her and looked up. It was Mai.

"Good morning, Del. I hope you are feeling better because your face is really looking rough. Anyway, we, I mean Kendra, Tameka and I were wondering what you were reading?" Del then saw the girls moving toward them. Del smiled and motioned toward the bunk across from her. The girls timidly sat down but were glad that she had asked them to join her.

"Good morning. Mai told me that you girls were wondering what I was reading. Well, I had a small New Testament in my jacket and I was reading it."

Tameka volunteered, "My grandmother would read to me from the Bible. I sure miss her." Mai and Kendra reached out to her. Del thought she should take this opportunity.

Del asked, "Tameka, would you like for me to read to you girls?" They all nodded their heads and so Del went back to the beginning of chapter five and read to the end, all twenty-six verses. When she finished Del looked up at the girls. They were weeping silently.

"Oh, I'm sorry, girls. I hope what I read didn't upset you."

Tameka said, "Oh no, Del. What you read didn't upset me. It was just talking about how evil men are and I've been experiencing that evil personally over these past several weeks. I don't want to be like those who kidnapped me. I remember how it felt to be good. I want to feel that again. I remember feeling some of those things, being some of those things, what did you call it, fruit of the Spirit?"

Kendra spoke up, "Yeah, that was it. They were love, peace, joy, kindness and there were several more but I can't remember."

Then Mai finished for her, "The rest were patience, goodness, faithfulness, gentleness, and self-control. There're nine fruit of the Spirit. These characteristics are what I memorized when I was younger. I wanted so much for them to instill the same character I saw in my Dad, especially after he left. But I've never understood why they are called the fruit of the Spirit. Do you know why Del?" All eyes turned toward Del who was having trouble keeping her mouth from falling open with astonishment.

"Well, from what I was taught at my church when I was your age, it means that only the Holy Spirit can plant these characteristics in us after we believe Jesus died on the cross for us and become Christians. In our own nature it would be impossible to have these godly characteristics without the Holy Spirit. We receive the Holy Spirit once we become Christians. That was how my pastor explained it. Does that make sense to you?"

Kendra responded, "My grandmother explained it to me almost the same way as your pastor. But it's still hard to understand. There were nine, right? Maybe we could talk about each one of the fruits for the next nine mornings?"

With a unanimous vote from all the girls, Del smiled and nodded. Then she said, "But girls we need to invite Rose and Gayle to join us."

Mai said, "Del's right. I'll ask them later after they wake up. But I don't think they'll be interested in learning what the Bible has to offer." Both Kendra and Tameka were agreeing with Mai.

Del just smiled at them. She saw a steward opening the gate with breakfast and said, "Look girls, breakfast is being served." They giggled and started walking toward the steward and once he had gone started eating their breakfast together. Del limped after them wishing she had some ibuprofen but silently praising and thanking God for His blessings.

Del then noticed Gayle speaking to a different steward through the fence. Gayle looked as if what she was telling him something that was extremely important and the steward's expression was one of severe panic. Del would have to tell the girls to be careful around Gayle, especially if she tried to act nice to gain their trust. She had seen this scenario played out many times before in her job. Gayle was a mole, a spy for L.R.

Javier was worried. He had just finished bringing breakfast to the girls when he saw one of them talking with Manuel. Javier shook his head. Manuel was a bad one, who had many times taken advantage of the girls they were shipping to England. No one seemed to care – as long as the girls didn't have any bruises or marks on them when they landed. After all, they were just going to be sold to the highest bidder. But Javier cared. His sister . . . but Javier couldn't think about her while he was at work. It hurt too much. He fingered the knife he always carried with him. *Someday, L.R.*

The wife of Patrick's previous boss called Detective Rankin to see if he had any more facts about her husband's assault. The detective unfortunately did not have anything new. She let him know that her husband was still in a coma. He told her he would get in touch with her if he uncovered anything else and that he was sorry that her husband's condition had not improved.

Victor was finishing off his report for the Captain when Will walked up. He sat down in the empty chair beside Victor's desk and waited until Victor spoke.

"Hi, Will. How's Clay?"

"He's OK. Have you heard anything about the ship's destination?"

"No, not yet. How are you holding up?"

"I've been better. I just wish I could do something! Were the creeps arrested able to make bail yet or are they still in holding? Oh Victor, you did make sure they were not put in the same holding cell with Patrick, didn't you?"

"Oh no!"

They shot out of their chairs, Victor grabbing his weapon. They ran as fast as they could to the holding cell. Will was not sure where they were going so he stayed behind Victor. They arrived at the lock-up and the uniformed policeman buzzed them through. They took the corner and Will almost fell down.

They saw a uniformed cop clubbing someone. As they got closer to the pen, both Victor and Will drew their weapons.

Victor yelled, "Police! Stop or we will shoot you!" But the cop kept beating Patrick. Will said, "Victor, don't kill him! We need him to talk."

Victor fired, and the uniformed cop fell back into the crowd.

Victor said, "Will, call 911!" Then he pushed the release for the locked door. "Where's the uniform cop who's supposed to be on guard duty?" He was not talking to anyone but just talking out loud in frustration because he had not prevented this nightmare.

Victor called Captain North and told him where they were and that he had shot a uniform cop because he was beating one of their witnesses and did not stop when commanded to stop. He also told him there was not a guard at the entrance.

Cap commanded, "Victor give your weapon to Will and I'll call for Internal Affairs to meet you there."

Will said, "They are both still alive but you need to stop the cop's bleeding. Listen everyone, stand back to let the EMTs through!"

Victor had taken his belt off and made a tourniquet above the wound area but then moved away from both injured men for the EMTs to work. He looked at Will and then down at himself - they were both covered in the victim's blood. Then Victor saw Cap and said, "Come on Will, we're finished here." Will followed Victor's eyes over to Cap and then followed him out of the pen.

Victor looked around the room one last time noting that neither L.R. nor his goons were anywhere among the remaining crooks. He thought, *You're slick but we'll still get you, L.R.!*

Liliana was one of the first people to arrive at the office, trying to lose herself in her work by catching up all of Friday's work. She had decided to shower and return to work since she could not sleep. Her message light was blinking. Most of the messages were work related except the last one. It was the police telling her about Patrick's admission to the hospital.

After hearing about her brother as well as her conversation with Will the evening before, her anxiety was worse than ever; now they had Del as well as Mai. As Will had suggested, she had been praying for God's protection and strength on their ocean voyage, and now she needed to pray for Patrick. Liliana thanked God for Will's hunch and that he had found them. She started to work through the different stacks on her desk.

L.R., Tiny and Face had been bailed out after their arraignment by L.R.'s lawyer. He dropped them off at the warehouse. After the lawyer drove out of the parking lot, L.R. turned to his goons. "Find Clay and kill him! I'll take care of things here once I have gone to get some food and beer. On second thought, you guys should wait to eat because you'll probably have a very long day trying to find him. While I'm gone, check out what that detective was looking for in the shipper's log. Oh yeah, you should also call and make sure that cop took care of that investor who stole my money."

Face nodded and said, "Boss I know you have everything under control but we wanted you to know whenever you get ready to blow this city, we want to protect you wherever you go."

"Thanks, Face, but there is no reason to leave. I've got so many of this city's leaders in my pocket those cops won't get near me. You guys don't worry but get busy checking the back of the warehouse and question everyone back there. We need to find out what the shippers remember about what the detective looked at."

The funeral home that Alma had hired for José's funeral saw his name in the morning newspaper. They called APD and asked to speak to the detective in charge of his case. They left a message to contact them once they were ready to release José's body and they would come and pick up the body for his burial.

Del was still hurting but she talked to the girls as they took turns cleaning up once they finished breakfast. One of the stewards had put clean, warm clothes near the gate in the fence. They seemed to have known the girls' sizes before they came on board. Del was both impressed and disgusted with the details of L.R.'s organization. How could anyone with such insight be so cruel and inhuman to such young, innocent girls? She thought, *Truly, power and greed destroy one's soul.*

Things were not moving fast enough for Will. He finally told Victor he had some things to do and could he call him when he found out the destination of the ship. Victor looked puzzled but said he would. On the elevator Will decided that this L.R. needed to be tailed and gave himself the job. Once in his car he headed for L.R.'s warehouse. Clay had told him that the building next door to his property was empty and was great for checking out the warehouse. Will brought his binoculars to watch his targets.

Once Will arrived he saw L.R. getting into a car. Just in case it was his, Will jotted down the make, model and license plate number. He thought, *Since Victor will be out of the investigation until Internal*

Affairs clears him, I've got to stay close to this guy. Will caught up to the car and followed at a reasonable distance. The car pulled into a restaurant and Will pulled into a gas station just down from the restaurant. He had a good view from his car, and took a few minutes to make sure Liliana had been contacted by the police and told about her brother Patrick's beating. She told him that the police had already called her about taking him to the hospital. Will just filled her in on some of the details the police had left out.

Alma had missed breakfast but was the first in line for lunch. She found an empty table in the mess hall. She was about to eat her first bite of food since the day before, when a cute, young stocky Hispanic steward asked, "Can I sit with you?"

"Sure thing."

"Hi, my name is Javier. I've taken some supplies to the women. I saw you get out of the same truck that they came in and I was wondering if you knew them."

Alma put down her fork, looked him over and said, "Why are you asking?"

"Well, I've been on several trips when we were carrying girls, and on almost every trip some of the crew thought they could have their way with some of the girls. I just thought you should know if you knew them."

"Thanks for letting me know, Javier. But what can I do to stop anything like that happening with these girls?"

"I'm not sure but I thought you might think of something if you knew them. If you did think of something I'd try to help you."

Alma sat thinking and said, "OK, if I do come up with something, how could I get hold of you?"

He took out a piece of paper, handed it to her, and then left. Alma quickly put the note into her pocket and began to eat. She willed herself not to look around the room to see if anyone was looking at her. She had learned a great deal from working for L.R. about dealing with criminals and thugs. But after a few minutes had passed she took a quick glance around and there was no one there. She finished her meal and went out onto the deck for a short time to enjoy the ocean view and blue skies.

After lunch Liliana told her boss the police had called about her brother's admittance into a hospital. She asked him if she could leave early to visit him but he told her just to go on and leave then. He told her to catch up the rest of her work on the next day. She called Will and left him a message that she was heading to the hospital to see Patrick and that she would call him as soon as she returned home.

L.R. left the restaurant with several bags and drinks. Will waited until he was well past the gas station before he pulled out to follow him. He seemed to be taking the same route back to the warehouse so Will took a short cut into the empty lot beside it. He jumped out of the car with his binoculars and hurried to the edge of the overlooking hill.

As L.R. opened his car door, Will could see Tiny and Face walking up to him. L.R. yelled, "Did you find that rat, Clay, yet?" Will could see that they were shaking their heads no. Will was torn between staying and finding out more information about the ship or going back to his apartment to take Clay to a more secure location. He chose the latter. Then as he turned towards his car, he heard L.R. order them to find Clay and to call him at his home after it was done. Once inside his car, Will called Victor to talk over this new information and to ask what would be the best, safest location to take Clay. Victor told Will he would meet him at his apartment.

Liliana walked into the ICU hospital room and almost screamed out in horror at the sight of her brother's face. He was black and blue, swollen, and hardly recognizable and there were so many tubes, so many wires hooked to monitors that she could hardly touch him. She finally worked her way around all the hospital equipment, took his hand and said, "Patrick, I'm here now. Please don't leave me!"

She saw him slowly close his fingers around her hand and then he squeezed her hand as though he was letting her know he was not leaving her. Liliana leaned over with tears flowing freely and kissed his hand. All her emotions from the past several days poured out. It was as if time had stopped and all she could do was pray, allow her tears to flow freely and succumb to all the horror from the past few days. It was just the two of them grieving and holding each other's hands, trying to deal with all their heartaches.

Del awoke from a nap at the sound of the dinner dishes rattling around on the trays as they were passed through the gate. She had propped herself up with pillows and she had slept soundly. It seemed colder than the previous day. They were probably crossing the colder waters of the Northern Atlantic. Before the steward could close the gate, Del asked if they could please get some more blankets and heavy sweaters or pullovers. He nodded and then locked the gate before leaving.

There was very little conversation during their meal. Del sensed the girl's melancholy mood, so she agonizingly stood up, thanked the girls for cleaning up and carefully turned. She then wished them a good night's sleep as she returned to her bunk.

Del could hear the different whispered conversations between the girls as she tossed and turned trying to find a comfortable position to sleep. She missed Will and she was feeling worse. Then she remembered what her pastor once spoke about, when you feel terrible give thanks. He said it would help so Del started giving thanks to God. It worked, she thought as she began to fall asleep.

Victor arrived at Will's as the sun was going down on a very long first day of the week. Will opened the door before he knocked and said, "Where have you been? We were getting worried that something had gone wrong at the precinct."

"Sorry about being so long. IA took their time getting to the crime scene and then their questioning lasted longer than I expected.

So have you guys figured out where you might go? If not, I may have an idea." Clay walked into the living room and greeted Victor. He turned and sat down in one of the matched pair of chairs opposite the couch. Victor and Will took a seat on the couch.

Victor continued, "Clay I was just telling Will that I may have found a solution to prevent L.R.'s capture and murder of you."

Clay sat forward in his chair. "Well? Spill it, Victor!"

"The New York Dock Master returned our call requesting the destination of the freighter. The ship is to make port next Friday morning, May 30th, at Southampton, England." Victor could see that Will was about to interrupt him so he continued, "Just wait, Will, let me finish. So once I'd been given this information, I thought of our old friend and one of the greatest detectives ever in Scotland Yard, Inspector Charles Wells. So I passed my idea by Cap who gave his OK. Then I gave Charles a call. Fortunately for us he was working late and still at his office. Boys, you're going to love this! Inspector Wells is not only interested in having you both to come and help, but Charles knows our crime boss, L.R. Gomez."

Will and Clay both jumped up out of their seats, fists pumping in victory as they shouted in relief and joy. Finally something was happening, something was going their way. Victor just sat laughing at them.

"Hold on boys, there's more!" They sat back down, leaning forward to catch every word. "Charles told me how he came to meet up with our L.R. which was a long detailed account that I can fill you in on later. The short version was in the late 80s, Charles had L.R.'s back to a wall after a long investigation but then out of nowhere his two goons showed up and killed three of his men and injured five others. L.R., Face and Tiny all escaped England. Charles can get enough warrants to put them away for life. The only problem is how can we entice L.R. to go back over to England?"

Clay's face lit up like a light bulb and he shouted, "That's why Alma was getting in the semi's cab! She'd somehow come up with a plan to get L.R. over to England. She knew he would never go back there without something so important to risk his capture. Wow! I knew she was up to something."

In one frustrated chorus, Will and Victor demanded, "Who is Alma and what are you so excited about?"

"Alma was L.R.'s right hand assistant for more than a decade. She knows L.R. better than anyone and she also saw L.R. murder José Ramos. They never said they were dating, but most of us had gotten the idea that they were. You could imagine how she felt after that! After Face threw Del into the truck's trailer, I saw Alma climb up into its cab. I also saw her face just after L.R. killed José and I've never seen Alma so angry. I'd bet anything she's already stirred the pot. Victor, you just need to get the cops to turn up the heat enough to get L.R. to leave Atlanta!"

"So boys, how quickly can you pack to fly to London?" Victor was grinning from ear to ear, but suddenly Clay looked panic stricken.

"I wouldn't miss this capture for anything, but Victor, I don't have a passport. Do you think your Inspector could get me through customs?"

"Clay, I'll give him a call back tomorrow with your London flight information and I'm sure he can work it out. So Will, if you could call the airlines while I go home to eat with my family, I'd appreciate it. Once I get back to the precinct, I'll call you and get the flight information. Will – wait, what is it?"

Will had a shocked look on his face. "It's my sister Elizabeth! I had forgotten that she is leaving for Paris in a few days, and I had volunteered to drive her to the airport! But if I'm in London, I won't be able to do that! I had completely forgotten until you said family!"

Victor slapped his friend on the back. "Will, you know you can count on your friends to help your family out! Just tell me what flight she is on and we'll get her to the airport on time." When he saw the big smile on Will's face, he continued with his original thought. "Will, you can tell me when you guys have finished packing and I'll send a squad car to pick you up. The officers can take you to the airport motel of your choice and then stay with you until you board your flight. And don't worry about Elizabeth. You have enough on your plate already."

They all nodded their heads in agreement, stood and went to work.

TUESDAY, MAY 20, 1997

Kendra, Tamika and Mai were curled up under a quilt at daybreak on one of the rear beds. Del was across the aisle also under a quilt with her Bible opened to the 5th chapter of Galatians propped up on her lap.

Del stared into the sleepy eyes of each girl and smiled back at them. "Good morning. I hope you were able to stay warm as the Northern Atlantic cold waters are keeping our area very cold. I'm sorry that Gayle and Rose decided not to join us."

Del held out the Bible to Mai. "Could you read the first part of verse 22 of the 5th chapter of Galatians."

Mai took the Bible and began to read out loud, "22 But the fruit of the Spirit is love… Galatians 5:22 (NIV) Is that where you want me stop?"

"Yes. What do you think God's love looks like? For example maybe like a parent's love."

Mai replied, "Yes, a parent's love is exactly how I picture God's love."

There was a short time of silence but Del could see each of the girls thinking through her question.

Then Kendra responded, "I believe God's love is different than human love. I believe His love is purer and more dependable than the love people show to each other." Kendra started to weep quietly, which kept her from speaking any more. Tamika reached out and put her arm around Kendra's shoulders. Del allowed some time for the girls to comfort each other before speaking again.

Del finally said, "You girls have been through some harsh circumstances that other girls your age will probably never experience. It's for this very reason that I think your idea of going through these nine fruit of the Spirit is so important. God's love will never hurt, criticize, lie, manipulate or assault you. Never." She then fell silent for them to absorb what she had just told them.

Mai asked, "Why can people be so hateful and cruel?"

"Well, the first part of this same chapter answers that for you." She reached out and took the Bible back from Mai and began to read out loud verses 19-21, "[19] The acts of the flesh are obvious: sexual immorality, impurity and debauchery; [20] idolatry and witchcraft; hatred, discord, jealousy, fits of rage, selfish ambition, dissensions, factions [21] and envy; drunkenness, orgies, and the like. I warn you, as I did before, that those who live like this will not inherit the kingdom of God." Galatians 5:19-21 (NIV)

"In other words, those who have not accepted Jesus as their Savior and Lord will live out their lives doing most of what I just read to you. There is no love associated with any of them. What do you girls think about any of what we've covered this morning?"

Del allowed some time to pass then bowed her head. "Let's pray silently, girls, and then I'll close in a couple of minutes."

"Lord Jesus we come to you this morning and ask You to teach us about Your love as well as the other 8 fruit of the Spirit. Help us to forgive the people who have hurt us and then fill up our hearts with Your love for them. We know this is impossible without you and we pray this in Jesus' name. Amen."

Del slid down under her quilt and rolled over facing the wall before breakfast came. She heard the girls sharing and laughing until she drifted off into a sound and peaceful sleep.

Victor was busy at his desk catching up on unfinished reports. He was glad that Will and Clay were able to buy London tickets on a flight leaving just after midnight. The uniform officers only had to take them to the airport and he would not have to report why he was requesting them to stay at the motel. They had made reservations for the same place he had stayed in London at the end of last year. Detective Charles Wells from Scotland Yard had been extremely helpful with the case of Will's sister. He would contact them tomorrow after they got settled.

Now all he had to do was talk to Jeffords and see what he thought about putting some persuasive pressure on L.R. Gomez. He was sure Jeffords had many tricks up his sleeve to help L.R. want to leave town sooner rather than later. Victor was finally starting to like this cat and mouse game with a seemingly untouchable crime boss.

Liliana arrived at work early to catch up on some of her work since her boss had let her go early the day before. Patrick had been badly beaten. It had been hard to see him like that but at least he was still alive. Will's friend Victor had posted uniformed policemen at his hospital room just in case. She did think that Patrick knew she had come to visit him. It was hard to know for sure. Even the doctors were not sure what he would and would not remember. She whispered, "God please protect Mai and Patrick. Amen." She wiped away her tears and then started to work on her stack of papers.

L.R. was slower than normal in his morning routine. He was sore and irritated from sleeping in the jail lock-up. Also to make matters worse, Tiny and Face had not been able to track Clay down yet. He thought, *I should have never sent Clay to get rid of the body. Now I've gotten myself into this mess with the cops. It's that investor who started all of this. I'll make sure he never leaves that hospital and I'll get the rest of his family for the trouble he's caused me.*

His thoughts drifted even farther back to Cuba. His father had been drunk and extremely angry at him. It was times like that when his words would not be stopped by his calculating mind. He started out by saying, "You are so much like your mother. She wouldn't stop pushing me either! But I took care of that the day I killed her."

L.R. realized tears were streaming down his cheeks and slammed his fist down on the table. He quickly wiped away his tears and brought his thoughts back to the present. He had learned that dwelling on that terrible moment would only bring more destruction. Even though he knew better he poured quite a large amount of liquor into his coffee cup.

It was already lunchtime but he was in no hurry to get to the warehouse. He had given the order that the whole place should be packed and shipped back to Miami by the end of the week. He knew the office would be in total chaos without Alma's guidance but he would never let her know he thought that about her organizational skills. He was sore about giving Alma the week off as well as trying to figure out where Clay was hiding. So for now he would continue to drink coffee and liquor, and stay away from the office for a couple of days.

Alma was wearing every warm garment she had brought but the cold winds off the Northern Atlantic cut straight through them all. She shivered all the way to her bones. She heard the door slam behind her and the small number of men in the tiny mess hall looked over at her. Alma had learned to ignore any effort at intimidation working for L.R., so she straightened her back, lowered her head and walked over to the food line to get her breakfast.

After Alma got her food, she turned and her eyes met Javier's. She thought, why not. So she headed toward the end of his table. Most of the other workers had eaten and gone to work.

"Can I join you?"

Javier took a quick glance around the mess hall and said, "Sure, why not."

"I've thought about the information you passed along to me. Are you still looking in on the girls?"

"When I am scheduled to deliver their food or supplies."

"Have any of the girls been attacked?"

"No. Although something has happened that the crew has heard about and none of them would try to do anything now."

"What?"

"One of the older girls has made some kind of request to the other steward. He wouldn't tell me what she said but he was really scared. He told me he had to be careful not to fall into some kind of trap. Her request was for him to contact someone back in the States. He was going to check something out this morning with her to confirm if she was being truthful."

"Did he tell you the name of the girl or what she looked like?"

"No. But I might be able to find that out."

"Only you must do this without drawing any attention to yourself. If she is who I think she is you could get killed, so you need to be really careful! Also from now on we cannot be seen with each other. I'm in cabin 3 that connects to 4 through the bath area. If you find anything out slip a note under the door of 4 and knock before you leave. But how can I contact you?"

"Down the hall there is a fire extinguisher inside a wooden box. There is a photo of an extinguisher in a plastic sleeve. Turn the photo upside down with your note behind it. When my girlfriend traveled with me this is how we would communicate. None of the crew ever noticed the photo being upside down. OK?"

Alma nodded, but she still had questions. She decided to come right to the point. "Javier, how do I know we can trust you? Why are you doing this to help us? Even when it might get you in trouble?"

Javier closed his eyes a minute. This was going to be hard. "OK, but no one else here knows about this. A couple of years ago L.R. kidnapped my younger sister." Alma nodded. Now it began to make sense. "He put her into sex trafficking in his Miami network. Eighteen months later my family received a call from the morgue. She died of an overdose of cocaine. She was fifteen."

Alma took his hand, squeezing it lightly in sympathy. Javier continued, "I've slowly moved through his network ranks and landed the job on The NY Derby. I knew who you were when you boarded her in New York. I knew something was up when you came on board with an elite group of underage girls. So I thought I would find out if you needed some help."

Tears were beginning to well up in Alma's eyes but she pushed them back and said, "You're not alone with someone special being killed by L.R. He murdered my boyfriend a week ago for nothing but bringing him a message. Right there, I decided that I would come up with a plan that would put L.R. in his grave. Maybe we can work together to make that plan a reality and maybe save the captives." They nodded in agreement but sat for just a moment, quietly sharing their sorrow, yet gaining strength from the other one's grief.

Alma stood to leave, thanked him, and left. She saw the wooden box as she went into her cabin. She could not believe that L.R. had sent his star informant along with this group of girls. Somehow he sensed trouble before it happened. *This could mean major setbacks for what I had planned! Javier is the messenger who has been sent to help me come up with a better plan. Someone must be looking out for me.*

Victor had called ahead to make sure Jeffords was at his desk and to ask if he had some time to see him. Jeffords was working on a pile of reports when Victor walked over to his desk. Victor just stood there until he looked up from writing.

"Hey Victor, what's on your mind?"

"Thanks for seeing me on such short notice."

Victor sat down and told him in great detail about Will and Clay flying to London and that Clay thought L.R.'s assistant, Alma, has somehow set him up. Clay was sure Alma was on the same ship as the kidnapped girls. Victor finally took a breath allowing Jeffords an opportunity to say something.

"It was nice of you to come over and update me but I don't see how any of this has to do with my homicide victim. What does this have to do with me or this case?"

Victor said, "Alma was your victim's girlfriend. Also our contact in London, Detective Charles Wells from Scotland Yard, has outstanding warrants from the 1980s for murder, racketeering, kidnapping, etc. on no other than L.R. Gomez." Victor sat back in his chair to watch Jeffords absorb what he had just told him. "Charles told me that he killed three of his officers."

"OK, you've got my attention now, but you'd better be sure about this London cop. So what do you need me to do?"

"Listen, this Detective Wells is the real deal. He'll get L.R. just as sure if it was our guys who were murdered. So, I was wondering if you could pull some of those tricks of yours to help Mr. Gomez want to leave Atlanta right away." Victor leaned back in his chair to watch the wheels turning in Jeffords' head. A huge smile began to grow on Jeffords' face and Victor knew he had thought of the perfect thing that would pressure L.R. to leave town. He could not wait to see what Jeffords had thought up.

Before Will and Clay had exited the plane's gateway, they were met by a uniformed police officer who said he was sent by Detective Wells. He escorted them through customs, retrieved their luggage and then led them out of the airport to his patrol car. It was cloudy and the sun was going down. He opened the trunk so they could put their baggage in. As Will and Clay climbed into the car, the officer said, "Detective Wells told me to make sure you blokes got through customs and to tell you he will ring you tomorrow. The detective also told me to drive you to wherever you have made your accommodations. So where to, gents?"

Victor was back at his desk working when his phone rang, "Detective Jones."

"Detective, this is Liliana. I'm a friend of Del Thomas and the sister of Patrick Cordero. I'm calling because I'm very afraid that the person who tried to kill my brother will soon be going back to the hospital to finish the job. Do you think you could help me find a place that will keep him safe until he's better?"

"Hello, Liliana. Yes, I know who you are. Will asked me to check in on you and your brother. Can I check around for some type of secure location like that and get back to you? I do understand your urgency and I'll call you back as soon as I can."

"Thanks so much. Del and Will have been so kind to me, when it's been very difficult for me. First my daughter being kidnapped and then my brother almost murdered, I would really appreciate anything you can do to help me out with Patrick." Victor quickly got her phone number.

Victor felt guilty as he hung up the phone. This poor woman was totally alone and he knew her urgency about her brother's safety was legitimate. Maybe he could ask his wife for some suggestions. She was very good at knowing what to do in situations like this and she did not have classes today. He dialed his home number.

Del once again noticed Gayle talking with the same steward she had talked to before. This conversation was even more intense than the previous one and a great deal longer. Whatever they were discussing, the steward left in a hurry, looking very distressed.

She must warn the girls the next morning before devotions. Then she asked God's wisdom for what she should do next about Gayle's actions.

Victor called Liliana back and told her that he had a possible solution but he had to make a few calls and talk it over with his captain. He wanted to know if she had any vacation days she could use if he got the details worked out. She told him she could probably get the rest of the week and maybe all of next off. So he told her to try and get with her boss about the days off and that he would call her later at her home.

Victor hung up and then called Will's mobile and he left him a message when he did not answer. Amy was going to see if her twin sister Anne could maybe check Patrick out of the hospital under her care. Anne was a doctor, so they would probably go for it. If she could, then he wanted to see if Will would allow Patrick and Liliana to stay at his apartment while he was in London. Once Amy and Will called him back, he then needed to see if Cap could find some money to pay for Patrick's transport to the apartment and his medical care until he was out of the woods. He felt like Cap could find some funds somewhere since it was a policeman who put Patrick in the hospital in the first place.

Liliana arrived home and began to pack enough clothes and supplies that would last for the almost two weeks she would be gone. Then she called her neighbor Mrs. Baines to let her know she would not be staying in her apartment. She asked if she could periodically check the front door for any messages and that she would call her and let her know she was OK. She fixed herself a sandwich and then just waited for Victor to call.

It was so hard to be in her apartment where the silence was deafening. She was glad she would be leaving and not having all the reminders at the apartment that she was without her sweet Mai. Also she would be kept busy caring for Patrick.

The phone rang and she answered, "Victor is that you?"

"No, this is not Victor, but it's someone to say prepare for your death." Then the line went dead.

Liliana slammed the phone down, grabbed her luggage, turned the lights out, and locked the door. She then ran down the stairs to Mrs. Baines' apartment where she fell into the open arms of her neighbor in uncontrollable sobs. Once Mrs. Baines could get her calmed down enough to find out what happened, she called Detective Jones and asked if he could send a uniformed policeman over to take Liliana to wherever he had set up. She then told him about the death threat phone call and he asked Mrs. Baines to please stay with her until the policeman arrived. She took his phone number and told him her apartment number and said she would take care of Liliana until the policeman arrived.

Victor hung up and walked over to Cap's door to see if he was on the phone or with someone. Victor tapped on the open door and asked if he had a minute. Cap waved him in and Victor quickly brought him up to speed and then asked if he knew of any money they could use to transport Patrick to Will's apartment. Cap told him to finalize any of the remaining steps and that he would find the money.

Once Victor returned to his desk, he answered his ringing phone and it was Amy saying Anne had worked out Patrick's dismissal under her care. She was arranging for the hospital bed, the ambulance and one of her visiting nurses who will ride over and stay with him overnight. Victor gave Amy the address of Will's apartment and said he would meet them there. Will had left a message saying it was fine for them to stay there and where his extra door key was hidden.

Victor then called dispatch to have one of the uniformed policeman pick Liliana up and drive her to the apartment. He told dispatch to let them both know about the death threat, the uniform cop needed to be careful picking up Liliana as well as relieving the uniform cop at Patrick's hospital room once he was picked up.

He put all his paperwork in a drawer and pushed his chair under his desk. As he left for Will's he stuck his head into Cap's office to thank him. He waved and told him he would be over at Will's apartment for the rest of the day.

Face and Tiny drove around the hospital until they found a parking place. They took the doctor coats from the back seat and put them on before heading for the rear of the hospital.

"Tiny, pull your tie up to your neck. We're supposed to be professional looking."

"OK. Boss was really wasted when he called. Wonder what that is all about?"

"I don't know but I know we better call back later with the news that the thief is dead."

"You are right about that. We're going to do what we always do by suffocating him with his pillow, right?"

"Yeah. Tiny, you deal with him because you are taller and stronger. I'll keep a look out for you."

They fell silent as they entered the hospital through the rear. There was no security yet because it was still visiting hours. They reached Patrick's floor and walked to the room number L.R. had given them. When they arrived at the room it was empty. Tiny asked a passing nurse about what happened to the missing patient. He told them that the patient had been dismissed. As they turned and walked towards the elevator Face quietly said, "You're calling Boss! I guess you calling his sister wasn't such a good idea."

WEDNESDAY, MAY 21, 1997

Victor knocked on Will's apartment door before seven with several coffees and a bag of donuts. Before anyone had answered the door, he heard someone greet him by name and he turned to see Anne, coming to check on her new patient.

"Hi Anne, I brought you a coffee and donut." Before she could answer, the visiting nurse answered the door and they went into the apartment.

Anne asked the nurse if the patient had adjusted well. She told the doctor he had begun a low grade fever during the night but the rest of his vitals were normal. Anne told her she would be relieved by another nurse at seven and asked her to tell them she would be calling in to have a prescription delivered to be added to the other medications administered through the IV.

"Victor, I'll have to pass on the coffee and donut but I appreciate you thinking of me. I've a surgery after eight. Also I want to pay for the twenty-four hour nursing service until there is no more need for that." Victor started to protest, but Anne shook her head and sighed. "It's the least I can do after everything that has happened."

Before Victor could say that her ex husband's crimes had nothing to do with her, or even thank her, she had turned and walked out the door. He thought he might have seen Anne's eyes begin to tear but he was not sure. So he turned to the nurse and asked, "Would you like a coffee and donuts?" A big smile came over her face and they walked to the kitchen to sit and enjoy the treats.

"Has Liliana woken up yet?"

"No, but she did go to bed very late last night. She was still upset over the phone call she received but I think by the time she went to bed she had settled down a great deal."

They finished their goodies and then Victor stood to go. "Thank you for coming in last night and taking care of these two. They've been through a great deal." She nodded her head and Victor left.

Del and the three girls were once again at the end of the bunk beds, under as many comforters as they could find. The storage area they were staying in had no heating and the Northern Atlantic was causing the temperature to get colder each day. They could see their breath when they spoke to each other.

Del began to read from her small Bible, "[22] But the fruit of the Spirit is love, joy... Galatians 5:22 (NIV) Like love, joy should be looked at as being different from human joy. Most of the time human joy is seen as the same as happiness but happiness most of the time relies on circumstances. So what is God's joy?" She suddenly started coughing and holding her side. Kendra handed her the glass of water by her bed and Del quit coughing.

Kendra spoke first, "Are you OK? You don't look too good."

Del responded, "Yes, I'm fine."

Kendra continued, "How you explained joy was exactly how my pastor taught us. Joy comes from within. You can't really explain where or how the joy rises up from within but it's just there. Kind of like when you are praying, worshiping and praising God for His care and guidance, then you realize that God's love and joy are bubbling up from within. It's those times that you are so glad you know Jesus and that He's in charge of your life no matter what."

Then Tameka said, "I have a hard time applying God's love and joy to what I've been experiencing over these past several weeks. I was kidnapped and taken to a motel room where one awful smelling man raped me repeatedly. After some time he was joined by several other men who also took turns raping me. Once they had finished with me they left the room. I quickly jumped into the shower and tried to wash away anything that remained of those who raped me. When I got out of the shower, I had no clothes because they had torn up everything I had been wearing when they kidnapped me. So I sat on the bed in a wet towel crying uncontrollably. I hate those men and all the men that have raped me since. I have no love or joy, at least not what you are talking about. I'm just empty of most emotions except shame. I would do anything to escape this life I've been forced into. Can you please help me to understand how I can experience God's love and joy?"

Kendra said, "I went through almost exactly what Tameka experienced. Except the part about being shameful and hating the predators. You see, I've asked God for His strength to forgive them and to move away from their evil life even though I'm still a part of it. I can't always do this but I keep working on it. You see, when I asked Jesus to save me at the age of ten, Jesus has been with me through these horrible experiences. I have experienced God's love and joy as it welled up in me through my prayers. Tameka, you can also ask Jesus to save you too. He loves you and gave His life so you can know Him as I do. Would you like to know Jesus?"

Del saw that Tameka was struggling and responded, "That's right, Jesus does want to know us and to forgive us, but sometimes we need to read more about Him in the Bible and pray more about the things people have shared with us about His love and joy. So let's do that now by praying; God please help us to understand about Your love and joy as well as how to forgive those who have hurt us. Help us all to hear Your voice and to respond to Your call once we understand all that we need to. Amen."

Mai asked, "Can we borrow your Bible for the rest of the day?"

Del handed Mai her Bible and then said, "Girls, thanks so much for your honesty and openness. It means so much that you trust me with your pain. So we'll meet again tomorrow morning. I've got to go use the bathroom." As Del walked away she heard the girls consoling one another and she thanked God for His presence with them that morning.

As Alma was leaving for breakfast, she saw the sign upside down in the little box and so she turned and went back to her room. She walked through the bathroom into the adjourning room to find a note that had been slipped under the door. It was from Javier. He wrote that his co-worker had made a call to the States and that the name of the girl who had asked him to call was Gayle.

She went back into her room closing the doors behind her and sat down on her bed. She could not believe how rotten her luck was for it to be Gayle out of all L.R.'s informants. She would find a way to work around her because she had what L.R. must regain, his mother's brooch.

Alma thought, *Gayle was so loyal because she had been deceived like so many of us. We thought L.R.'s gifts and kindnesses were because he cared about us. Although in reality he was only using them to gain control. Gayle like so many of us wanted to please him because we thought he liked us. Over ten years of my life was dedicated to someone so evil and it took losing José for me to see L.R.'s treachery. I'll do whatever it takes to make sure he never hurts anyone else.*

When Victor arrived at the precinct he had a voice message from Detective Jeffords. He was letting him know that his plan of pressure would be taking place after lunch at his department's interrogation room with L.R. and his lawyer. Victor looked at his watch to see if he had enough time before the meeting. He knew he should let Cap know what they were up to. He pulled out a yellow note pad from his desk and began detailing the events since Patrick's assault.

Liliana slept soundly for the first time since Mai had been kidnapped. She felt safe for the first time, and knowing the nurse and Patrick were in the apartment with her had helped. She had heard a great deal of activity in the apartment but she stayed behind her closed door. She just needed to gain some perspective. There had been such heartache and not enough time for her to adjust.

She picked up her Bible and turned to Psalms 23. Her mom had read this to her many times growing up. She read the verses over and over until she fell back to sleep.

Will stumbled out of the bedroom and found Clay in the suite's living room, hunched over a coffee maker. *He looks terrible,* thought Will, *and I probably don't look much better.*

Clay turned and gave Will the thumbs up. "Look! I figured out the coffee maker. They have weird stuff over here. But I'm just glad they have coffee – I was afraid all they would have to drink was tea." He made a face of disgust at the thought, and Will laughed. *It felt good to have something to laugh about, even something so simple.*

"They do have coffee, and a lot more. We'd better get ready so when Charles calls, we can meet with him right away. I remember some place down the street where we can have breakfast." He thought for a moment. "Wait, cancel that. What if he calls my mobile while we're in the restaurant? I don't want to be talking strategy in the middle of a noisy breakfast crowd. I'll leave my mobile with you, and go down and get some breakfast to go for both of us. I'll go to the place I went the last time I was here."

Clay grinned. "Now you're talking! You can take the first cup of coffee, and grab the first shower so we don't waste any time. Here, take this." He handed the mug to Will.

Will had wasted no time in getting ready and out the door. He returned with enough food for breakfast and whatever snacks they might need before getting the call from Charles. But when he entered the suite, Clay's face told him some bad news was coming.

"Charles called. He's all backed up with some time sensitive work today, and can't meet with us until tomorrow."

Will just stood there, trying to take it in. *They had dropped everything, cut through all kinds of red tape, gotten special permission to let Clay travel without a passport, and now Charles can't meet with*

141

them until tomorrow? He put the bags of food down on the coffee table. Clay was shaking his head.

"And, it's even worse. He can't meet with us until teatime tomorrow. That's in the afternoon, right? What are we supposed to do until then? Visit the queen?" His voice had dropped into sarcasm for that last sentence, and Will knew how he felt.

He dropped into a chair and closed his eyes, trying to sort through his emotions. Suddenly it just felt so hopeless. Del . . . but he couldn't think about her, couldn't let himself think about what might be happening to her. It wouldn't do any good, and would just make him crazy. He got back up and paced around the living room. "I've got to do something, Clay. I can't just wait around here for teatime tomorrow. I know we can't do anything to help get L.R., but I can't just hang around here, doing nothing!"

Clay nodded. "I know what you mean. I've been sitting here, trying to read the Bible, but I am feeling too antsy to get through even one chapter. Maybe we need to get out of here, take a walk, get our energy worked out."

Will stopped pacing and his shoulders relaxed a little. "I think you're on to something. I feel all messed up about the time. We should probably try to get in sync with this time zone as fast as we can, so we can be 100% when we start working. And as long as we're walking, maybe we can go see the changing of the guard. I thought that was the greatest ever the last time I was here. You know what? I just remembered that Charles put me off the last time as well. Maybe it's the Scotland Yard way? You know he's really a great detective. You'll see when we meet with Charles tomorrow." He looked down at the breakfast food. "We should probably eat something, and then get some exercise." When Clay reached for a breakfast sandwich, Will laughed. "And one of us still needs to hit the shower!"

Victor had given thumbs up as he passed his desk on his way to the observation room connected to the interrogation room where L.R. and his lawyer sat. There were a couple of other guys observing that Victor did not recognize. Victor made his way into the corner that gave him a direct line of sight into L.R.'s face.

Jeffords entered the room with his partner, Detective Dennis, and they took the seats directly across the table from them. Jeffords carefully placed the file folder down in front of him and looked L.R. square in his face with his well known 'I've got you' expression. Then he waited for the lawyer to start protesting their treatment by being brought back to the precinct.

"Detective, why have you brought my client back here?"

"We are in the process of taking statements of eye witness accounts of your client, L.R. Gomez, killing José Ramos." With that he opened the folder.

"You don't need my client here for that process. We are leaving."

Victor shifted his weight; *Come on Jeffords, quit messing around.*

"Not yet. I have some questions I need answered. Do you have an employee named Clay Stevens?"

Then L.R. spoke for the first time, "No. He's been fired."

"When Clay Stevens worked for you on Friday, May 9th, did you tell him to get rid of the body of José Ramos?"

"Don't answer that question, L.R.!"

"You are unwilling to answer my questions regarding your commands to Clay Stevens, and with Gomez's lack of cooperation, we feel he could be a flight risk. So I guess we'll just have to get an injunction from the courts to freeze his assets."

Victor started laughing as he watched L.R.'s lawyer grab him as he lunged across the table for Jeffords. *Well, I think he finally hit the subject that will get L.R. to leave town.*

"Come on, L.R., we are leaving. Detective, you just try and get that injunction."

Jeffords started laughing out loud as L.R. and his lawyer left the room. "I guess our interrogation is over." He then turned to the one-way glass and held out his hand with a thumb up. Victor was the only person left. He could not help himself from punching the air with his fist. "We've got you now, Gomez!"

Mai was finishing her dinner when Kendra asked, "Have you heard how Del has started to cough? I've heard that kind of cough before and it can be bad."

Gayle said, "She's just been running her mouth too much." Then she started laughing, but Rose just stared at her.

Mai reached for Kendra as she started to lunge for her. "She's not worth the trouble, Kendra."

"Yeah, you just wait and see if we aren't worth it."

Kendra sat back down and looked at Mai, questioning her comment. Mai just shrugged her shoulders and went back to eating her dinner.

THURSDAY, MAY 22, 1997

L.R. walked into his office before seven and slammed the door. He saw a package on his desk. As he sat down at his desk he picked it up. He noticed no name under sender. L.R. tore the box open and his shadow box fell out with a note. He turned to look at his wall. The space on the wall where it had hung was empty. He sneered and growled while removing the note. It read:

"L.R., I stole your mother's brooch. If you want it back, you'll have to come find me in England! Alma."

He cursed, "OK, Alma. I think you've started something that you may regret and end up like José. Face, Tiny come in here, now!"

"Yes, Boss."

"I want you guys to call the warehouse down in Miami and tell them to find Alma Hernandez. I think she's visiting her parents. Tell them to put her on the first truck to Atlanta. Pick her up and bring her to me."

Tiny shifted his weight and carefully said, "Boss, I saw her take the truck to New York Harbor last week. I'm not sure but I think she is on the same freighter as the shipment."

L.R. once again screamed out a huge series of curse words and then asked, "That freighter, was it headed to England?"

"Yes, Boss."

"OK then, you boys go home and pack your bags. I'll give you a call later and let you know where to meet me."

"Yes, Boss." They both left his office.

It was then that L.R. saw his answering machine blinking. It was one of the stewards on The NY Derby. "Mr. Gomez, I hate to bother you but one of the girls, Gayle, gave me this emergency message. She said that you had to meet the freighter when it docked in Southampton, England because there was something very wrong with this shipment. Sorry for bothering you, Mr. Gomez, but she insisted that I call you." Then he heard the click of the disconnection.

L.R. opened his drawer and took out the binder with all the shipping information. The NY Derby was to make anchor next Friday morning, May 30th. He put that binder and several others into his large briefcase. Then he pulled the duffle bag of cash and a packed suitcase out of his closet and neatly stacked the money into two large leather satchels.

He dialed the phone number of his private pilot and told him to quietly prepare his jet for a trip to London but not to file a flight plan. He told him he and the boys would be there shortly. He stood, picked up his suitcase, satchels and briefcase, and looked one last time around the office. He turned, walked out of his office, down the stairs and out of the warehouse. Once in his car he called Tiny's mobile phone and told them to meet him at the Peachtree-DeKalb private airport as soon as possible. He then dialed his CPA in Miami and told him to move all his money out of the U.S. by five today, into his other banks in Europe and the Caribbean. After giving him his mobile phone number, he told him to leave a message on his mobile and he would call him back on a clean phone. L.R. told him to let him know once all the money had been transferred.

Victor was waiting on the main road near L.R.'s warehouse. He waited a couple of cars back and then pulled onto the road to follow his car. He took the secondary roads and that was just fine for Victor. L.R. wove through the North Atlanta streets and neighborhoods until he turned into the Peachtree-DeKalb private airport. Victor just kept on driving until he came to a donut shop. He parked and went in to buy a coffee and donut to celebrate their victory. He called Jeffords once he found a table to share the good news; they had tricked him into running. Jeffords said he would try and get their destination the following day and once he got it he would give him a call.

Once he arrived back at the precinct, Victor called Detective Charles Wells in London. He did not get him but he left the message about L.R. Gomez leaving Atlanta and heading his way. He told him that once he got more information about the flight he would call him back.

Del, Mai, Tameka and Kendra once again met at the end of the beds for their morning study. Del asked if they remembered to bring the Bible with them. Kendra took it out of her sweater and reached out to give it to Del. But Del said, "Kendra would you mind reading the Galatians 5 passage?" Then Del started coughing and had a hard time stopping.

Mai asked, "Are you all right?"

"I'm OK. I just have a cold. Kendra, if you don't mind."

She then read the passage. That morning they would be talking about the third fruit, peace.

"Thanks, Kendra. Questions to maybe help us get started - what is the difference between how the world sees peace and how God's peace is seen?"

Tameka spoke up, "I'm not sure what those differences are, but I sure would like to have some peace in my life."

Kendra said, "The world sees peace as the opposite of conflict or strife but God has several aspects of peace. The one I think about the most is that God's peace is a state of mind or being complete in God. I know I keep coming back to this but the only way we can get God's peace is to believe that Jesus died on the cross for our sins. Then the Holy Spirit comes to live within us. He shows us God's peace, love, joy, and peace can only be experienced through Jesus."

Tameka replied, "I think you are right. I read through some of the different gospels yesterday and Jesus tries to tell the people exactly what you just said, Kendra. I'm so sad and bitter because of all that has happened to me since I was kidnapped. I don't want to feel like this anymore. I want Jesus to be in my life so I can experience those fruits. What should I do?"

Del replied, "Tameka, that is a great question. So let's read what the Bible says. Mai could you read Acts 16:30-31."

Kendra handed Mai the Bible and she read, "[30] He then brought them out and asked, 'Sirs, what must I do to be saved?' [31] They replied, 'Believe in the Lord Jesus, and you will be saved—you and your household.' Acts 16:30-31(NIV) Wow, that doesn't seem too hard to understand." Mai looked up to see Tameka crying and Kendra and Del smiling.

Del asked, "Tameka did you tell Jesus that you believe that He can save you and that you are sorry for your wrong doings?"

Tameka in a voice barely audible, "Yes and for the first time in my life, I feel loved and at peace."

Then with one flow of movement, Kendra and Mai flung their arms around Tameka. Del just smiled and bowed her head in praise and thanksgiving.

Gayle and Rose looked down the aisle at them and Gayle shook her head in disgust. Rose turned away from Gayle as she had tears in her eyes about to flow down her cheeks.

Before they broke for the morning, Del said, "Girls I don't want you to worry but I think Gayle is trying to get word back to her boss. She's been speaking to one of the stewards the last couple of days. So I want all of you to be very careful about what you say to her. OK?" They all nodded their heads in agreement with Del.

As the girls walked back to their beds, they could hear Del coughing again. They looked at each other in concern for her.

Liliana was in the kitchen early preparing some breakfast for the nurse and her. As they sat down at the table, Liliana said she wanted to bless the food.

"God, I want to thank you for this place, food and wonderful care givers for my brother. Please bless us and heal Patrick. Amen."

Before they could start eating they heard some noise coming from Patrick's bed. The nurse hurried over and realized he was trying to remove his ventilator tube. She quickly touched his hands and said, "I'll help you remove it." He looked at her and stopped moving around.

The nurse retrieved a large sterile piece of gauze, placed it at the base of the tube and quickly pulled the tube from his mouth. Patrick began coughing up mucus, and the nurse handed him some gauze. She raised the head of the bed so Patrick was sitting upright. She handed him more gauze and he wiped his mouth from coughing up some mucus. He continued to cough and wipe his mouth for several more minutes. He finally began to breathe easier and without coughing.

Then he whispered, "Wow, Sis, I didn't know you could pray." They all started laughing. This caused him to start coughing again but they could tell by his expression he was doing better.

Alma stood in line for lunch. The food wasn't great, but she wasn't there for the fine dining. She was still trying to adjust her plans after learning that Gayle Simpson had sent word to L.R. Gomez. She was sure he had already left Atlanta to fly over to England and land at some remote airfield. She knew he would be waiting at the dock for this freighter's arrival. *Well, enough about them! I'm going to sit here and eat my lunch while looking out at the beautiful blue ocean and bright sunshine.*

Detective Charles Wells had been seated at a table for three. This was the same tea room they had met in last winter. Will shook Charles' hand with a big smile on his face and then introduced Clay.

"Charles, I can't thank you enough for your great work on my sister's case last year. I hear from Victor that you've run into L.R.

Gomez before. Could you bring Clay and me up to speed on your dealings with him?"

Charles took a swallow of his tea, then he began, "It's nice to see you once again as well, Will. Why don't you tell me what you and Clay know of this villain first?"

Will waited while the server took their orders and then said, "Clay, you should go first about your background with L.R., OK?"

Clay started his story with José's murder and finished with fleeing to England so they would not be able to kill him. They all had finished their hot drinks so they just sat until Charles had absorbed all of Clay's information. It was almost five and Will could tell Charles needed to leave. He had started looking at his watch about half way through Clay's account.

Will once again remembered his first encounter with Charles and how much better his performance had been once he had finished clearing his calendar. He could then better concentrate on their case; they had once again just dropped in on his week. The freighter was not arriving until the following week. Even though it was difficult for Will, he suggested, "Look Charles, it's pretty late, we can hear your account of L.R.'s criminal activities another time. Just let us know what we can do to help you."

"Yes, you are correct. I do need to return to the Yard. If you gents can entertain yourselves through the weekend, I'll be able to get these pressing matters off my desk."

Will tried to once again let Charles know he was the lead investigator, and continued, "Sure, there is plenty to do here. Clay has a long list of places he would like to go. So we'll just look for your call Monday."

They all stood, shook hands and left the tea room. It had started to rain, so Will and Clay hailed a taxi to take them back to their hotel.

It was late afternoon in Atlanta and Detective Paul Rankin checked his voice messages for the first time. It was the one of the first messages from early that day.

150

The message was from Mrs. Hill, "Detective I'm calling to inform you that my husband, Jason Hill, passed away early this morning. This has been extremely difficult for me and my family. I hope now that it's murder, you'll be able to spend more time in finding my husband's attacker. Please keep me informed of any changes in this case."

Rankin just hung up the phone after listening to the message. He sat there for a couple of minutes to gather his thoughts and picked the phone up to leave a message for his boss. This case would be sent over to homicide.

As Detective Wells made his way back to Scotland Yard, he played back each of the details Clay Stevens had recounted for him. Even though Detective Victor Jones had left a message that L.R. Gomez would soon be arriving in England, he did not want to cause Clay any more anxiety than he already had. But one thing Wells did know, the evil man he had known in the late 80s had become even more sinister. Sex trafficking using underage girls was a new low, even for L.R. He had to be stopped during his time in England. Victor would call him with the flight information and once he had found out Gomez's whereabouts, he would tell Will.

The lights had been turned out for over an hour, when Kendra woke up abruptly. She sat up in bed to gather her thoughts. She had heard someone call her name.

It was after she sat up that she heard someone struggling to breathe. She jumped up and shook Mai, "Mai, I think something is very wrong with Del's breathing. Get up and help me."

They made their way to Del's bunk by feeling each bed. Kendra asked, "Del, are you OK?"

"Kendra, touch her forehead and see if she has a fever."

"Mai, she's burning up!"

Then Mai took Del's shoulder and shook her with no response.

"We need to tell the steward that Del is unconscious from being sick."

They both made their way back to the gate. They started shouting until one of the crewmen heard them and came to find out what they were shouting about. They told him that Del was unconscious and needed a doctor. He opened the gate and turned the light on. Everyone started fussing about the light being turned on and waking them up.

Mai said, "Listen, tell the doctor that she had a really bad beating the past Sunday morning. She was kicked many times around her chest and she's been struggling to breathe ever since."

He followed the girls to Del's bunk. He realized right away when he saw how pale she was and how she labored so to breathe that there was a problem. He called for some help on his two-way radio. A few minutes went by with everyone talking at the same time. Then two other crew members came in with a stretcher, put Del on it with all her blankets, and left, locking the gate behind them.

Kendra and Mai called after them that once they found out what was wrong with Del to please let them know.

FRIDAY, MAY 23, 1997

Javier was surprised when they brought one of the girls into the infirmary on a stretcher. Although, looking at her more closely, she was certainly older than those other girls. He helped the doctor and the other assistants for a couple of hours to get Del's vitals under control. They had finally warmed her up with hot water bottles and started an IV with some fluids and a broad-spectrum antibiotic. The doctor also tightly bound her ribcage and treated the many bruises on her face and body. Both her breathing and fever began to stabilize. It was after one a.m., so the doctor told Javier to come wake him in a couple of hours unless she started to get worse. He told the others to go back to bed.

They all left except for Javier. He worked overtime with the doctor so he could fulfill the infirmary's requirements. Once he fulfilled them he could start working for the Doc and leave the steward/crane operator position. The whole time he had been working for the Doc he had never seen someone so sick. He guessed the guys on the ship worked out so much on their jobs that they did not get sick as much. They were used to the cold, harsh weather of the Northern Atlantic because of the different crossings but these women were not. There was no heat in their area, just what would work its way down from the crew's quarters.

Maybe he should get Alma in on this so this sick lady could be moved to her adjourning room. Then she would not have to go back to the cargo hold. He sat down and wrote Alma a note about what had taken place in the infirmary. Then she could read it and make up her own mind about what she wanted to do.

In the cargo hold, Kendra, Mai and Tameka had huddled together to pray for Del. They spoke in low voices not to bother the other two girls. Before they prayed Kendra told them about how she woke up. She told them she thought it was God waking her up and they all agreed with her. They prayed for the doctor and that Del would respond to his treatment. They also asked God to heal Del so she could quickly come back to them and thanked God for being with her. Then they went back to bed.

Will awoke with a jolt. He was sweating and breathing as hard as if he had just run five miles. He could not explain his state of urgency about Del. He went to the minibar and took a cold bottle of water out of the refrigerator. He drank the whole bottle without stopping. He shank down into one of the oversized chairs, not being able to shake his despair.

Clay walked out of his room and saw Will sitting with his head in his hands and asked, "What's wrong, Will?"

Will jumped and said, "Clay you surprised me! Did I wake you up?"

"No, I woke up with a real burden to pray for Del. What about you, why are you awake?"

"Are you are messing with me? I was jolted awake with real fear for Del. What's going on?"

Clay could hear the fear in Will's voice. He had been praying for an opportunity to continue their conversation about knowing Jesus. So Clay prayed for God's leading and sat down on the couch across from him.

"What do you think is going on with both of us waking up with real concerns for Del's safety?"

There was a fairly long time of silence and Clay just prayed for Will's understanding of God's plan for him.

Will finally broke the silence, "Clay I can't shake this feeling that Del is in real trouble. If she was here she would tell me to pray but I'm afraid I might lose her. What am I to do, Clay? I don't know much about praying."

Clay could feel the fear in Will's voice, and could feel the burden to pray still strong in him. "Praying is just talking to God. You don't have to use fancy words, like those ministers in church sometimes do. Just talk to God as if He was right here in the room with us. Tell Him what you're feeling." Clay waited until Will nodded his head. "Would you like me to start?" Will didn't say anything but looked so relived that Clay almost laughed, but bowed his head instead.

"OK, here goes. God, thank you for waking us up knowing that Del needed our prayers. Right now we lift her up to You, knowing that she needs Your help. We don't know what she needs help for, but You do. We know you can help her, and we ask you to help her, right now. And we thank you for waking us up to pray for her, and we thank you for helping her." Clay looked over and saw that Will was looking more relaxed. Maybe the prayer was helping him, too. "Will, go ahead, and when you're through I'll finish up."

Will cleared his throat. "God, I feel like You know what's going on here a lot more than I do. I am just starting to get to know You, and don't feel as if should be asking You for favors right off the bat. But since You woke me up to pray for Del, I guess it's what I need to do. So I'm asking You to give her whatever she needs. It must be important, since you woke us up so we could ask for it. And I am trying not to be worried about her, but I am worried. I am trying to trust You to keep her safe, and maybe this prayer is part of it. So, here it is, I'm praying to You to help her, and I am praying to You to help me not be worried, to know that You are taking care of her." He looked over at Clay.

"God, thank you for waking Will and me up. Thank you for Will being willing to start trusting you. And thank you for taking care of Del. In Jesus' name, amen." He looked over at Will and somehow was not surprised to see tears streaming down his friend's face.

"Clay, I've never done anything like this. I have no idea what just went on, but for the first time in days, I am not afraid for Del. I know she will be all right. It's like I can breathe again." He wiped his face with some tissue and blew his nose. "I didn't know how tense I was until all the tension left me. What just happened here?"

Clay prayed he would know the right words to say and then began, "I think you just took your first steps to having a relationship with God. You are feeling peaceful, right?"

Will nodded. "Like nothing I have known before. It is amazing. But you know about this, right?"

"Yeah, for me it was when I was a teenager and I was going to the same young people's group at Del's church.

"I guess I had been hearing the youth pastor's teaching for almost a year. We had studied many of the books in the New Testament and I saw many of the guys in the group change. It was a positive change in each case. Then one Sunday evening the pastor spoke about the disciple Matthew. He told us how most tax collectors during this time period cheated most everyone.

"[9] As Jesus went on from there, he saw a man named Matthew sitting at the tax collector's booth. 'Follow me,' he told him, and Matthew got up and followed him. [10] While Jesus was having dinner at Matthew's house, many tax collectors and sinners came and ate with him and his disciples. [11] When the Pharisees saw this, they asked his disciples, 'Why does your teacher eat with tax collectors and sinners?' [12] On hearing this, Jesus said, 'It is not the healthy who need a doctor, but the sick. [13] But go and learn what this means: 'I desire mercy, not sacrifice.'[a] For I have not come to call the righteous, but sinners." Matthew 9:9-13 (NIV)

"Will, I had already begun to steal from people. So this story about Matthew hit me hard. I had seen others change as a result of telling Jesus that they believed Him. I knew God was showing me that I, too, needed to believe that Jesus also died for me. I knew in my heart that I was like Matthew cheating people, and I knew I needed to follow Jesus like Matthew did. So that night when the youth pastor asked if anyone wanted to ask Jesus to change them, I stood up and told everyone I needed Jesus to save me. The pastor prayed for me and some others who stood. I also prayed silently for Jesus to take my life and to change me.

"That night when I got home, I knew Jesus was there with me. I had never known such peace and joy. I knew I was different." Clay glanced at Will. He seemed to be taking it all in, nodding his head. "But once I graduated from high school, I quit going to church. I started hanging around the thieves I once ran with again. So for a long time I turned my back on what I once had with Jesus. I would hear Him calling for me but I would never listen because I liked having all that money. But then L.R. told me to get rid of José's body and I did what he said because I was afraid of what he would do to me if I said no. Will, after I threw my friend's dead body into the river, I was overcome with guilt and sorrow for what I had done to my friend. I couldn't get rid of the sound of his lifeless body hitting the water. I got so drunk but nothing would take that sound away until I picked up my old Bible and read some of my favorite passages. I then told God I had been so wrong not to follow Him instead of trying to get rich. I asked Him to forgive me for not standing up for my friend and to help me do whatever I had to do so José would not have died for nothing.

"When I finished talking to God, I knew He had forgiven me. I also knew I would have to call Victor even if it meant that I would go to jail. After I had set up a time to get with Victor, I realized I wasn't hearing José's body hitting the river anymore. God had taken my guilt and betrayal from me. I promised Him I would do whatever I needed to do and I did. Now I'm in London sharing my failures with you." Clay shook his head, as if a little bewildered at what had happened. "I am so glad I am back to my life with God, but I'm just so sad about the wasted years I lived for myself. And all the people I hurt during that time."

Clay waited silently, praying that Will would know what he should do about Jesus. In the silence Clay could hear Will's sighs. Then he heard him clear his throat.

"Clay, thanks for being so transparent about your life. I don't know God like Del and you but I want to. So would you mind if I said some things to God out loud?"

"Sure, I would like that."

Will cleared his throat one more time and said, "Jesus, I want You to take my life like You have with Del and Clay. I believe that You came here to show us the Way to God. I don't know You well yet, but I want to know You and to learn how to live the way You want me to. Please forgive my shortcomings so far. Please help me to understand what You want me to do."

The two men sat silently, both feeling the peace of God.

It was just after six when Liliana opened the door for the doctor.

"Hi Dr. Kalski, it's good to see you. I think Patrick is doing much better, thanks to you."

"Hi Liliana, and please call me Anne. Well, let's take a look at Patrick."

Patrick was sitting up in bed eating his breakfast. Anne examined him and then said, "Patrick, you are a very lucky man. Very few people who were beaten as brutally as you were survive and those who do survive have brain damage or some other kind of life changing handicap. Your arms and legs took most of the hits, saving your head and internal organs. It was very clever of you to curl up into a ball like you did. It saved your life. We'll take another look at your right arm once you've had more time to heal, the cast will protect it for now. We'll know from the x-rays that we'll take when you come in for your first office visit, if surgery will be required but for now just take it easy and get well."

"Thanks Doc, for everything. Liliana told me you have been very generous with my case."

"You're welcome. I will keep the nurses through the weekend

and when I see you Monday we'll decide if you need them any further." Anne gave a quick smile to them all and then she was gone.

Liliana came over and gave Patrick a hug and said, "Patrick, God has given you another chance. I hope you'll live differently once you finish your prison time."

"Liliana, I'm so sorry! I'm sure Mai was targeted because of me. I really do want to change and I'm not just saying what I think you want to hear. If it wasn't for your friends, I would be dead."

The nurse said, "Patrick, you need to rest now, so I'm going to give you something so you can relax."

In seconds Patrick was asleep and the ladies went back to their cold breakfasts.

Victor arrived at work later than he wanted to. It had been a very long week, especially not knowing who was being paid off by L.R. Victor was not sure how these people would respond once they found out L.R. and his money had left Atlanta. He just needed to keep his nose in his paper work and act ignorant.

He had already brought his stack of files down a good bit when the phone rang.

"Detective Jones."

"Victor, it's Adam Jeffords. I've got the location of where L.R.'s jet landed in England."

"Great job! Let me find my notebook. I'll take down the information and give Charles a call in London."

Alma was on her way to breakfast when she once again saw the sign upside down. She turned the sign right side up, took the note, and went back to her room. She wondered if this was going to be an everyday event. Once in her room she read Javier's note about this sick woman and her first reaction was that she did not want to get involved. Then she remembered the man running along the dock and wondered if the older woman with the girls was somehow related.

She answered his note offering to help out with the sick woman. Although she reminded him she did not want any unwarranted attention. Alma put the note back in the box and continued on to the mess hall for breakfast.

The steward pushed the girls' breakfast through the gate and quickly closed it. Mai asked him, "How is the lady you took to the infirmary?"

He just looked at them and left.

Gayle walked back to her bunk and said sarcastically, "Why do you care. She's done nothing but stick her nose into our business."

Mai looked at the other girls and shook her head no, so they would not respond to Gayle's remark.

Kendra was not going to take any more of Gayle's sarcasm this morning, "Gayle, just because you are the boss's favorite, don't get too cocky in this flea trap because you are very much outnumbered! Just keep your mouth shut regarding Del, understand!"

Kendra stood about three inches taller than Gayle and she knew Kendra would not think twice about enforcing her threats. So Gayle finished her breakfast without any more lip.

Rose had her back to Gayle and gave Kendra a slight smile. Kendra nodded her head to acknowledge Rose's gesture.

Once the girls finished their breakfast and chores, they went back to Del's bunk.

Mai said, "It'll be difficult to find out any information about Del's condition. So let's just pray together until we hear something." The other two girls agreed and they began to pray for Del.

In the infirmary, the doctor examined Del who was better but not out of the woods yet. She was still unconscious but her vital signs were better. He told his assistant to watch her closely and report any changes to him. Then he left for his office.

Victor gave Liliana a call to let her know that L.R. had gone to England, so Patrick was safe. Also to prepare her for his return to jail once he was released by Anne. He told her to enjoy their time together and not to worry about him anymore.

Detective Wells was working diligently to clear his desk. He had spoken to Victor about the small airport between Kidlington and Oxford where L.R. Gomez had landed. It was an hour and half drive northwest of London and he recalled that he had dealt with the Chief Constables there in the late 1980s. Detective Wells was never surprised at the habits of his opponents, they would usually return to what was familiar. Gomez had a network of contacts around Oxford. It was a location that had direct routes to two of his very important costal shipping cities, Portsmouth and Southampton.

Gomez knew that the Thames Valley Police (TVP) covered four large counties. Even though their police department was one of high standing, the amount of coverage would be difficult for any law enforcement agency. It was where his three officers had fallen during the sting that the Yard and TVP had executed against Gomez's network. He had heard that in 1991 a new Chief Constable had been appointed. He was sure they would remember that sting because they also had officers injured. Wells was sure they could find the car rental agency that Gomez used that morning. Wells then put a call through to the new Constable to get the rental information.

Clay and Will had gotten a late start that morning, since they had been up in the middle of the night. They decided since they couldn't do anything at the hotel room, to do some walking again. The walking helped their bodies get in sync with the time zone difference, and there was plenty to see that helped take their minds off Del and L.R. Will was especially enjoying feeling the peace of God that had settled on him after his prayer in the middle of the night. It made the waiting bearable.

They got back to their suite just in time to shower for dinner.

Clay had grabbed the shower first, which gave Will time to think about the phone calls he had gotten that day. One was a message from Victor letting them know that L.R., Tiny and Face had arrived in England that morning. The other message was from Charles giving them the car description and tag number for the vehicle L.R. rented at the Kidlington RAF airfield. Will had not told Clay about L.R. being in England.

Will thought it ironic that they had left the U.S. for England to keep Clay safe and now his predators had also arrived in England. He would allow Clay to enjoy his dinner before sharing the phone messages. Once again Will prayed for Del's safety and protection. He really wanted to tell her about believing in Jesus as the Son of God and how he now understood what she had been trying to tell him about her love for Jesus. For now he would just pray for their safe reunion. He heard Clay tell him to hurry up, that he was starving..

When Javier arrived at the infirmary, he was surprised to see their newest patient sitting up in bed. His counterpart, whom he was relieving, was feeding her some hot broth. She still looked very pale and weak with the IV still running.

"Hello, my name is Javier, and I'm very glad to see you sitting up in bed."

"Hi, I'm Del, and I think I'm finished so I can lie down once again."

Javier signaled that he would take it from there, and slowly let the bed down, keeping her head still elevated slightly. "Is that better?"

"Yes, thank you. After I sleep some I might finish the broth. I'm still not feeling well."

"Well, I think you should sleep as long as you want. I'll be here if you need anything."

Del was sound asleep by the time he returned from placing her broth in the small refrigerator they had in the back room. Since Alma was OK about Del using the adjacent room, he would see what the Doc thought about the idea. He made sure Del's covers were properly secured to keep her warm and then started working through his duties.

L.R. was phoning the contacts he knew from the late eighties with not much luck. He just needed a couple of men who knew how to handle themselves in a firefight. He found one who was going to see if another guy he knew could help out. He had already purchased a clean mobile phone and had given the new number to his contact, Toby.

They had gotten a room at one of the inns he knew from before, south of Oxford. Tiny and Face had eaten and turned in after a few drinks. He had stayed in the pub waiting for his contact to call back. They had gotten a large vehicle, a navy Toyota 4Runner, big enough to seat six. It was new with four-wheel drive capability just in case they had to get off the main roads. By the time Toby called him back he was very drunk but he still was able to take the contact information. He told Toby it would be from Tuesday to next weekend and he would make it worth their time.

SATURDAY, MAY 24, 1997

L.R. was so hung over he was having difficulty making the time he told Tiny and Face for breakfast. He made it though and drank mostly coffee and ate a roll. The guys knew he was hung over so they said very little to him. He just kept focusing on Alma's betrayal and the look on her face when he would be there waiting on her as she left the Derby.

Javier was scheduled for duty that morning as the steward to take the girls their breakfast. He had written Del's friends a message letting them know she was doing much better and would probably be staying with one of the passengers for the rest of the voyage. Del had described the girl she wanted him to hand deliver the note to, Mai. She had also told him to be as discrete as possible because they had an informant among them and described her to him. He followed her directions to the letter, leaving without the informant knowing what he had done. Javier was impressed that Del had figured out what he knew as a fact about the informant. He would let Alma reveal that fact once she thought Del was ready.

Liliana asked the nurse if she thought Patrick could move from the bed to the couch. They both helped him over to the couch and propped several pillows behind him. He realized how sore his legs and back were in moving around for the first time, but he knew it would help him heal faster if he worked his muscles.

Liliana put a tray full of his favorite breakfast foods on his lap. Patrick looked up at her. "What's the special occasion?"

"Well, I know the food in jail is not very good, so I wanted to spoil you before the doctor releases you. So enjoy and remember to eat and drink slow."

"I appreciate you making all this for me, thanks."

"We're also enjoying the food, just at the kitchen table." She touched his hand and smiled as she went over to eat with the nurse. He was having a hard time controlling his emotions. It had been a long time since he had enjoyed this kind of attention. Like Liliana told him, he ate and drank his food slowly and enjoyed each bite.

After breakfast Mai, Tameka and Kendra went to Del's bunk at the end of the row of beds. They read some from the Bible and then softly Mai read the note the steward gave her. "Del is doing much better and wanted you girls to know she would probably not be returning to the cargo hold. A guest will be looking after her where she will have heat and the doctor can look in on her. If you would like to write her a note, I can take them to her but without anyone knowing. Javier."

Mai stuck the note into her pants pocket and asked the girls if they wanted to thank God and pray for continued healing for Del. So they started praying and softly thanking Him for His grace and healing.

Victor really hated giving up his Saturday with his family, but Jeffords had left a message on his mobile asking him to meet him at his precinct. So instead of enjoying this beautiful, clear, crisp day, he was driving in to meet Jeffords. Maybe it would not take too long at the precinct.

Jeffords was pacing back and forth by the windows on his floor. Victor walked over to him and said, "What's up?"

"Thanks for coming in on your day off, Victor. I think you'll understand in a minute. I got a call from Detective Rankin late last night. He was the detective in charge of Patrick's case. He told me that Patrick's boss, Jason Hill, died from his injuries this week. From Rankin's investigation he does not think Patrick was the one who assaulted Jason. Rankin's opinion is mainly from circumstantial evidence as he can't see Patrick inflicting those kinds of injuries Hill received because he was just not strong or big enough. Yet all the concrete evidence points to Patrick. Victor, I'm taking over the case and I'm going to have to charge him for the murder of Jason Hill.

"Victor, this really changes Patrick's situation. I must move him from his present location to the clinic in Fulton County's jail. I'll do whatever I can to keep him safe."

"Adam, L.R. has left the country but I don't know if the bounty for killing Patrick has been rescinded. My guess is that it hasn't. How can you protect him when there's probably over a dozen criminals in that place who know about L.R.'s bounty on him?"

"You know my hands are tied on this, I've got to move him. So where is he? I'll send a couple of uniforms with the ambulance. Victor, I'm really sorry."

Victor slowly moved towards Jeffords' desk and gave him the address of Will's apartment. Then he dialed the phone number and gave Liliana the bad news. By the time he reached his car to go home, Victor was really distressed about this whole mess. On one hand L.R. was walking into a trap but on the other hand he couldn't believe the terrible luck Patrick had. What could he do to help this poor guy out? Victor could not prove it, but he was sure L.R.'s two goons were the ones who assaulted Hill to get the information. Yet Victor did not have one piece of evidence or proof to back up his theory.

Detective Wells picked up his messages. One of them was from the Constable from TVP. The vehicle information he had given him was now incorrect. The vehicle had been returned and their sources did not know anything else. He had telephoned other sources but he had not had any luck concluding, "As this villain of yours is very clever."

Charles hung up the phone after hearing this bad news. How was he going to tell Will and Clay that he had lost L.R. who was in England, and might destroy them both? He had to find this villain before he could carry out his destructive plans, he must do this.

That morning Clay and Will had decided to just stay around the hotel. The walking tour the day before had made them both sore. Clay had gone to the exercise area to work out some of his soreness.

Will wanted to talk with Del so badly. He was so worried about her and there was nothing for him to do but pray. Then he thought, *I could write her a letter and tell her about all that has happened.* He pulled out the desk drawer and found some paper and a pen.

Dear Del, Clay and I are in London staying at the same place I did at the end of last year, St. Ermin's Hotel. I came to the New York Harbor and almost got to the freighter before it left. I miss you so much!

I feel like you've been gone for a really long time but in reality you've only been gone for little over a week. So many things have happened since you left; I decided to write you a letter about them.

This case we're all involved in has taken many weird and crazy turns but we can talk about that later. I want to tell you about this past Friday's early morning. I woke up around two a.m. with a dreadful feeling that there was something very bad happening to you. I went to the minibar to get a bottle of water when Clay walked out of his room. He asked me what I was doing up so early. So I told him about waking up with such a bad feeling about you. You're not going to believe this but he had also gotten up because he was concerned for you as well.

So I asked him how it could be that we were both awakened with concerns for you. He basically said just to talk to God as if He were right in the room with us. So we did – he started, then I said some things and then he ended. And now I understand what you meant about the peace of God! I knew God was taking care of you. After that Clay told me about going to the same church when you guys were in high school and how he came to believe in Jesus. Then how he had gone back to crime for many years until L.R. made him dump José's body and how dumping his friend's body had caused him to return to his faith in Jesus.

The main point I took away from his story was about the Bible story told by the youth pastor that he had heard the night he believed in Jesus. The story was about a tax collector who was asked by Jesus to come and join him and his disciples. That night this tax collector threw Jesus a party. Many of the leaders of the time were very critical of Jesus for hanging around with the tax collector and his friends.

Del, for the first time I saw that I was like those leaders who were criticizing Jesus. I realized that I was judging people of faith just like they did in the story. This judgmental attitude was something that I had buried deep within me so people couldn't see what I was thinking. I realized I had buried these judgments throughout my time on the police force. In the story Jesus was eating with the same kind of people who killed my wife. They were the same kind of people that I put in jail for terrible crimes. Why would I want to be a part of a religion that forgave these kinds of people?

Then Jesus told these leaders that he had come to heal people who knew they were sick. Jesus said the tax collector and his friends knew they were sick and the leaders did not. Del, I was sickened about how I had been judging these kinds of people when all the time they knew they had a problem and I didn't.

So I asked Clay if I could pray with him. He was more than glad to do that so I started and told God how I had been wrong and that I wanted to believe and take Jesus as my Savior. Del, I understand now why you had concerns for my spiritual life. I've never experienced this kind of peace and joy in my life after praying with Clay. You were so right to wait and to pray for me. Thanks so much for your commitment to Jesus and for waiting for me to believe! I miss you and love you so much. Will.

He pushed the paper back as tears were dripping off his face onto the desk. *God, please bring Del out of this mess alive, please God.*

Rose was listening to Gayle complain about the other girls, for what seemed the hundredth time. She was really getting frustrated with someone she had admired for some time now. But seeing how the other girls treated each other was causing Rose to have second thoughts about Gayle's character.

After dinner Del was going to be taken to a room, not back to the cargo hold. She guessed that she needed to be looked after and one of the guests had offered to keep an eye on her from her adjacent room. Javier bundled her up in several blankets before he put her in the wheel chair. The doctor told her that the fever was down but she still needed to take the pills he gave her. He also told her to keep warm no matter what. Del supposed that was the reason Javier was bundling her up so.

Then he rolled her out of the infirmary onto the desk and the cold wind almost blew her out of the wheelchair. She could tell he was hurrying to get to the elevator. Once in the elevator he said, "Did you get too cold?"

"It just hurt a little to breathe, but I'm OK."

He pushed her chair down the hall and stopped at a door and knocked. A woman with kind eyes opened the door. Javier introduced them.

"Del, I want you to meet Alma. She will be in the adjoining room and will look in on you from time to time. I'm going to give her your door key as you probably won't be going anywhere without her. But enough introductions, I need to get you into bed."

"Javier, I'll open the door for you."

Before Del could even say hello Javier and Alma were tucking her into the room's bed. Someone must have made up the bed and warmed the room. Javier excused himself by telling Del to call him if she needed anything and gave Del his extension before leaving.

"Del, I'm right next door with the bathroom doors open so I can hear you if you call. Javier already gave me your medication with a schedule of when to take them. So give me a shout if you need anything and we'll talk tomorrow."

Del could only wave and tell her thanks before she had gone back into her room. She was more worn out than what she thought she would be from such a short trip. Between the warmth of the room and the exhaustion of her trip, Del found herself falling asleep, thankful to these two kind people she had only known for such a short time.

Alma stuck her head in the bathroom and she could hear Del's slow but deep breathing of someone sleeping. She thought her new suitemate had a pleasing smile and for someone as sick as she was seemed very nice. Alma would give her the medication later as well as check her temperature. Then she went back to her book.

SUNDAY, MAY 25, 1997

After an early breakfast Will and Clay returned to their suite to gather what they needed for their walk today. They had decided to go to Piccadilly Square and see what plays had a matinee. They had just stepped into their room when Will's mobile rang. It was Charles, telling them that the car L.R. had rented was returned. The police could not find any other record of him renting another vehicle. Charles said he was going to do everything he could possibly do to track L.R.'s whereabouts. There was nothing for Will and Clay to do at the moment.

Will ended the call and flopped down in one of the overstuffed chairs. He shook his head in disbelief. "How can we plan a sting to save Del and the others without knowing where he is?"

Will looked up to see Clay pushing his hand through his curly hair. Clay asked, "What's wrong?" Will went ahead and told him the bad news.

Victor was in the kitchen before six fixing a pot of coffee. This new charge against Patrick had really done a number on him. He was normally able to put things like this to the side but he was not being very successful at the moment.

The coffee was finally made, so he was at the counter pouring the coffee into a mug when he heard someone enter the kitchen. He turned and saw his beautiful wife walking toward him. She gave him a big hug and said, "Can you fix a mug for me while I put a couple of cinnamon rolls on a plate?"

"My pleasure and can I ask why are you're up so early?" Victor brought over two mugs of coffee and joined his wife at the kitchen table. Amy took his hand and squeezed it.

"I sensed my husband was struggling with something more so than usual. Do you want to talk about it?"

"Well, usually I can put most things out of my mind until I need to do something about them. I'm not having much success with this huge case we're all trying to solve. You know the officer I shot to keep him from killing one of the criminals? Well the criminal's name is Patrick and he's now being charged with a murder that we think he didn't do. Amy, I can't figure out how I can help him and why I feel so obligated to resolve it." They just sat eating their rolls and coffee while mentally working on how they could help Patrick.

"Victor, could you see if Cap would give you permission to follow up on some of the leads regarding Patrick's case? If he gives his OK, maybe you will find out some more information that could prove your theories. While you're working that angle, I can ask Anne if during her research on defense lawyers if she came across someone who had success in his murder cases."

Victor's expression and body language changed immediately and he jumped up to give his wife a big kiss and hug. "Sweetheart, what would I do without you?" Then he was gone to change and shower.

"I'm glad I could help you out." She then started cleaning off the table with a big smile on her face.

As the girls moved down the aisle to read the Bible and pray, Rose approached Mai.

"Mai, I was wondering if I could join you guys this morning."

Mai turned around and saw the fear in Rose's eyes. She put her arm through hers and said, "We would love for you to join us, right ladies?"

Kendra and Tameka looked over at Rose and at the same time replied, "Yes, we would love it."

Rose's face lit up with a big smile as she joined the small group of girls. Mai took a quick glance back at Gayle and if her expression could kill, they would all be dead. Mai knew Gayle would take Rose's actions as an act of betrayal, yet she was so happy that Rose had made a step away from Gayle's influence. Although she also felt that they all would be hearing what Gayle thought before they got to England. Mai then turned her attention to Kendra who was reading something from the Bible.

L.R. had wanted to eat at his favorite restaurant in London ever since he arrived. He let the boys know that he was going to London to eat. He felt his life would not be threatened because he was sure no one knew he was in England, except Toby, and he would take his handgun with him. If they wanted to they could join him but he was allowing the boys to have the day off. They thanked L.R. for the invite but they had found a poker game that accepted their last minute entry fee. L.R. told them he would be late returning and not to lose their shirts.

Alma's schedule really had not changed that much. She had given Del her medication and brought her the trays of food that the cook had prepared for her but Del mainly just slept. In fact, Alma started to think they would never get a chance to talk. There were just a few more days on this freighter and then she would be running for her life.

Victor had received Cap's permission to re-visit the work of Detective Rankin but from his desk and with discretion. So he asked records if they could photocopy the investigation reports from Rankin's work on Patrick Cordero. They told Victor to come by in a couple of hours and it would be ready for him to pick it up. He told them to put Captain North's name down as the officer who requested the file.

Victor had also called Liliana back and told her that they were working on a plan to help Patrick out. She had cried and Victor had tried to encourage her about the good news of receiving permission to re-investigate the evidence against Patrick. He had told her he would keep her posted on any new evidence. Liliana had thanked him for his help but he could tell she was struggling in Will's apartment by herself.

Will and Clay had liked the play they attended. They were walking out of the theater when Clay pulled Will back behind the ticket kiosk. Will turned around and said, "What are you doing?" Clay just pointed at someone passing the theater. Will understood because he saw that it was L.R.

"Clay, he doesn't know me, so you stay here. I'm going to follow him from a good distance. Maybe he's leaving and I can get the information on what he's driving." Clay looked like he was going to be sick but nodded his understanding.

Will slipped out of the theater just in time to see him turn right. He jogged until he had a good distance between them. Will stayed close to the shops in case he had to sidestep into one of them. It looked like L.R. was returning to his car, so Will just kept his distance. Sure enough he paid the parking attendant and Will pulled out his little notebook that he always carried. He watched L.R. slip into a 1997 navy Toyota 4Runner and then wrote down the tag number as he drove away.

Will made his way back to the theater and found Clay right where he had left him. His color was back to normal and Will told him he had all the car information Detective Wells would need. They quickly returned to the hotel, gave Wells a call and left a message with all the vehicle information.

"Well, Clay, you handled it as well as possible, I mean if I had almost come face to face with the man who wanted to kill me, I probably would have thrown up."

"Sorry to disappoint you but I barely made the men's room." They both started laughing uncontrollably about the whole encounter.

Patrick was now a patient of the Fulton County Jail. Detective Jeffords had assured him that he would be safe but when he looked at the mirror's image of his face at what had happened at the police station, he was not very optimistic. He just hoped Liliana's friends could work another one of their miracles.

Alma had put Del's dinner on her desk because she was sleeping. It would not spoil because it was only a sandwich and fruit. Soon she heard her moving around in the bathroom and figured it would be OK to check in on her. Alma waited until she was finished in the bathroom and then knocked on her door leading to the bathroom.

"Yes, please come in as I've wanted to thank you for all your wonderful care."

"How are you feeling?"

"If I could stay awake long enough, maybe I could figure it out. I'm able to walk around but I'm still not sure of myself. Your name is Alma, right? Just checking to make sure I remembered correctly."

"Yes, that is right. I'm glad you are feeling better. Maybe all that sleep has worked."

"You're probably right about that. Have you heard anything from the girls in the cargo hold?"

"Yes, in fact I have a couple of notes for you. I guess it's from them." Alma handed the notes to her.

"Oh thank you. I've been very concerned for them. I always felt that as long as I was with them, the crew would at least keep their distance but I can't be sure that was what took place."

"If you feel strong enough and don't mind me asking, how did you end up with the girls?"

"Yes, I'm feeling well enough as eating seems to help. Before I answer your question could you please tell me your connection to these girls and this freighter?"

"Yes, you should probably know what my role is concerning them. I've worked in the office with L.R. Gomez for over ten years. Finally he did something that made me decide I couldn't work with him any more. I've done something that will make him follow us to England, where I hope he can be arrested for his crimes. I just hope it works. Now I've been honest about my connection, now it's your turn."

"OK. One of the girls that was kidnapped is the daughter of my friend. She hired my boyfriend, a PI, to look into the kidnapping. A high school friend came forward and gave us information about when the girls would leave Atlanta. He helped me find the truck - it was about to leave. So I decided to join the girls."

"Your boyfriend was hired to find your friend's daughter?"

"Yes."

"This is really interesting. So did your friend involve the police?"

"No, she didn't, but my friend who showed me the location contacted the police."

"Del, I think you need to know that I'm in no way connected with this crime network anymore, well since I quit, anyway. In fact since my old boss killed my boyfriend, maybe we can help each other catch my old boss, L.R. Gomez."

Del's eyes widened and she sat up in her bed and said, "Alma, I'm so sorry for your loss. Our high school friend said he was a wonderful person. Although are you serious about helping catch your old boss?"

"Yes, Del, very serious. In fact I need to give you something because it will be safer with you. I'll be right back."

Alma went to her room and then returned with a satin pouch. She opened the pouch and took out one of the most beautiful and expensive pieces of jewelry Del had ever seen. Alma placed the piece into the pouch and handed it to Del.

"Why are you giving this to me? These look like real diamonds and rubies! It's too expensive just to be carrying it around."

"Yes, you are right about its value, but the most important thing about the brooch is that it belonged to L.R.'s mother. His devotion to the piece is beyond anything I have ever seen. It is the only thing in the world he cares about. I knew by taking it he would do anything to get it back, even return to England."

"Why are you trying to get him to go to England?"

"He was almost captured in England in the late 1980s by a joint sting. He killed several officers associated with the sting and barely escaped. He swore he would never return to England. So I knew I had to take the only thing that would make him return, the brooch."

"So what you are telling me is that you believe he will be waiting for the freighter when it docks?"

"Yes, I believe he'll be waiting with a great deal of fire power supporting him trying to get his mother's brooch back."

"You and I must come up with a plan for the girls, you and I to leave this ship before she docks on Friday morning. I guess I need to start walking around a lot more to get my strength back."

"I think that you have a brilliant idea! In fact I may have someone who is part of the crew that will help us."

Alma stuck her hand over Del's body and Del quickly took her hand to shake it. They both had huge smiles on their faces as Alma helped Del out of the bed to begin her walking regimen.

MONDAY, MAY 26, 1997

L.R. was still agitated about who he thought he saw in London, Clay Stevens. *If it was him, why would he have traveled to England? How could Clay have any connections in England? Even if he was trying to escape me, why go to England?*

He was just becoming more irate the more he tried to figure it out. So for now he would let it go so his subconscious could work on it. He had practiced this process most of his life. Quietly he said, "Mother, I will get your brooch back! You can count on it."

Victor arrived early to phone the contacts from Detective Rankin's notes but he first called the lawyer that Anne had suggested. He was not there yet so he left a message to call him back as soon as he arrived. Then Victor told him that the accused man's life was in real danger.

Then he called Jason Hill's boss to see who Jason would have reported an angry investor to, he called the liquor store where Jason was murdered to see who was working that evening, and finally he left a message for Jeffords to call him when he had a few minutes to talk over the case.

Del accompanied Alma that morning for breakfast in the mess hall. Del asked for food that would help her regain her strength and a lot of it. When they sat down Del looked at her plate and then over to Alma, who was having a hard time not laughing.

"You've got to be kidding. How could anyone eat this much food at one sitting?"

"Well, you asked him and he gave you what he thought you wanted. Maybe you can take some of the food to snack on in the room." Then they both started laughing uncontrollably.

Rose joined the girls once again to pray and read the Bible. She prayed especially for Gayle and for wisdom on what to say because she looked like she was going to blow up. The others prayed for Gayle also and for Del's healing. They had heard nothing since the initial note and they were really worried.

Will answered his mobile - it was Charles. He could not believe that they had seen L.R. and gotten the vehicle information but he was genuinely glad. Charles let them know that until he could get a pinpoint on his car there was not much they could do at the Yard. He did ask Will to call Victor and update him on the case and Will told him he would give a Victor call.

Victor heard back from the lawyer, who had gotten the case information and told Victor he would try to bail Patrick out as soon as possible. He felt he could get him out especially since he had been assaulted in the lock-up of the APD. This fact would give him leverage to shed doubt that jail could do any better in protecting him. The liquor store manager called with the person's name and phone number who had been working that night. There had been no callbacks from Jeffords or Jason Hill's boss.

Victor decided to call Jeffords back but before he could pick up the phone it rang.

"Detective Jones."

"Hey Victor, this is Will. How's everything with you? Is Patrick doing any better?"

"Hey Will, things here have gotten complicated, how about you? Has Charles come up with a plan to arrest L.R. yet?"

"Well he has put a BOLO out for L.R.'s car and he's working on a plan to pick him up. What's gotten complicated? Is Patrick OK?"

"Well physically he's doing better because Anne has been taking care of him. Although, Patrick's boss died and Jeffords charged him with his murder, arresting him yesterday. Patrick is in the infirmary of the Fulton County Jail. Wait, before you start yelling at me, I just spoke to a defense lawyer that Anne recommended and he thinks he can bail him out."

"OK, but Victor remember what happened at the precinct, don't take too long. We'll call you back tomorrow to check Patrick's status and give you more of the plan we've come up with."

"Thanks Will. Talk to you tomorrow."

Victor told Cap he was going over to talk to Jeffords and he would return as soon as he could. "If anyone drops by from the Review who wanted me, tell him I will return soon." Cap nodded and Victor headed outside. On the way to Jeffords' building he had a thought. Maybe he should call the clerk at the liquor store first to find out if he remembered what he sold to Jason Hill. He quickly placed the call. The clerk had sold Jason a large bottle of one of the most expensive bourbons. Victor smiled as he took down the brand from the clerk. *Finally, some progress!* Victor thanked him and gave him his phone number in case he remembered anything else. He then walked over to Jeffords' building.

The girls were slowly moving toward the front of the cargo hold when they saw Gayle stationed between them and their bunks. Mai moved to the front of the group and stopped.

"L.R. is going to hear about your little morning gatherings. You can count on it!"

Mai felt someone take her hand and pull her closer into the group. It was Rose, with Kendra beside her.

Kendra spoke first, "Gayle, my heart breaks at the lies that you believe. You think L.R. cares for you but in reality he only cares that you are one of his most productive recruiters. If I'm not mistaken, you recruited Rose. L.R. only cares about money and power. He will destroy anyone that gets in his way. Girl, you need to take a step back and see him for who he is and to be sure he doesn't have anything to do with love or kindness."

Gayle looked a little shocked – Mai thought she might have been surprised to see these girls talk back to her.

Rose touched Kendra's arm and she stepped back to let her come forward. "Gayle, I'm sorry if I've hurt you in any way by meeting with these girls. I never wanted to hurt anyone like I've been hurt. You know my family was nothing but a bunch of drunks and thieves. In fact, as a recruiter you look for girls who have terrible families because we are so hungry to be loved by someone." Gayle opened her mouth to say something, but Rose didn't stop to let her.

"Gayle, I don't have a family who cares, but now I don't have any self-confidence, I'm a year behind in school, and the dream of having a husband and family is gone. Sure, don't get me wrong, the money for nice clothes and jewelry is great. I'd never get any of that from my family. Yes, I get to go out with rich, classy guys, but what am I giving up?

"Some of the girls I've run into are really sick from sexually transmitted diseases and they are so addicted to drugs." The other girls nodded as Rose went on. "Both STDs and addiction make you way too thin and also make it easy for you to catch other illnesses causing you to die too young.

These girls are so afraid to say anything to their pimp because he might beat them up, or worse, be left behind with no way to make any money except by becoming a street walker. I also saw the girls who got pregnant. The pimp demanded either they get an abortion or leave. The ones who got an abortion were really messed up and the ones who left had no job and a baby on the way. No words can describe the heartache I felt for each of them."

Mai could see Gayle's face begin to redden. At first she thought Gayle was red-faced from shame, then she saw the anger in her eyes. Rose must have seen it, too, because she softened her voice. "I really love you like a sister, Gayle, but I don't want to be a part of this lifestyle anymore. I made high grades in school. I had dreams of becoming someone who could help kids coming up in a family like I did. I want to get them to a safe place so they would have more choices. Now my choices are very limited.

"You see, I saw a way out, I mean, that's what I saw in these three girls who came out of solid families. They have hope and kindness that I've never seen or known before except by you. Don't think I'm fooling myself, I know I'll have nothing if I can escape this lifestyle but now I know with God things could change for the good."

Mai saw that Gayle was shaking with rage, and hoped she could give her a way out. She stepped to the front and said, "Gayle you're a really smart and clever. L.R. knows this and he uses your gifts and talents by protecting you, giving you things and money. He is only going to use you as long as you're doing exactly what he says, and still look young and pretty, but once any of those things change he'll drop you like a hot iron or kill you because you know too much about his network. I understand all of us have been spared to some degree because of our appearance and age. This is why we are on this freighter because in Europe L.R. knows he can get a higher dollar amount for each of us than in the U.S. We are nothing but a classy high dollar product, like a thoroughbred horse that runs the Kentucky Derby.

"You can tell L.R. whatever you want to tell him. We understand that L.R. is not in charge of our futures, God is. Gayle, we would like you to know that you, too, can do something else. I'm sure you also had dreams about your future. It's possible for any of us to fulfill the dreams we once had."

They all fell silent and waited. Gayle clenched her fists, and then slowly unclenched them. She took a deep breath, and then turned her back on them while she spoke softly, "You guys will be killed once we dock."

The girls looked at each other and then returned to their bunks.

Victor's string of luck was continuing when he saw that Jeffords was at his desk.

"Hey Adam, how are you?"

"Sorry I haven't called you back. It's been really crazy this morning. What can I do for you?"

"I was wondering if you had found any more video of the parking lot for the evening of Jason Hill's assault."

"No. We've canvassed the area to make sure there was not another camera rolling that was focused on the parking area. We found nothing."

"Adam, I want to ask you for a favor and it's going to sound like a waste of your time but could you get a warrant to search Tiny and Face's apartment?"

"What for, they've left the country?"

"Like I said, it would sound like a waste of your time. I talked to the liquor store clerk who waited on Hill that night. He sold him a large bottle of expensive bourbon and if what I think went down that night I think that same bottle could be in their apartment. I know it's a long shot but if you would do this and if you found the liquor it could be enough firm evidence that Patrick didn't commit this crime. I'm not sure, but I think this liquor is so expensive it could have some code that connected to the liquor store."

"You've given this a lot of thought and you've convinced me. I'll see if I can get a warrant since I'm investigating Ramos' murder too. I'll let you know what I find."

"Thanks Jeffords! I owe you."

Del had slept through dinner but Alma had brought a sandwich back to the room that she could eat later. Alma had been thinking about how they could get off the ship before it docked early Friday morning and she wanted to talk it over with Del.

Alma was remembering the low middle deck of the ship. If the deck was close enough to the water, and if Javier could find them an eight-man inflatable raft and a two-rung rope ladder that could hang over the side, they could escape this ship before she docked. Everyone would be sleeping early Friday before daylight when the Derby entered the bay. This meant very few crew members would be on deck, allowing an escape unseen in the darkness.

Another item Javier would need to take from the infirmary was a strong sleeping aid to put in Gayle's evening drink so she will not create a scene when the girls leave the storage hold. Alma smiled, nodded her head and thought, *Yes, this escape plan could work. I just need to see what Del thinks once she wakes up.*

Thinking about how crucial Javier was to her plan, Alma remembered the crushing pain in her heart when José was killed. She was beginning to feel something for Javier but the grief and pain was still too close. She needed his help but did not want to hurt him.

Jeffords got his warrant to search Face and Tiny's apartment and sure enough, they found the same size and kind of expensive liquor. He took a Polaroid photo close up of the bottle's numeric information and then wrote it up to be placed in the evidence lock-up. Then he sent a uniform to the liquor store where Jason Hill had been assaulted. Jeffords directed the uniform officer to get a written statement from the manager swearing that the bottle was their stock sold to Hill. If it was, then he was to call him with a statement.

Jeffords went back to the precinct to file his report on the search. The uniformed officer called him and told Jeffords he had the sworn statement that it was the bottle of expensive liquor that Hill had purchased. He thanked him and told him to include the statement with his report. Then he called Victor to tell him his hunch had been right. He was dropping the murder charge and he was calling the county jail to have Patrick Lopez released into the custody of his lawyer, at a much lower bond. Jeffords received a huge thank you from Victor and for helping Patrick's sister. Jeffords told Victor he would be sending the case back to Detective Rankin.

Patrick's lawyer was already at the jail when the call came through from Jeffords. Patrick was released and wheeled out to an awaiting ambulance without anyone assaulting him in the jail. Liliana was ecstatic when Patrick was brought back to Will's apartment. She thanked God for the blessing and that she now could take care of him without any threats.

Before he left for England, L.R. had issued a high dollar reward for either the whereabouts of Patrick Lopez with his sister Liliana or their capture; an informant inside the Fulton County jail had called one of his men. The informant had heard Patrick was going to make bail soon, so he told his man to wait outside the jail and to follow his ambulance. He had to be disguised so he would not be recognizable. This way he would find out the location and tell L.R. where Patrick went and collect the reward to use in bailing out his leader. The informant's man did as he was told, and was able to follow Patrick's ambulance.

Will and Clay received a call from Charles that he had found L.R.'s vehicle and that he would pick them up in ten minutes in front of their hotel. They quickly changed into some warm clothes and boots that they had bought. Clay had also purchased a cheap mobile phone and an airtime card, pay as you go service for twenty pounds. They had given Charles the new mobile number. No one knew what was about to go down, and in case they were separated they needed to be able to communicate. They decided to wait outside in case he was early.

Charles was right on the dot, driving an unmarked Mercedes sedan. Will climbed in front and Clay got into the back. Charles filled them in on the trip to the Oxfordshire area. TVP had spotted the vehicle outside of a pub that hosted the Monday night high stakes poker game, a weekly event.

TVP had surrounded the pub with plain-clothes detectives and roadblocks manned by uniformed Bobbies. "They're waiting for us because we're the only ones who know what L.R. and his goons look like. Actually the more chaps that leave, the better it is for us."

The remainder of the trip was spent in silent mental preparation for what was about to happen. They had been driving over an hour when Charles came to the first roadblock. The pub was in a small village between Oxford and Kidlington. Charles pulled his vehicle off the road and then they all got out of the car, the two Americans following close behind Charles.

The officers directed them to the lead for this raid/capture, Inspector in charge, Owehn Chapel. Charles walked up to Chapel and introduced himself, then Will and Clay. Chapel pointed out the pub telling them the location of his detectives.

"Wells, the Chief Constable suggested that since the three of you know these criminals that you lead the way to point them out to my team."

"Chapel, these crooks will not give us any time for introductions. Your team will just have to follow our lead. Clay, I suggest you stay here for now. Your testimony is worth more than being killed in this raid. Will, here's a protective vest and an assault rifle, or would you prefer the pump action 12 gauge shot gun?"

"I prefer the shotgun, thanks."

"Chapel, you and your men flank us as we enter the pub and game room. We will go for the key players, if your team could disarm any of the other players. Tell your team in the rear that we're engaging now."

Clay stayed back as they quickly moved to the front of the pub. A quick glance through the front window, then with one movement the company of constables led by Charles and Will pushed through the heavy door and back to the game room. Will shot the lock off and they pushed through the door. Will saw Face and Tiny sitting at the game table. He moved quickly toward them before they could pull their pistols. Charles was right with him as he hit Face in the head with the stock of his shotgun; Charles pushed Tiny to the floor still in his chair, putting his foot on his neck and rifle in his

189

face. The others on the TVP team arrested the remaining criminals. One detective was hit by a stray bullet, but it was just a flesh wound above his elbow. The raid had been extremely successful. With a final count of all the criminals to be jailed, there was one casualty and no fatalities for everyone involved.

Clay was at the spot where they had left him. As Charles and Will walked toward him, he asked, "Where's L.R.?"

Will said, "Look Clay, he's probably at his inn and we'll get that location from either Face or Tiny. Don't worry, OK."

But Clay saw the exchange of worried expressions between Charles and Will. As they followed the line of vehicles to the headquarters of TVP Clay prayed silently, *Please God help us find L.R. and put an end to all the misery he has created for the last forty years.*

Del had stayed awake long enough to eat her dinner and listen to Alma's plan of escape. Alma told her that her face was healing well. Before she fell back asleep Del let her know it sounded like a good plan and that she hoped all the sleep she was getting would heal her ribcage and lungs. Alma turned off Del's lights and just figured she had done too much the day before. She had to get stronger for this plan to work.

Once in her room Alma wrote a note for Javier spelling out each step of the plan as well as for him to let the girls know, by a note, that a plan of escape was in the works, and to be careful around Gayle. She asked him if he was all right with what they had asked him to do. If he did help them he must leave with them or L.R. would kill him. She turned the sign upside down and left the note. She went back to her room and went to bed.

TUESDAY, MAY 27, 1997

Just after midnight the bartender told L.R. that he had heard about a raid at the big weekly poker game. He thought that L.R.'s two bodyguards had been arrested. L.R. was extremely drunk and yet he thanked him for letting him know. He went upstairs and went through both his room and theirs before checking out. He made sure he had packed everything that could be used by the cops.

He waited outside of the inn until Toby picked him up. He had called him to let him know he needed him now instead of in the morning and that he would receive a thousand dollars in cash if he could pack and make it to the inn in ten minutes. Toby made it in under ten, and L.R. put the cash in his hand when he got into the car. Toby would take a hit on the exchange to pounds but he needed the money and he knew not to challenge him. L.R. told Toby that they needed to drive toward Southampton because something came up that he had to arrive earlier than planned. The cash made Toby satisfied with the earlier time.

It was close to one a.m. when Charles realized they were not going to get any information from Face or Tiny. Once they got to the route back to London, Will said, "Charles, would it be OK to let Victor know we captured the two goons but not L.R.?"

"Of course. Also let him know we'll keep him abreast of the changes in the case."

"OK, thanks."

He called Victor's mobile and got his recording. He left a message updating him on the evening's raid but that they didn't have L.R. yet and also gave him the phone number of Clay's new mobile, just in case.

Charles dropped them off at their hotel and told them not to plan on going to the Yard the next day. He would call Will's mobile if anything came up.

At that moment they both were happy to oblige his wishes so they would be able to sleep in. They both thanked Charles and let him know they wanted to help in any way they could. They went to their rooms and fell into bed as soon as they turned off the lights.

The girls were still moving slowly that morning because it had been so cold during the night it was hard for them to sleep. Mai was already up to get her breakfast. Javier was on the steward schedule to deliver breakfast to the girls that morning, and passed a note to her. She looked behind her and saw there was no one looking, so she slipped the note in her pants pocket. She nodded to Javier as she turned and went back to her bunk. She would read it to the others at the prayer time.

Javier responded to Alma's note by letting her know that he wanted to be in on the plan. He wrote that he would not have any problems stealing the items she mentioned. He also wrote that he had passed the plan on to Mai that morning. He let her know if she needed anything else just to tell him.

Alma picked up the note on the way back from breakfast. She was beginning to realize that Del was not going to be strong enough to climb down the rope to the raft. She knew it would irritate Del to change the plan for just her but it had to be done.

Alma knocked on her door and heard Del tell her to come in. Alma put her breakfast on the table and sat down on the sofa bench.

"Del, I'm glad you are feeling better but I've been thinking."

Del interrupted her mid-sentence, "I know what you're going to say next, so I'll say it for you. I'm not strong enough yet to get off the ship as we've planned. I've been trying to come up with some type of alternative for me. What do you think about using my illness to get off? What if Javier reports that I've asked to be taken to the hospital as soon as the ship docks? He could put the rope ladder back, roll me off to a waiting cab with all of our things in my lap and he can tell the doctor he needs to go with me. This will take any suspicion away from him for your escape.

"What if L.R. starts up the ramp before you two can make it off the ship?"

"Well, I thought about just waiting for him to board first with Javier preparing me for the descent. He would have his back to L.R. and I could be slumped over as he attends to me. This way we control the circumstances and once he has passed by us we head down the ramp to the cab."

"You're taking a big chance. L.R. is very observant. He'll remember the two of you."

"Yes. But he has never seen us before and he cannot see who we are when he passes by because of the position of our heads. We will have picked you and the girls up and will be on our way to the train station before he might become suspicious. It's a chance we'll need to take unless you can think of something else."

They fell silent as they both went through the different scenarios. Then Alma nodded in agreement.

"OK, I'll write Javier another note with this new addition to our plan. Hopefully the doctor will buy it and he'll be able to call for a cab to be waiting or we'll be as good as dead."

"Yes, but send a note to the girls to start praying for God's protection for both parts of our escape plan. I've seen God work like this many times before - to keep the foolish blind to what is right in front of them."

"I'm not that familiar with God but I'll trust your experience with Him. Now we need to keep working on getting you stronger.

While you eat your breakfast I'll write Javier and then we'll take a walk around the rooms as well as to the wooden box."

Victor picked up his messages from the weekend as soon as he arrived in the office. He had not updated Cap about these reports, so he pulled out his yellow pad and began his department's summary of the last two days including his message from Will.

Once he completed his report to Cap he finished the paperwork on the shooting of the uniformed officer. This was the last step to being cleared. He had heard from Jeffords this same officer had given a detailed written report on L.R. Gomez, once he realized that he was going to be charged. Jeffords told him that he should be placed on active duty once all the reports had been filed with IA.

L.R. and Toby had found an out of the way inn about halfway to Southampton. Toby had not been able to contact his friend who was going to help them out. It would be up to them to take care of things Friday morning when The NY Derby and Alma made port.

They had finished lunch and Toby had left to take an inventory of their ammunition and guns. L.R. had already gotten a jump start on his drinks during lunch. Now he sat, drinking his liquor, his rage simmering, waiting for the arrival of the Derby.

Will's mobile was ringing. It was Charles.

"I spoke to Chapel earlier and we've decided to release Face and Tiny since we could only hold them for twenty-four hours. This way we can follow them and hopefully they will lead us to L.R.'s location."

"Charles, I understand you're limited on your choices for them but they are very clever and I don't think they will go near L.R."

"I'm sorry, Will, this is all we can do at this point. If we have to we can drive to the port when the freighter arrives Friday in Southampton. You can be sure L.R. and his thugs will be there waiting. I've got to go. I'll call you if anything changes."

Will hung up and fell into the nearest chair. *This is terrible. We captured them and now we are letting them go. Unbelievable! I can't tell Clay this now. If he asks I'll just have to lie.*

Victor had finished all his reports, so he called Anne to see if she could drop by Will's apartment to check on Patrick. She did not answer so he left her the message as well as thanking her once again for helping out. He looked at the time and knew he needed to call Will back. He reached his mobile and told him about finding the expensive liquor in Face and Tiny's apartment. Jeffords was going to try and talk the prosecutor into charging them with Jason Hill's murder. Then Will gave him the bad news about capturing Face and Tiny but then because of his lack of evidence Charles released them. He hoped they would lead them to L.R. Victor hung up as disappointed as Will.

Face and Tiny returned to the inn in L.R.'s vehicle. They went to the bar to find L.R. but the bartender told them he had left once he knew they had been arrested. They asked if he had left a phone number where he could be reached but the bartender did not know.

They went to their room and could tell L.R. had removed any evidence before he left. They packed up, paid for their room and left. Once they got into the car they just sat for a minute.

"Face, he must not want us to try and contact him or he would have left a phone number. What do you think? Should we go to Southampton?"

"Maybe it's a setup. I mean letting us go. You know in the movies they let people go so they can follow them. I don't know though."

"Yeah, you could be right. Well what would Boss do? He would want to get rid of this car, so let's go to London and drive around for a while to see if anyone is following us. If they are then we can lose them and then get rid of the car."

"How will we meet up with L.R.? We know he'll be at Southampton Friday morning, so we'll disappear for a couple of days in London. Then Thursday afternoon we'll take the train to Southampton. What do you think?"

"Yeah, that sounds good. Do you think they have barbeque in London? I'm starving."

"Let's get to London and lose the cops if they're following us. Then we can find somewhere good to eat."

"OK."

They drove to London and lost the cops even before they got there. They found a station for the trains and the underground transport called the Tube, parked the car in the lot with keys in the console, and boarded the Tube to the restaurant area a local had suggested. When they found a seat both of their stomachs started growling.

Anne knocked harder on Will's apartment door but no one came to the door. She had a late dinner engagement, so she would telephone Victor that she had gone by to check on Patrick but no one answered. She then left after one last try.

Charles phoned Will to tell him they had lost Face and Tiny in London. He told him if he received any good news before the next day he would let him know. Will ended the call and looked across the room at Clay. He could see the tension building in him.

"OK Clay, let's go find a pub to eat and grab a few beers. I'll fill you in once I've drunk a couple of beers."

Clay followed Will out of the room and down the street to the pub they had been in earlier. This place served cold American brand beer because of so many American tourists staying in the high-end hotels around them. American tourists were not used to the room temperature beer that was served to locals. Once Will had finished a couple of beers he updated Clay on the many dead ends in their investigation. They ate and drank in silence.

One of Javier's shipmates saw him looking through the emergency/rescue area.

"Hey idiot, what are you doing in here? You don't have clearance for this area."

"Sorry, someone bet that I couldn't find out how many rafts there are in this area. I'll leave now and pay the guy off."

"Don't let me find you near this area again or I'll get you fired!"

Javier barely heard him say the word fired as he was running as fast as he could to his next job. He did not think this guy knew his name because he was a part of security and he had never dealt with any of them before. This would make it more difficult to steal the raft, rope ladder, etc. He would let Alma know with his next note. Maybe she could think of something to help him out but he should steal the sleeping pill that night just in case.

Victor had stepped away from his desk. When he returned he saw his message light blinking, so he picked up the message. It was Anne telling him that no one had answered the door at Will's apartment. She would try to catch up with him later.

Victor asked Cap if he could send a couple of uniforms over to Will's apartment. They could get the manager to open up the apartment if no one answered because Liliana took the key earlier. Cap called dispatch and told them to send two officers to Will's address.

It seemed like everything had fallen apart. He had to get back out into the field, so he called IA to find out how much longer his case would take. Their answer was non-committal and he was not surprised.

The two uniform officers reported back to Cap once they forced the manager to allow them to enter. The apartment had been trashed and there was no one there.

Cap told Victor what they had found and told him to turn the information over to the detective in charge of Patrick's case. Victor went back to his desk and phoned Detective Rankin. He answered and Victor filled him in on what the uniforms had found. The case had just escalated to kidnapping. Victor let Rankin know he would help him as much as he could from his desk. Rankin told him he would let him know once the apartment had been investigated and got the address from Victor before he hung up.

Victor asked Cap if he could head on home and Cap could tell he was discouraged. He waved goodbye to Victor and he was gone in a flash. Cap shook his head, *This was the strangest case he had seen in a long time, although his experience had shown him that everything falls apart just before the crooks do something stupid and are caught as a result of their arrogance.*

Patrick moaned each time he moved and Liliana continued to whimper. The masked assailant had bound their hands and mouths, put a hood over their heads, and driven them to an unknown location. Their hoods had been removed before they were locked into a dimly lit, rank, filthy room. Patrick tried to reassure his sister but he could not lie very well. He knew his fever was back and he was feeling lousy again. At least their assailants had removed their bonds.

"I'm really sorry, Liliana, that I've brought so much pain and suffering your way because of my crooked dealings. I've realized it's not just your own life you ruin, but also the people around you." Then he fell silent as his body slumped to the side. He could hear Liliana's screams as if she was very far away, then he passed out and heard nothing.

WEDNESDAY, MAY 28, 1997

Alma walked to breakfast with Del holding onto her arm. It was the first time since Monday that Del had been out of the room. They picked up the note from Javier when they walked past the wooden box. They sat alone once they had served themselves.

"What did he say, Alma?"

"He was looking at the rafts and other equipment and security saw him. He made up some lie and fled; but he believes security will be watching that area with more frequency. He asked us if we had any ideas on how to take the items we need."

There was no one around them and so they just sat silently thinking as they ate their breakfasts.

Del spoke first. "What if I go to that area and act like I'm fainting?"

Alma grinned. "Well, I think that is an interesting plan, to attract their attention to allow Javier to get the rope ladder and raft. Although, since you and Javier will be putting on an act the day we dock, I think I should be the one who gets to act out some damsel in distress kind of diversion. What do you think, Del? Am I up for the job?"

"I think you are perfect! I might even get out of bed to watch your act, or maybe not. I think it's time for me to return to the room, please."

They both laughed as they left the mess hall and Alma held Del's arm on the return trip to their rooms.

Mai met with the girls later than normal that morning. Once again the cold temperature of the cargo hold was hampering their sleep. Also Gayle's moody personality had been shifted into high gear. They were concerned for what she might do.

Mai asked, "How are you doing, other than cold?"

The other girls looked at each other, and Kendra spoke for them all. "We're ready to leave this freighter whatever might happen during the escape."

"OK then let's ask God in our prayers this morning for His safety and His strength."

They all held hands and prayed.

Victor had an extremely difficult time concentrating on work. He was truly finding it hard to get any work done. He just sat looking at his pile of filing. Then his phone rang. It was Rankin.

"Victor, we caught a lead on the Lopez kidnappings. Would you like to come over?"

"Boy, would I. Tell me again where your office is?"

Victor let Cap know where he was going on his way out.

Will and Clay had hung around their suite most of the morning because they were tired and frustrated. The investigation was slow and then when it looked like there was going to be a break, things just fell apart. Clay was the first to snap out of their bad mood. It was not going to help just sitting around the room dwelling on what seemed to be L.R.'s victories and the law enforcements failures. He suggested that they get out and walk around some. They might find an interesting restaurant to eat lunch in. Will agreed and they headed out to get some lunch.

L.R. and Toby had decided to stay put until the next day. L.R. just stayed in the pub. Toby was still trying to find a few more guys to meet the freighter but he had not scored. He had seen L.R. drink before but never like this. He decided to leave him alone but he told the bartender to give his mobile a call if L.R. started asking for him.

Alma went to the box and left the note for Javier spelling out the new plan. They felt it should take place that evening if it was a good time for him. Alma felt they needed to try it out early - just in case it did not work, they would have time to figure out something else. They both thought it was a good plan, giving enough time for Javier to get into the area, steal the needed items, and depart.

When Victor arrived at Rankin's desk, he could tell something had happened. He just stood back and waited until Rankin spoke to him.

"We got a call from the jail early this morning letting us know that someone heard one of the inmates barking out orders to someone on the pay phone. They just now called us back with an address. Would you like to tag along?"

"Yes. I'll stay out of the way and thanks."

Rankin and his team left the precinct with Victor right on their heels. They exited their cars as soon as they came to a complete stop. The neighborhood was like one of many neighborhoods in Atlanta where the homes had started as high-end houses, but the original owners had sold them and fled to the outer suburbs. The new owners were only interested in how much rent they could make from their tenants, with no questions asked. The neighborhood had become a haven for illegal activities of all kinds.

Rankin quickly directed the team to go to their assigned positions around the house. Moving to the front door, he gave the command to enter over his radio. Victor was on the street side of the vehicle in front of the house. He listened for any gunfire but heard nothing. It was hard for him to sit on the sidelines but until IA made their decision, he was stuck just watching.

It had been several minutes since their entrance when he saw Rankin helping a very distraught Liliana out the front door. He

201

waved Victor over to help him out with her. He reached the porch just as Liliana fainted and scooped her up. Victor carried her to one of the cars and put her gently into the back seat. An EMT vehicle pulled into the driveway. He watched them enter the house and then went to the driver's door to lower all the windows for Liliana. By the time he had done that, the EMT guys were rolling Patrick out on their gurney. He caught Rankin's glance and knew Patrick was in bad shape. Following Rankin was a uniform officer escorting the kidnapper to his patrol car.

Rankin walked over to Victor and asked, "How is she? She hasn't regained consciousness yet?"

Victor shook his head no. Rankin called over one of his team and told him to drive them to the same hospital as the EMT vehicle. Victor climbed in the back seat and put Liliana's head on his leg. The detective closed the windows, turned on the air conditioner and emergency lights, then followed close to the EMT vehicle as it left the driveway.

Victor could see where the EMT vehicle was heading and so he called Anne to let her know. He asked if she could call ahead because Patrick was not doing well and now they thought Liliana was in shock or something. She had fainted at the crime scene and had not regained consciousness.

Face and Tiny decided to not go outside of their inn. They had found a small inn not far from the restaurant they had eaten dinner the night before. There was also a tube station within walking distance. It was better if they did not draw any attention their way. Tomorrow evening they would take the tube to the Victoria train station. From there they would take the train to Southampton.

It was getting close to dinner time. They decided to clean up and head over to the restaurant area. They could walk around and check out the other restaurants. They had only eaten snacks and their stomachs were already rumbling.

Will and Clay had just gotten back from eating dinner when Will's mobile rang. Charles was letting them know that he had made contact with the Southampton police and they were working on a plan to meet the freighter. Charles suggested that they pack their things and be ready to check out the next day once all the details had been finalized. Will ended the call and told Clay what Charles had said. For a moment they just stood and looked at each other. Finally, some good news! Will was both excited and nervous.

"OK, Clay, the chase will start soon. It won't be pretty, you can count on that."

Clay nodded. "Maybe we should take some time to pray. When I couldn't get the sound of José's body hitting the water, I read some from the Bible and asked God to help me put his murderer behind bars. So far He's shown me the way. What do you say?"

"I think we are only going to catch this slippery snake with God's help!" He nodded to Clay. "Would you start us off?"

They bowed their heads and after a few moments of silence Clay began to ask God for the help they needed. After some time they said amen and felt His peace.

Anne had called one of her classmates who worked at the hospital. The doctor met them at the entrance of the ER. Patrick and Liliana were taken to separate stations and the nurse pointed the way where the detective and Victor were supposed to wait.

As they walked toward the area, the detective told Victor he had to leave and that he hoped they would be OK. He also told Victor that he would update Rankin. Then Victor phoned Cap and left him a message about what had taken place. He also told him what hospital they had been taken to. Victor told Cap he would stay until the doctor gave him an update. He also let Cap know that he did not drive here and that someone had to come get him.

Del had decided to stay behind, even though she had wanted to observe Alma's performance. Javier had confirmed where he would be waiting near the location of the emergency gear. The setting sun provided the perfect lighting. After Alma went out the door, Del started to pray for them and the success of the diversion.

Alma moved to the farthest place on ship from the area Javier would enter. She looked around to make sure someone would hear her screams. Someone was working on the crane just far enough away not to see her but he would hear her. She prepared herself by ripping her blouse and slapping herself hard in the face.

Alma fell to her knees, screamed at the top of lungs, then yelled out, "Help me! Please someone help me!"

By the time the crane operator reached her, tears with black mascara were running down her cheeks, her hair was messy, and her whole body was trembling.

"Are you OK? What happened?"

"I need to speak to your security!"

He removed his receiver and requested that Security and medical personnel report at once on the main deck by the crane. Then he just said over and over, "They're coming."

Two men rushed over. "I'm security, what happened here?"

"I was admiring the sunset and someone attacked me from behind. When I screamed and this kind man came to my rescue, they ran away."

"Did you see their face?"

"No. I tried to turn after they knocked me down, but I didn't see anyone." Alma shook harder thanks to the cold wind. By then someone from the infirmary had arrived and both security guards asked that he take her to the infirmary.

Alma grabbed one of the legs of the security guard, screaming, "No please don't leave me, he might try to get me if you leave!"

"We'll escort you to the infirmary just to put your mind at ease."

The infirmary aide helped her to stand, "Do you think you can walk?"

"Yes with some help, I think I can. Only if it's slow, as I think I twisted my ankle when he pushed me to the ground."

"We'll take it nice and easy."

Alma leaned heavily on the aide, limping the whole way. At each step she would look back at the guards with a fearful expression on her face.

Once they arrived at the infirmary, security told her she would need to fill out a report of the attack once she felt up to it. Alma shook their hands and thanked them for staying with her. They nodded their heads and left. The infirmary aide sat her on one of the cots and told her the doctor would be in to see her soon. Once he left, Alma looked at her watch and grinned. She had given Javier enough time to take what they needed. She lifted her fake sprained foot onto the cot and relaxed. Her performance had been a success and she would tell Del about their victory once she had confirmation from Javier.

Victor had gotten a favorable report on both Patrick and Liliana from their doctor. The doctor told him that dehydration was their primary concern. Victor gave the doctor his card and added his mobile phone. The doctor told Victor that he would keep him updated. When the uniformed officer arrived he went back to the precinct with him.

When Victor got to his desk, he could see that his message light was blinking. He picked up his message.

It was from Will and Clay. Will wanted him to know that Charles would be picking them up the following morning. They would be going south to the Port of Southampton. If he needed to talk with him, he should call his mobile.

Victor checked to see if Cap was free and Cap told him to come in to give him an update.

"The doctor thought that dehydration was the Lopez's primary concern and he told me he would keep me updated. Although now after hearing that the fight in England was moving to the dock, I'm really concerned for all of them. I was really hoping that L.R. and his gang would have been arrested before this. The docks are his backyard, giving him the advantage."

"Look Victor, you know when things look their worst, something unexpected usually happens. Del is very smart so don't count her out.

"Changing the subject, I heard from IA and they told me that their investigation into your shooting was about to be closed out. It may be by tomorrow and you'll be able to go back out into the field with a clean slate. I thought you could use some good news right about now."

"You're not joking with me, are you, Cap?"

"I'm telling you the truth."

Victor jumped up and shook Cap's hand and then shot out the door, looking about as excited as he had been since the shooting.

Alma had managed to convince the doctor that she had been attacked. He gave her a sleeping pill so she could sleep and finally released her. Alma grinned all the way back to her room but noticed the sign in the box was upside down. She opened it, put the sign right side up and took the note.

She peeked in Del's room and was excited to see that she was awake.

"How did it go? Did you fool them?"

"Yes. I have to say it was one of my best performances. Also look what was in the box."

They both giggled as Alma unfolded the note.

"Javier wrote that he got all we needed with extra time to spare."

Del grinned. "Great job, Alma!"

"Our plan was successful. So maybe we should turn in early as tomorrow is our last day to eat and walk."

"You're right. Thanks for carrying all the weight of our escape so well and that's also from the girls."

Alma gave her a thumbs up and left. Del's light went out immediately and Alma knew she had stayed awake just for her report.

She was very impressed with Del and her inner strength. Alma was glad she had agreed to help her out. She still had not asked Del about the handsome man who tried to stop the freighter in New York. The time had never been right to share the story with her. Hopefully soon, maybe tomorrow she would tell her.

Alma wrote a note to Javier to ask if he could let Mai and the girls know that their plan was on schedule for early Friday morning. Also, to please remind the girls, they should be careful not to give anything away to Gayle that would cause her to become suspicious. This could keep her from drinking her dinner drink that had been mixed with a sleeping pill. She told him that she had another sleeping pill if he needed it.

Victor went by the hospital before going home. Patrick had been put in ICU just to make sure nothing flared up from his brutal beating. Victor found Liliana sitting up in bed and he was very pleased to see her doing so much better.

"Oh, Victor, how nice of you to come by. Have you heard anything about Mai?"

"Liliana, you look so much better. How are you feeling?"

"I'm OK. I just miss my daughter so much. The doctor gave me some medications after hearing me describe these past couple of weeks. The doctor felt the medications would help with all the emotional trauma. I sure appreciate everything Will, Del and you have done for Patrick and me. Thank you for coming by to see me."

"As soon as I hear anything about Mai, which will probably be this weekend, I'll let you know. You should go back to Will's apartment when they let you go from here. I don't think you will have any more problems. The goons that kidnapped you have now found out that L.R. Gomez left the country and there is no reward money from any of his bounties. The word will now get around on the streets. No money means that no one will be taking any risks. They will have also heard about your kidnappers being charged."

"I'll talk to Patrick before I decide. It's easier at Will's than my place. There are so many reminders of Mai at my place."

"Well, you need to get your rest, so I'll head out. Here's my business card with my mobile phone number on the back. Call me if you need some help once you've been released."

"OK, and thanks again, Victor."

Victor gave a final wave as he walked out. He did not know how Liliana was holding up as well as she had been. If one of his children had been kidnapped by these human traffickers, he would be crazy and depressed.

You know God, I don't bother You very much with things, but if You could keep those kids, Mai, Del, Will, Clay, and Charles safe, I sure would appreciate it. Thanks.

THURSDAY, MAY 29, 1997

L.R. and Toby were packed and eating breakfast before seven. Toby was amazed at how well L.R. could function after his alcoholic binges. L.R. was in the car waiting on Toby. He wanted to drive the few remaining kilometers to Southampton to reserve the hotel, De Vere Grand Harbour, which he stayed during the late eighties. Early summer vacationers would book the Harbour first because of its high ratings.

Mai and the girls met before breakfast. They knew this would be the last time they would pray and read from the Bible together. They had really grown close during their time on the freighter and they had seen L.R.'s rage erupt on girls who had tried to escape. They never saw them again. So they once again read and prayed that the escape plan would succeed. They went over Javier's last note one more time and then prayed they would not do anything that would tip off the already enraged Gayle. Each girl brought her fear to God, and when they broke for breakfast each of them had received a blessing of peace.

Will and Clay did not wait for Charles' call to check out. Will knew that things were going to pick up as the day went forward. He wanted to have a calm breakfast with Clay to encourage him as much as he could. Will was not sure if they could capture or eliminate L.R. He seemed to be surrounded by men willing to die to let him escape justice.

They were early enough to eat breakfast in The Tea Lounge and they asked the hostess for a table on the outside balcony. The view was just of the hotel's entrance, but it was nice to be outside. They ordered the full English breakfast.

Del asked Alma if she could bring her breakfast back to the room. Del thought she had walked too much the day before and she was feeling drained. Alma said she would also bring her breakfast back so they could eat together. She returned quickly with their food on a tray.

"OK, dinner is served." Alma steadied Del as she moved from her bed to the table.

"So did you sleep soundly last night, Del?"

"Not really. I think that's why I'm more tired today. I need to walk some more today. Maybe after I eat I'll feel better. How about you?"

"No, I didn't sleep much either. I kept running our plan over and over in my mind. I'm bothered about you and Javier staying on board until the freighter docks. Yet I know you don't have the strength to go with us. I just feel like something bad is going to happen."

"Well, let me bless our food and our travels. Lord Jesus, thank you for my new friend Alma. I really don't think the girls and I could have set up this great plan of escape without Javier and her. I pray you bless our food and protect us over these next thirty-six hours. Amen. Let's eat."

They began to eat. They ate quickly with not much conversation. As they were finishing their coffee Alma readjusted her weight and her chair whined.

"Del, I'd like to tell you something. I've wanted to tell you as soon as you became my neighbor but I felt you needed to get better before I told you. So here goes, before the freighter left New York I saw you with the girls as you boarded. Then just before we were pulling away a handsome, tall blond man came running after the freighter as if he was going to try and jump over the water. A longshoreman grabbed his arm and started telling him off as the freighter went toward the Atlantic. Del, I think he was trying to find you. Do you know who I'm describing?"

"Alma, you're not teasing me, are you? That really happened?"

"No, I wouldn't tease you about something like that. He was really in New York. Who is he?"

"I'm sure that was Will. He's my PI boyfriend who is working Mai's case." Del sat up straighter, her eyes shining. "Do you know what this means? Will, Clay and Victor are working this case from the U.S. In fact I bet Will and maybe Clay are in England working with a detective from London's best, Scotland Yard." Del could not contain herself any more. She jumped out of her seat and took Alma's hands, shaking them up and down like a child. Then she returned to her seat, a little pale.

"So you're telling me that you think your friends are working this case with the Yard? Oh Del, that means they will meet this freighter also. Boy, this is going to be a very interesting day and a half. I need to warn Javier that there might be some fireworks tomorrow when you get to your cab."

Long after Alma had left to write a note to Javier, Del was still bubbling over with joy.

Face and Tiny waited at the train station. Their train would leave later that afternoon to arrive in Southampton that evening. They would take a cab to the hotel where L.R. stayed when he was working in England. Face saw an interesting looking restaurant and talked Tiny into going to lunch. It would help the time pass.

Victor continued to work through his stack of filing. He was hoping to hear from IA but it was already late. He did talk to Liliana earlier. She had spoken to Patrick and they both would like to return to Will's apartment if the detective in charge of his case approved it. Victor had left Rankin a message to see if he would sign off on the transfer. Victor had given Cap an update and he had not heard anything from Will.

He was clearing his desk to leave when his phone rang. It was IA notifying him that he had been approved for fieldwork. They were sending their findings to his Captain. Victor thanked them and hung up.

Victor stood in Cap's door grinning. When Cap looked up he smiled and told him he had just forwarded IA's report to him. Cap returned his badge and firearm, and Victor thanked him and went back to his desk. His computer had not been shut off so he pulled the report up and printed it. Then he finished shutting down his terminal and left. He wanted to go through the report with Amy.

As he walked out of the precinct he hoped everything was OK with Will. Maybe he would hear something later that evening. He did not realize how much he loved his field job until now. He grinned the whole way to his car.

Charles picked up Will and Clay closer to lunch than breakfast. The drive out of London to Southampton had been smooth riding until they were about to go through Winchester. There had been a terrible automobile accident at the intersection of another major highway. All lanes were blocked and from the looks of things the accident had just happened. There were emergency vehicles behind them trying to get past the line of stopped cars and trucks.

Charles shook his head. "Well chaps, I think our trip was just extended."

"Will this delay interfere with your plan?" asked Clay.

"Hopefully not. We'll just wait and see."

Charles pulled out a folder and began jotting down some notes. Will and Clay got out of the car to get a better view of the crash. It was a bad wreck involving multiple vehicles. They thought that most of the emergency personnel were on site working with the wounded.

Clay got back into the car as Will walked down closer to see if he could help out.

"Charles, do you think this plan will work? It's not easy to be so close to L.R. with them trying to kill me."

"I hope so. Clay as you well know, L.R. is a very dangerous criminal. No one is clear on who else will be with him. I would not be truthful if I didn't tell you, we are planning, but with this bunch no one knows the outcome."

"Thanks for being so honest. I hope I wasn't intruding. It's just that I'm so nervous being so close to him."

"It's quite all right."

The door opened and Will slipped into the front seat.

"It's a really bad accident. Several people injured and a couple of fatalities. Unless you know a way around this area we're going to be here for a long time."

"No. There isn't another way and we are in the midst of so many other cars. I fear we will not make it to the station in time for their planning session."

There was not any other conversation during the three-hour wait or the rest of the trip. They were all disappointed about missing the planning but went straight to the police department. Clay seemed better as the day went on. They were brought up to speed by the detective in charge, Shane O'Malley. O'Malley gave them directions to an inn that was clean and reasonable.

L.R. directed Toby to the location of the hotel De Vere Grand Harbour. The beautiful hotel was still there but it had changed ownership. It was now called the Grand Harbour Hotel.

They parked and went into the hotel. It was not the weekend so they still had a suite looking out over the bay available for the one night. The bellman retrieved their luggage and led them to their suite. Toby tipped him and L.R. went over to the suite's mini bar and made himself a drink. Then he went out onto the balcony overlooking the bay. Toby went to his bedroom to take a nap.

L.R. drank his glass of liquor and fixed another. Back on the balcony his anger smoldered toward Alma. *How could she have done this to me, especially after buying her the forged immigration papers! I trusted her with running my offices for over ten years. Then she takes the one item that I cherish above everything else, how dare she. She's going to pay and pay dearly.* He went back to the room's mini bar and made another drink. He got his luggage and went to his bedroom.

Toby was awakened by a pounding on the suite's door. He opened the door and to his surprise there stood Face and Tiny. He stood back to let them in just as L.R. came out of his bedroom.

"Hi, Boss. We made it."

"Boys, I've never been so glad to see you. I wondered if they would have to let you go and if they did I knew you would know where to find us."

"Yeah, the name has changed but our taxi driver knew this place by its other name. So what's the plan?"

"Have you boys eaten? We were just getting ready to go eat. We can go over the plans once we've eaten."

"Sounds great to us. We're starved!"

"Well, come on then, I knew a place that served the best food in town. That is if they're still there."

Alma was anxious about the escape so she went for a walk on the deck, first wrapping her ankle with the ace bandage just in case she saw anyone. She could start limping if she was noticed. Most everyone was asleep but she was too nervous to relax. She was concerned for the girls, Del, and even Javier. He had been great helping them out like he had done. She knew L.R.'s rage. Even though it would be directed toward her, they would suffer the same fate.

She had heard Del praying many times since she moved in. Maybe there was something to her prayers. *God I don't know You but Del says You know me. Well, please help us tonight and keep everyone safe.*

She heard footsteps behind her and turned around to find Javier standing there, just smiling at her.

"You scared me to death! What are you doing on deck?"

"I should ask you the same thing. Only you are here for the same reason I am. This escape could get ugly and we both know it. So we are both out here walking our jitters off. Right?"

"Yeah, you're probably right about that. Is everything ready for the first phase of our plan?"

"I gave Gayle her special drink and the girls gave me a quick wave when she wasn't looking. So yeah, I think we are good to go. The first part is not what bothers me. It's after I call for the cab, it's the part when Del and I are just waiting on deck to go down that gangplank and then into that cab."

"Yes, I also agree with you that this part of the plan is the weakest. Especially since we found out that the Yard might be waiting along with L.R. and his goons. But this was our only choice with Del being as sick as she is. You guys will pick us up where we decided, right? Then on to the train station once you've picked us up."

Javier nodded. "I hope there won't be anyone chasing us. We're just going to get on the next train that will be leaving the station, headed north, right?"

"Right, and hopefully it will leave soon after we get there. I'm sure that we won't have a great deal of time before L.R. tracks us there. It's going to be a close race and I just hope we'll win. Even if something unexpected happens I'm going to beat him, no matter what. I hope you've gotten that but for now we stay with our plan. I'll see you in a couple of hours right down there with the girls!"

"That's the place. Yes, I've heard you and I feel the same way. See you soon."

They waved goodbye and went back to their rooms. *Yes, please God, You must help us or we'll all be dead!*

FRIDAY, MAY 30, 1997

Javier released the girls first. Gayle never moved a muscle the whole time they were gathering their things. Once on deck they could see another woman near the side. They looked upset until Javier introduced them to Alma.

Mai asked, "Where's Del?"

Javier looked at Alma who answered, "Del is not going with us. She's still so weak from her infection. We've got it taken care of and I'll explain once we are far away from this freighter. Now we need to leave so we don't go past the spot we've picked out to go ashore."

Javier climbed down the rope ladder that was on the starboard side of the freighter and held it for each of them. Once everyone was seated and had a lifejacket and oar, he climbed back up the ladder. Alma waved and he untied the raft then pulled up the rope ladder. He waited until they had reached a good distance from the vessel before he left. He checked the deck that no one was there and then made his way to the place below deck where he had chosen to hide the rope ladder. As he went down the steps he could hear the engines whining down as they got closer to their docking position.

He retrieved the wheelchair and his backpack and put the rope ladder under the same blanket that was hiding his things. Earlier he had also used the freighter's radio to arrange for the cab when the operator had gone to the bathroom. Javier mentally went through his list of things he must do before heading to Del's room. Everything was complete except what he could not control - the wait on the deck as The NY Derby docked. He would have to deal with that as it happened so he gathered the equipment up and made it to Del's room without anyone seeing him.

Charles, Clay and Will had checked out of their inn and were on the way to the police station. Once they arrived Detective O'Malley led them to the conference room where there was coffee, tea, and breakfast cakes. While everyone was eating and putting the final details of the raid together Will excused himself and went outside the precinct.

He called Victor's mobile that woke him up and told him what was happening.

"Victor, if I'm killed please let Del know how much I love her. I wrote her a letter and it's stuck inside my carry on with my passport and other papers."

"Will, I'll tell her but you just need to stick to your training no matter what anyone else is doing. Good hunting!"

Then O'Malley called everyone together and went over the final preparations.

"We have notified the port police in case we need to call them in on the confrontation. I asked that they have a vehicle at the parking lot's entrance just in case these guys get past us. There will be two small trucks with different port logos. There are only two buildings near the dock, so the trucks will have to stay near the loading area. This is a real disadvantage because the buildings are a good distance from the freighter. This means we'll have to stay inside the buildings and trucks until we see the hostages disembark the vessel.

"Teams one and two, you'll be hiding in the trucks at the outside end of each building in the loading docks. Team three will be in the building closest to the freighter with Detective Wells, Will, and me. Clay, you stay in the building until it's safe. Once we see the hostages we will all move in from the three positions at my command. Everyone will be given a radio. Listen, no chatter, only directions and new tips. Also everyone wears a bullet proof vest so pick one out of the box over there. There are no exceptions on this because of the distance from the buildings/trucks to the freighter where we'll be in the open.

"Detective Wells has warned us that this L.R. Gomez and his associates are armed and extremely dangerous. So stay alert and follow our lead. Any questions? Well done, the freighter will be arriving soon so get your vests and report to your team leaders. Let's get these guys with limited damage."

O'Malley nodded for Charles and his team to join him. They went over to him and waited for his next command. Will could not believe he was finally going to see Del. So much had happened and he could not wait to see her but O'Malley was right about taking out the criminals first. Then he could think about reuniting with Del.

L.R. and his henchmen drove to another restaurant that he remembered had a great breakfast. Once their breakfast was served and the boys had almost finished L.R. once again went over the high points of their plan.

"OK boys, we've got to do this right the first time, so listen very carefully. Face, the crew knows you so you grab one of the crewmen that knows the freighter. Then tell this crewman to show Toby where the girls are locked up. Toby, you frighten the girls with death if they don't obey you by showing them your pistol. After they understand what you told them, you bring them up on deck. Face, you go tell the captain that I want the freighter unloaded and fueled by two this afternoon. Tell him in no uncertain terms that this is my order and he must make it happen. If he asks about what to tell the port authorities, tell the captain to put them off with some excuse.

"Toby, you should be up on deck with the girls by then, so Face you help him out with taking the girls quietly to the car. There is no parking on the dock so make all this happen very quick. That way Tiny and I aren't hassled by the cops. Any questions? No. OK, men, let's go."

Once they arrived at the dock, L.R. directed Toby to drive

between two storage buildings in front of him as he drove through the parking area. Once they were on the other side, they were actually on the dock but it was an area as big as a small parking lot. It was made of concrete and a fifty-foot wide pier went straight out into the harbor for a quarter of a mile. Small freighters like L.R.'s could dock on either side of the concrete pier because they had their own crane/lift to unload their cargo into waiting trucks.

L.R. directed Toby to stop right were the pier started to stretch out into the water from the large vacant area. The only buildings around were the buildings they drove between. From where they stopped they had a clear line of sight in any direction just in case cops showed up. L.R. was taking his usual precautions, just in case it was Clay that he had seen in London.

Alma was at the rear of the raft steering them with one of the oars. It was almost daylight and there was still a good ways to go, about a quarter of a mile against the current. She could see the effects from the girls having been locked up for ten days - they were already tired.

Alma said, "I'm getting pretty worn out. Maybe we could just not row for a little while."

Kendra responded, "That sounds good to me. What about you guys?"

It was unanimous. Alma thought since everyone was taking a break maybe this would be a good time to go over the details of their escape.

"OK, this is a good time to bring you girls up to speed. Pretty soon we'll be able to see the spot where we want to go ashore. There is a school close by with mostly farmland that surrounds it. We'll hide the raft and we won't look suspicious walking on the side of the road. Don't speak to anyone no matter what. As soon as Javier and Del get away from the freighter they will come and get us. Javier told me that he had arranged for a cab to meet the freighter, so as long as we are walking toward Southampton we should run into them.

"We will go to the train station and take the train going north to Swindon. We need to stay together at all times because there are different people who want to catch us. Everything should go as planned as long as we stay together and don't panic. Questions?"

"What if we need to go to the restroom?"

"Well, we can all go to the restroom and Javier can stand outside guarding us. OK let's get going again so we don't attract any port patrol once the sun has risen."

It seemed as if they had all gotten a shot of adrenalin because they were really putting everything into their rowing. Maybe they realized their lives did depend on getting to shore as soon as they could and probably my life depends on it, too.

The tugboat had almost finished its job of docking The NY Derby. The crew were securing her and letting the gangplank down to the dock. Javier was squatting down in front of the wheelchair that Del was sitting in. She had their baggage on her lap with a blanket covering it all. She was wearing a hoodie that Alma had given her and she was leaning over and moaning softly. No one seemed to care that they were there.

"Del, the cab just drove up. Stay like you are but hold on."

Javier knew time was short to make the trip to Alma and return to the train station not far from the dock. He stood up and went behind the wheelchair. He released the brakes and started to wheel her onto the gangplank. Suddenly two large men came out of nowhere, blocking them from going down, so he abruptly stopped. Del almost went flying down the gangplank without her wheel chair.

While righting herself her hood fell off her head, she looked up and Face was reaching out to steady her. Their eyes met and each recognized the other. The brooch she had in the satin waistband became very heavy. She moaned as she leaned over into her lap. The men stepped off the gangplank onto the freighter.

Javier thanked them as he wheeled Del down the gangplank. He helped her into the rear of the taxi, putting their bags on the floor at her feet. He wheeled the chair back onto the deck, folded it and leaned it against the wall then he ran back to the cab. Javier told the driver to take the bridge over the river Itchen and he drove away, passing the parked vehicle at the end of the pier.

Face knew this was the lady he had put on the truck in Atlanta but he had never told anyone. He thought it had not mattered but now here she was, leaving. If L.R. found out about this he would kill him. He hesitated as he looked over his shoulder at the cab. Then he walked toward the cargo hold. Toby was looking at him but he ignored him as they walked down the stairs to get the girls.

"Javier, look back at the freighter. The big guy who kept me from falling, is he looking after us as if he's trying to get information off the taxi?"

"Yes, he is. Who is that?"

"That's L.R.'s bodyguard who put me on the truck with the girls. L.R. is here and I know his bodyguard recognized me. He's going to tell L.R. that he saw me. Oh Javier, I've ruined our escape plan. But he didn't say anything to stop us, why?"

"Del, they were going to find out we had escaped when they go down to the cargo hold and Gayle is the only person there. We'll just stick to our plan."

Detective Wells observed the waiting car and pointed it out to O'Malley. Wells told O'Malley that he was sure that it would be L.R.'s car waiting to retrieve his victims of sex trafficking. When they did not pursue the cab, Detective O'Malley radioed the team to allow the taxi to pass, so not to blow their cover. O'Malley got the cab's tag and owner so he could check it out after the raid, then re-focused his attention to the freighter and the vehicle.

L.R. was becoming impatient; it had been long enough to retrieve the girls and especially Alma when L.R. saw Face and Toby dragging a tousled Gayle behind them on the gangplank. L.R. told Tiny to back the car up to the gangplank.

As Tiny reached the area of the gangplank he turned his head back toward the front of the car and said, "Boss, there is a boatload of cops running toward us."

L.R. opened the back door as they reached the car. Once inside they closed the car door and Tiny accelerated toward the middle of the line of cops. They scattered everywhere as he drove away. A port authority vehicle headed out in pursuit. Tiny knew where to go and lost them in just a few blocks. He was on a rural route on the way out of the city before any of the other cops could be dispatched.

Then L.R. turned around with his pistol pointed at Gayle's head. Gayle was directly behind Tiny.

"Where are the rest of the girls, Gayle?"

"I'm not sure. Somebody drugged me."

L.R. leaned toward her enough to touch her temple with the pistol, "You'd better clear your head quickly."

"I think I overheard them say, train to Wales."

He pulled the pistol away from her head and was turning back toward the front of the car, when Gayle opened the door and rolled out of the car.

"Did she get up, Tiny?"

"No, Boss."

"Good, Tiny, let's get off this rural road and take the throughway north to the train station in Swindon, then maybe on to Wales."

Face moved over to where Gayle had been sitting and slammed the door shut. Then he thought, *I can't tell L.R. now, that I threw that lady on the truck with the girls going to New York Harbor. I've got to come up with a good enough story before telling L.R. about her. So I'll just keep my trap shut until I can figure it out."*

O'Malley called out, "Everyone all right?"

Will replied, "We're OK." Then he helped Charles to his feet and looked around to see everyone standing up. Charles looked long at the route L.R. had taken. Then he went over to O'Malley who was walking around checking on his officers.

Charles shook O'Malley's hand and said, "Thanks so much, O'Malley, for your time to help us. I hope everyone will be all right. It looked like he was heading north so we'll be on our way. If you wouldn't mind keeping an eye on this freighter just in case they come back, it would be brilliant."

"We can keep an eye on her for you. Careful Detective Wells, those villains will be watching for you."

Charles walked back over to Will and said, "We're off. Let's find Clay and my car."

Del took off the hoodie and put it into her sac. Javier looked at his photocopy of the map of Southampton, and once the driver crossed over Central Bridge, he asked, "Please take Portsmouth Road; then take a left onto Hamble Lane; then right onto Bridge road. After the next bridge take a right onto Barnes Road that will dead end onto Brook Lane; take a right until it will change its name to Newtown Road. We are picking up our friends who were visiting the Wesley Superyacht Schools yesterday. They told us they would walk until we met up with them on the road. Once we pick them up please take us back to the Southampton Central railway station."

The driver drove until they saw them walking toward the cab on Barnes Road. He pulled over to let them get into the cab. Javier had asked the cab company to send a van. Javier got out and moved to the front with the driver, and the women filed into the rest of the van's back seats. Once everyone was in the taxi they turned around to go back to Southampton. Alma looked at her watch. Somehow they were much later than she had planned, about an hour and a half. They had missed their trains going north so they had to change to their second option.

"Javier, it's much later than we wanted it to be and I think we should go to Hertz off West Quay Road instead of the train station. OK?"

Del and Javier both nodded their heads in agreement. Then Javier told the driver they had changed their mind and for him to take them to the Hertz Car Rental off West Quay Road instead of the railroad station. It took another forty-five minutes to arrive at Hertz. As the girls climbed out of the van, Javier paid the driver and thanked him.

Alma gathered the girls into a huddle. "OK, everyone, we're here so check around where you were sitting and make sure you get everything around you. Mai, would you please help Del and make sure she finds a chair inside. Whatever happens today you stay as close as you can to Del and get her to the hospital as soon as you are able. Does everyone have everything? Good, let's go inside."

On the way inside, Alma gave Javier enough money to pay for the rental. She did not have any kind of legal papers or a passport to rent or anything, so he went to the counter and asked if they had a van or large SUV they could rent. They had both and the van was cheaper and used less gas.

On her way in to the rental office, Del had seen a pay phone right outside the building. This might be her only chance to make a call. She had to let Will know that she was OK. She really wanted to call Will, but knew their emotions would get in the way. Either he would have too many questions, or she would break down in tears, whichever happened it wouldn't work. She knew she wouldn't have much time, she needed to give Victor and Will information they needed, and she knew that Victor could get a message to Will. She didn't want any arguments with Alma or Javier about calling, but she had to get word to Will that she was OK. She got her chance when all the girls went to the bathroom. Javier was standing guard, but was not looking in her direction. She stood up quietly and walked out. Javier never saw her. As she walked she calculated the difference in time zones from the clock on the wall behind the service desk. She knew Victor would already be at work. By the time she got to the phone most of her energy was gone. She had to make this quick so she could make her way back inside before passing out. It was another thirty minutes before they were on the throughway headed north to Wales.

When Victor got to work he was grinning ear to ear. Finally he could go back out into the field. He sat down at his desk and was flipping through the current investigations when his phone rang.

"Detective Jones."

"Yes this is Detective Jones. Can I help you?"

"This is the international operator wanting to know if you'll accept a collect call from England."

"Yes, I'll accept the call."

"Oh Victor, I'm so glad you are at your desk. This is Del Thomas and I need to get a message to Will. I think he's here in England. Can you help me?"

"Yes Del, he's in England, and boy am I glad to hear your voice! Of course I can help you. Shoot."

"Tell Will that I'm alive and I'm traveling north to Wales in a van full of young girls who have escaped from L.R.'s human trafficking operation. We also have two very important witnesses. We hope to leave the van and catch a train from Swindon, England to Cardiff, Wales, I have relatives there.

"I've got to go as L.R. and his goons are following us. Please tell Will that I love him. I'll try to call you once we reach the Swindon railway station. Thanks Victor, goodbye." Del weakly made her way back to her chair before anyone came back.

Del hung up before Victor could say anything. It was not like her. Her voice was hardly audible but he went ahead and pushed the button for another line. Victor thought out loud, "The two of them call me and give messages to give to each other but they hang up before I can tell them! Crazy the both of them." He dialed Will's mobile but it went straight to voicemail. Victor left each of the facts that Del had entrusted him on both numbers of the mobile phones. He also left her message that she loved him on both mobiles. He placed the receiver back, leaned back in his chair, shook his head, and softly said, "Man, there's a storm about to be unleashed in England. God help them all!"

A car pulled up to the spot where Gayle lay on the ground. Gayle looked in the direction that they were headed to make sure L.R. had not stopped. By the time the women who had stopped got to Gayle, she was sitting up and looking at the minor cuts and scrapes on her hands and knees.

The older woman asked, "Dear, are you all right?"

"I think so." Gayle stood up and realized that her right ankle was swollen.

The younger woman reached out to steady her. "Would you like a ride?"

"It looks like you are headed north, but could I bother you to take me to the Southampton Central Police station?"

The older one replied, "Of course we can. We're actually not that far from the station."

The younger woman helped Gayle to the back seat of their car and said, "When we saw you roll out of that car, we thought you would be dead. It's quite amazing you are not injured more than you are."

"You are right about not being hurt more but I think I'm going to be really sore tomorrow." That got a smile out of the two women. "I really appreciate your kindness in stopping to check on me as well as taking me to the police station."

"That's quite all right."

Alma was glad the girls were finally sleeping but then she looked back at Del who was not looking well at all. *This escape has weakened her more than I thought it would. It's got to stop for them all. I wish we could just drop them off at a police station but most of us don't have any papers. The cops would just throw us in jail because we have no proof.* Alma turned back around and secretly vowed that it would end soon.

Javier was watching Alma in the rearview mirror and he saw something flash across her eyes that he did not like. He would need to watch and make sure Alma did not do something stupid.

"How long will it be before we reach the Swindon railway station?"

"It's about a two hour trip and we been driving about forty-five minutes. Why don't you try to sleep?"

She nodded her head in agreement and smiled.

Charles was driving north and asked, "Are you gents hungry? I am and since we don't have a clue where to go next, I know a restaurant not too far from here that serves decent food. We can get it to go and eat in the car. What do you say?"

Clay said, "I'm in, what about you Will?"

Clay heard no response and turned to look at him in the back seat. Will had his mobile phone to his ear and it looked like he was listening to his messages. He had told Clay earlier his best reception was in the hotels and on the larger highways because there were more towers.

Will lowered his phone and said, "You guys aren't going to believe this! Del called Victor and asked him to call me. She and several others are in a van traveling to the Swindon railway station. They are going to take a train from there to Wales because she has family there. Can you believe our luck?!"

"Sorry Clay, we'll have to bypass lunch. Will, did she tell Victor that she would call him back?"

"Yeah. She told him she would try to call him from the train station. Why?"

"L.R. has done very well with hunches through the years and I bet he will go to Swindon as well. There is a reason he's done so well through these past thirty-five years. They need to be warned that he might try to snatch them there. Can you call Victor back and let him know that they need to be warned?"

"Sure thing."

Then Charles called the Swindon Police. He knew one of their detectives there and he asked to speak with him.

Clay leaned back into his seat, sighed and thought, *Here we go again. Oh Lord Jesus please help and protect us all.*

L.R. told Toby to park at the back of the Swindon railway station. Once he had found a parking place and parked, L.R. cleared his throat.

"OK, this is a long shot, but I believe this is the closet station from Southampton to take the only train line that goes to Wales. So check your guns because this time we're not coming back unless we have the girls and Alma.

"Toby, you stay here and make sure the coast is clear. Face, you and Tiny walk down to the last entrance and move through the terminal toward me. I'll go into the first entrance. OK boys, let's finish this and get out of England."

They got out of Toby's car, checked their weapons to make sure they had extra magazines and then went to their assigned positions.

Toby watched them leave and then disappear around the front of the station. He quickly put the car key in the ignition, grabbed his backpack that had L.R.'s payment from when they first met, and took the rest of his weapons. *L.R. is too hot headed for me. I don't want to die and so I'll take the chance of leaving. They're either going to die or go to prison and I don't want any of it.* Then he broke into the fastest run he could to catch the next bus to Oxford.

Del and Mai were seated in the main terminal. The others helped pick the trash out of the van before Javier returned it to Hertz Rentals. They came back into the main terminal and found where Del and Mai had saved some seats around them. It was Friday so there were a good number of travelers in the station.

Just as Alma began to sit down, she saw Face and Tiny moving toward her through the crowd. Alma looked over her shoulder to see L.R. *This will get out of hand and innocent lives will be lost. I've got to end it now even if it isn't what we planned.*

She lifted Del out of her seat, hugged her and whispered, "Face and Tiny are behind you coming this way and I'm sure that's L.R. walking this way. Use every ounce of strength you have and take the girls to the restroom, lie if you have to. I will never forget you."

She then pushed Del in the direction of the women's restroom and turned her head to find L.R. She backed away from Del and moved carefully through the crowd, making her way toward him. She could see Del demanding that all the girls help her to the restroom. Alma had worked her way behind L.R. with the help of the crowds, took a quick glance back and saw them turn the corner without Face and Tiny seeing them.

Alma made her way again using the crowd and came up on L.R. from behind. She put her arm through his and whispered, "If you want your mother's brooch you'll follow me without a scene."

L.R. smiled, turned with Alma and then together they left the station.

Javier was climbing into the van after completing the cleaning the rest had started when he saw Alma leave with L.R. He quickly made a U-turn and followed them as they turned the corner. Javier waited and watched from that corner. They got into a car and pulled out, leaving the station and Javier followed him, several cars back.

L.R. returned to the same route he had just taken north but he headed back south. Javier stayed several cars behind him. He guessed he was going back to Southampton to take the freighter out of England.

From the balcony of the train station, Clay saw Del and the girls head in the opposite direction that Alma took. Then he watched with disbelief the heroic action of his friend Alma, as she surrendered to L.R. followed by them leaving the station.

Ever since José's murder, Clay had seen Alma on the truck and thought she had a plan of some kind or something to stop L.R., but he had hoped it would not mean her giving up her life. Yet Alma, probably to save the others, had just walked out with the vilest person he had ever known. Clay was sure L.R. would kill her. He bowed his head, *Lord Jesus please protect my friend and bless her for her bravery.*

Clay opened his eyes to see the multitude of police officers surrounding Face and Tiny, with Charles and Will following a small distance behind. Face and Tiny bolted in different directions, each heading for the station's exits.

The posse divided and half of the police followed each criminal in the two directions. Charles went with the team headed to the back and Will went with the team that went out front.

Clay went to the front of the station to see what happened to Will's team. Tiny ran back and forth through the parked vehicles. One of the detectives had a bullhorn and it looked like he was commanding all the civilians to hit the ground. Tiny, Will and the rest of the policeman were running with their pistols pointed to the sky. Then he saw several other policemen running toward Tiny from behind. They had him trapped. Clay could see Tiny's body language and he could read that he had no intention of going to prison. As Clay turned away he was sure that like Tiny, Face would do the same. He then walked back to the stairs leading to the main floor where he had seen Del and the girls disappear. Clay had seen enough death to last a whole lifetime.

As he reached the alcove he ran into one of the girls. He held out his hands so she would see he didn't have a gun, and introduced himself.

""I'm Clay Stevens. I'm the one from Atlanta who told Del where to find you girls. Where's Del? What's going on?"

"Thank God you're an American and a friend, I'm Kendra. We need a doctor right away. Del's collapsed in the women's restroom and we can't wake her up."

Just then Will came back into the station and Clay whistled loudly. Will turned and saw Clay waving him over. He ran over to Clay.

"Will, this is Kendra and she says that Del has collapsed in the women's restroom. What should we do?"

"Clay, you find Charles and tell him to get an emergency vehicle here STAT! I'll go with Kendra and see what I can do. Clay, GO! Lead the way, Kendra."

Kendra ran ahead of Will and pushed opened the restroom door. He ran in behind her. Mai had Del's head in her lap and another girl was holding her legs up on her knees. Will kneeled beside Del and took her hand. Her pulse was slow, her skin was pasty and damp, and he knew she was in shock. The air was stale and stagnant in the restroom, so Will scooped her up in his arms and moved her out into the alcove where the air quality was better. He heard the girls questioning who he was and why he was moving Del.

Kendra said, "This is Will and he's OK."

Clay and Charles came around the corner with a couple of uniform policeman. Charles gave the men some directions and they started moving the crowd out of the alcove, including the girls. Clay went with the girls to make sure they knew what was taking place and that nothing else would happen to them.

"Charles, elevate her legs. She's in shock. How long before the emergency personnel will get here?"

Charles had looked at his watch and was about to tell Will the time, when several uniformed police came around the corner leading the EMTs with their gurney. Charles moved back as soon as the female attendant took Del's head. Will moved over to where Charles stood.

"Will, these medical teams are the best. They will take Del to hospital. Would you like to go along?"

Charles looked over and saw tears running down Will's cheeks. He went over to the officer in charge and told him something. Then he spoke to the lead EMT. Once they had established an IV line with fluids running they put Del on the gurney. The lead EMT motioned for Will and he followed them.

"Will, I'll take care of Clay and the girls. Call me once you know something and we'll meet up."

Will waved back to let Charles know he heard him. Then Charles thanked the officers and turned to go find Clay. He saw Clay and the girls sitting among the other travelers. Charles walked over to them and Clay stood to meet him.

"How's Del?" The girls all turned to him, their expressions ranging from fear to pleading.

"Will and Del have gone to hospital. Once Will knows something, he'll phone me. So is this everyone remaining from Del's group?"

Mai answered, "No. We're missing the two key people who planned our escape, Alma and Javier."

Clay said, "Well, I don't know about Javier but I saw Alma heroically give herself up to L.R. They left together about the time Charles and the other policemen entered the station."

Charles waved over one of the uniformed policemen and told him something, then turned back to the little group. "This is what we are going to do. Clay, you and the girls will go with this nice officer. He'll take you to an inn so you can clean up and get some food. I'm going to follow up on Alma."

Charles turned and left the train station. Clay tried to calm the girls down as they followed the officer out of the station.

Once they were out of Swindon driving south on the interstate, L.R. swung his left hand across Alma's face, throwing her body up against the door. Her body went limp and slid to the floor like a rag doll.

"You just wait. You thought you could outsmart L.R. Gomez? You'll find out what happens to people who have tried that in the past."

L.R. took a leather pint flask of alcohol out of his jacket and drank liberally. He returned the leather flask and laughed mockingly.

Alma woke with a jolt from the pain in her ankles and wrists. It took her a few seconds to realize she was in a freighter's cargo hold. She was chained to the wall by her ankles and wrists.

"No wonder they hurt so badly. Well Alma you're in a pickle now." Then she realized that she was not alone.

L.R. walked out of the shadows. "That you are, Alma. Where's my mother's brooch?"

"I hid it on The NY Derby."

"Where?"

"I'll have to show you."

"OK. I can work that out."

Then with no warning he repeated the same powerful slap to Alma's face. Once again she was thrown back into the concrete wall unconscious. L.R. stared at her for a few seconds, then turned and walked away, laughing contemptuously as he had done before.

It took many times for Gayle to tell her story to several different detectives before she was taken to Detective O'Malley. Gayle's physical wounds had become very painful during the time it took to meet O'Malley. Not only had her physical wounds begun to hurt during her four-hour wait but also her emotional state had taken a hit. Kendra, Mai and Rose had been right about L.R. How could she have believed him - but she was now at this precinct to make up for those shortcomings.

Detective O'Malley sat across from Gayle at the interrogation table.

"Gayle, I'm Detective O'Malley. I've heard you've had a difficult time getting the attention you've needed. I assure you I want and need whatever information you are willing to give me concerning L.R. Gomez. But first you look like you are in pain. Can I get you something to help?"

"Thanks Detective O'Malley. I'm glad to finally meet you, but I think we are running out of time if you want to capture him. If you could ask someone to bring me a cola and a couple of ibuprofen that would be helpful."

He waved a uniformed officer into the room and asked him to

bring Gayle the items she asked for as well as a sandwich. He then turned his attention back to her.

"Gayle, please give me the information that you have come such a long way to share."

"Briefly, I'll tell you about my role with L.R.'s network. Then you'll understand how I could have this information. I've been L.R.'s best sex trafficking recruiter for the last couple of years. I was on the freighter you boarded to make sure nothing happened to the underage girls that L.R. was going to sell to an elite buyer in Europe. But many things went wrong on the voyage here and they escaped before we docked this morning. They drugged me and that's how L.R. found me this morning.

"Once they had me in his car, L.R. put a pistol to my head and I thought I was going to die. Then he was momentarily distracted. I knew I did not have much time, so I opened the car door and rolled out of the car. I did not move until I was sure he was gone. Two very kind women stopped to help me and I asked them to drive me here."

Gayle paused to open the cola to take the medication. She drank most of the cola with a couple of bites of sandwich and then looked at O'Malley.

"All right, Gayle, I'm now ready to listen to what you think is the best way to capture L.R."

"OK, then. L.R. is one of the most brilliant people I've ever met and that's why he's never been captured. He won't return to the freighter you went to this morning. You need to get the manifest from the Harbormaster and look to see if any other freighters belong to him. He usually has a couple of freighters in the same port city for occasions just like this one. If you have a Coast Guard they need to be ready to pursue him. I'm sure he is moving toward international waters as we speak."

"Thank you, Gayle."

O'Malley rose and left the interrogation room, barking off orders to the outer room full of waiting officers and detectives. Gayle picked up her cola, leaned back in her chair and said out loud, "Get out of this you…" cursing a series of foul names to finish her sentence.

Detective O'Malley and his teams sped toward the docks. He had delegated orders to other detectives to telephone Her Majesty's Coastguard, Port Authorities, and others. His detectives would call O'Malley and their new HMCG contact on their mobiles once they have found the information on the other freighters that L.R. owned.

As they were driving to the harbor, O'Malley received a call from Detective Wells.

"O'Malley, this is Wells. I've got some important information regarding L.R. Gomez." O'Malley interrupted him.

"Yes Wells, we had a tip regarding his return. The Harbourmaster and HMCG are seeking another freighter that he owns and that he may use to escape. Where are you?"

"I am coming your way about fifteen minutes from the harbor. O'Malley, he has a hostage or maybe two. He nicked them at the Swindon railway station. Can you ring me once you know anything?"

"Yes, and hurry."

Alma was jolted awake by the freighter's movement. She once again tried to gain her senses about her surroundings. She remembered and searched the area for L.R. He was not there, to her peace of mind. Her face, wrists, and ankles were throbbing and painful. She moved her back up against the concrete wall. The pain she experienced with each movement was terrible.

She then turned her attention to her surroundings. She realized she was not on The NY Derby. Then she remembered that L.R. always told her to schedule two to three freighters at the same port. She had always thought it wasteful until now.

The motors were not at maximum rotations so she figured they were not yet in international waters. Once he reaches those waters outside of Britain's jurisdiction she would be dead.

When O'Malley and his team reached West Quay Road at the harbor's entrance, they pulled over to the side. His mobile rang and he answered, "O'Malley."

"O'Malley, Wells here. I'm almost to the harbor. Do you have any more details?"

"Wells, we're on West Quay waiting. Make your way here and you can wait with us."

"Roger that, O'Malley."

Charles was almost to West Quay when he saw the same trucks and cars they had been in earlier that morning. He pulled in behind the last car. It had been a very long day and he could not believe that this crook was going to escape once again.

O'Malley's phone rang. It was the Harbourmaster, giving him directions to the dock where they could board the HMCG's Cutter, and stating just O'Malley and one other could board. O'Malley rang Charles.

"Wells, O'Malley here. Have you arrived?"

"Yes, I'm at the rear of your line of vehicles."

"Jolly good. Hurry to the lead vehicle. We've been cleared to board the HMCG's cutter."

Wells got out of his car and rushed to O'Malley's car. He knocked on the window and it opened.

"Wells, into the back, hurry."

He opened the car door and got into the back seat. They sped toward the dock. The HMCG's cutter was waiting for them. O'Malley led Wells up the gangplank where a lieutenant met them.

"Sirs, follow me."

He led them up to the pilot's area and before they arrived the cutter was racing away from the harbor. Once they entered the lieutenant led them over to a highly decorated officer.

He stood and said, "Good evening officers, welcome aboard. I'm Captain Winters. The Harbormaster said one of you could relay details concerning the freighter and her personnel that we are pursuing." O'Malley gestured to Wells to answer.

"Good evening Captain. I'm Detective Wells from London's Yard and I've been working with Detective in charge O'Malley since yesterday to pursue and capture L.R. Gomez, who is wanted for murder in both our country and the States. My team pursued him from this port to the Swindon railway station earlier today. His two bodyguards were killed but L.R. Gomez escaped with one hostage and maybe two. I've encountered this criminal in the late eighties when three officers lost their lives. He is armed and very dangerous."

"Thank you, Detective. Do you know anything about the hostages?"

"Yes Captain, one woman in her thirties, Alma Hernandez, and one steward named Javier, also in his thirties, from the freighter that they arrived on earlier today. We do not know for sure if Javier is on board or his last name but he's the bloke that helped the captives escape."

"Thank you, detectives, for coming on board. Now please follow the lieutenant. He'll lead you both to a safe place of observation. The HMCG will pursue and capture your criminal."

L.R. returned to the cargo hold where Alma was chained.

"Well, Alma, it's time to take a walk on the deck."

He removed his pistol from its holster and held it to her temple. She nodded her head that she understood. He re-holstered his weapon and unlocked her chains. Then he dragged her until she could right herself, running after him to the deck.

The freighter was out of the bay, speeding out into the North Atlantic. L.R. pushed her toward the port side of the desk. Alma noticed there was no one on deck. *He could always make sure there was nobody to witness his murders, except when he murdered the love of my life, José Ramos.*

As L.R. moved closer to Alma, pressing her closer to the edge of the freighter, she saw a shadow rushing toward them. Then she recognized him, it was Javier. As Javier reached L.R., Alma jumped sideways down onto the deck. Javier plunged a long bladed knife into L.R.'s spine and pushed him over the rail into the North Atlantic, holding onto the knife as the man went over the rail. He looked at Alma and helped her up to her feet. She moaned out loud.

"How did you get here, Javier? If it hadn't been for you . . . Thank you!" Then she hugged him.

Javier held her gently. "I saw you and L.R. leave the train station and I followed you here. Then I snuck onto the freighter, but are you hurt? I didn't hurt you, did I?"

"I'll tell you later but I hear voices heading our way. If you have a plan to get us out, let's go."

Javier took her hand and led her to the other side of the deck where he went down a rope ladder and into a raft. She was right behind him even though every step was agonizing. Once in the raft, he cut the rope with the same knife he'd killed L.R. with. The ocean was very rough until the freighter passed them but calmed down after that.

Javier clipped several flashing lights at different spots on the raft. He looked thoughtfully at the knife, then threw it overboard. Then he sat down beside Alma and put her hoodie around her shoulders. Alma leaned into his shoulder and started crying.

"What's wrong, Alma?"

"I'm OK. It's just fear and tension coming out."

"It has been a long day and boy I'm glad I saw L.R. shoving you through the train station doors. You know it was my pleasure to bring the final blow to the man who killed my sister, as well as save you."

"Thank you so much, Javier. None of our plan could have worked without you. You knew I needed help on The NY Derby even when I didn't. Everything you did guaranteed that L.R. Gomez will never murder anyone else. Although here comes Her Majesty's Coastguard, so what do we tell them?"

"How about the truth, without the part with the knife? I

rescued you from him trying to throw you overboard but then he fell overboard in the skirmish."

"That sounds like a good alibi to me."

They both took each other's hand and waved for help with their other hands for the HMCG to come rescue them.

EPILOGUE

Mai, Kendra, Rose and Tameka where escorted to Del's hospital room by Will. Del was sitting up in bed brushing her hair. She had showered for the first time in days. The girls entered the room smiling and squealing as they circled Del's bed.

Mai asked, "How are you feeling, Del? We were so worried about you!"

Del smiled even larger and responded, "Much better now, and Will told me that you girls were the ones who rescued me in the train station. Thank you so much."

Kendra replied, "Del, it was everybody chipping in. Did you hear how Alma and Javier are the main heroes? Alma surrendered to L.R. and Javier followed them back to the Port of Southampton. Javier stowed away on the freighter and then saved Alma's life. L.R. went overboard during the fight.

"Del, we and all the other young girls caught up in his sex trafficking are free. We can go home. We can't thank you and the others enough and with Alma's help most of the girls in his network will be freed! I also telephoned my aunt. She was so excited to hear from me and when I told her Rose didn't have anyone to go home to, well, she wants Rose to come and live with us." Del looked into the tear-streaked faces of all the girls and started crying as well.

"Girls, oh how I love you, and there are some things I want you to take with you when you return to the States. Each of your recovery time from all of these traumatic events will be difficult and long. I encourage each of you to find a church that teaches the Bible as well as seek out some type of counseling. Also that you won't give up on yourselves no matter how bad you feel. Will, could you pray and thank God for his love and provision in each of our lives over these past several weeks."

They all took each other's hands as Will began to pray. Knowing it might be the last time they would be in prayer with Del, after everything they had gone through, made each girl realize how much they had to be grateful for.

Mai called her mom on Will's mobile. Liliana was overwhelmed with joy to hear her daughter's voice. Mai told her she still had to give her statement to the police but she would be flying home with Del, Will and the others later that week. Mai told her mom not to worry, everything was OK now and that God had taught her many things. Liliana started crying and agreed that God had taught them both a great deal.

Detective Charles Wells questioned Alma and Javier as well as the crew from the freighter about L.R. falling to his death. There were no witnesses of the incident, and with the medical report of Alma's injuries from L.R.'s beatings, no charges were pressed from the Yard. Alma and Javier were cleared of any criminal involvement.

Detective Wells requested Alma, Del, Javier, and the girls give their statements of what took place during their voyage. Also Clay and Will were asked to give their statements regarding their involvement with L.R. Gomez and the steps that led up to their leaving the States. Once their statements were taken they were free to leave the U.K. Gayle Simpson was also free to leave the U.K., but Detective Wells advised Detective Jones to watch her closely once she arrived back in the States. She had given a statement, and had committed no crimes in the U.K., but Charles thought once she returned home she would just resume her previous illegal activity, with some other partners.

The Yard extended their thanks to the victims, the fellow detectives in TVP, Southampton Police, Swindon Police and especially Her Majesty's Coast Guard who deferred any legal matters to the Yard.

Del and Alma discussed with Charles what they should do with L.R.'s brooch. He suggested that they sell it and give the money to all the victims' families, including the officers that L.R. had killed in the late eighties. They thought that was a great idea and asked Charles to send those men's addresses to Victor, his official contact in the States. Then he would contact the proper personnel to dispense the funds.

Once Detective Paul Rankin updated the authorities regarding Patrick Cordero, he was charged with a lesser crime. Detective Rankin also updated the widow of Jason Hill that the two men who murdered him had been killed during their arrest.

Javier wanted to know if Alma could use his help with putting together the information the police could use to prosecute every level of L.R.'s human trafficking network. She would love Javier's help with the work but she also wanted to know him better. He thought that was an even better idea.

Clay was escorted to the airport by Detective Wells. Wells cleared him to return to the States without his passport. He also thanked Clay for his courage throughout their pursuit. Wells told him it had been his detailed information that led to the case's conclusion. He also told him that Detective Victor Jones would meet his flight and that he would not be charged for his involvement with José's murder.

Once Del was out of the hospital and she had started to meet with Detective Wells, Will met her for lunch and brought his letter.

After lunch Will asked Del if he could read her something and she smiled. Will read her the letter he had written and Del cried.

After Will saw Del's response to his letter he knew what to do. He sat there, enjoying the moment just staring into her beautiful blue eyes. Then he walked over and knelt down, reached into his pocket and drew out a little black box.

He opened it. "Del will you marry me?" He looked up and now her eyes were welling up with tears and he smiled at her.

"Oh Will, I would love to be your wife." The tears were streaming down Del's cheeks as Will took the ring out of the black box and slid it onto her left ring finger. She held her left hand out in front of her and gasped, "Oh, Will, it is so beautiful!"

Will stood up and gave her a big hug, then a kiss, and returned to his seat. "We can talk about any wedding plans once we get home. I just want you to know how much I love you Del. Also to thank you once again for waiting for God to work in my life, you were right about waiting. Right now you just need to heal and gain your strength back."

"Oh Will, I love you so much. I'm sure we need to move though many things before we plan the wedding but you have always been the love of my life."

They ordered some coffee and dessert, savoring each moment together.

RECOMMENDED BOOKS, ARTICLES AND/OR WEBSITES

Books:

Stolen: The True Story of a Sex Trafficking Survivor
By Katariina Rosenblatt, PhD and Cecil Murphey – October 7, 2014

Rescuing Hope
By Susan Norris – January 1, 2013

Forgotten Girls (Expanded Version): Stories of Hope and Courage
By Kay Marshall Strom and Michele Rickett – June 28, 2014

Articles / Websites:

NEW YORK - 14 Years of Slavery b/c Sex Trafficking

Largo Project from the Investigative News Network > Juvenile Justice Information Exchange > News > Victim of Sex Trafficking in U.S. Tells Her Story
By Theresa Fisher | January 23, 2014

What you need to Know, Sex Trafficking and Sexual Exploitation; A Training Tool for Mental Health Providers

By: Arizona State University School of Social Work; Office of Sex Trafficking Intervention Research – ASU_Sex_Trafficking_STIR_ASU_Brochure.pdf

Dominique Roe-Sepowitz, MSW, PhD, Director, STIR

Kristine Hickle, MSW, Associate Director of Research Development, STIR

Angelyn Bayless, Director of Communications, STIR

Teen Girls' Stories of Sex Trafficking in U.S.
By - ABC News - http://abcnews.go.com/Primetime/story?id=1596778 &page=1
Note: This report has been revised to clarify that the man Miya says lured her into prostitution was charged with pimping and pandering only in connection with the minor with whom he was traveling.

Diane Langberg's Link: Video - The Blight of Domestic Sex Trafficking: Choosing Sides.
http://globaltraumarecovery.org/the-blight-of-domestic-sex-trafficking-choosing-sides/

CPSIA information can be obtained
at www.ICGtesting.com
Printed in the USA
FSOW01n0626181216
28519FS